The Urge

A Devil's Rules Series Novel

CL Gibson

First My Blue Horse trade paperback edition September 2018.

Manufactured in the United States of America.

ISBN (hardcover) 978-1-7326720-1-7
ISBN (paperback) 978-1-7326720-0-0
ISBN (ebook) 978-1-7326720-2-4

My Blue Horse Publishing
more information at *ChristiLGibson.com*

For you Honey.

My Dean, My Sweets

Acknowledgements

I wish to thank my editor, cover artist, and dearest friend, Patricia Childers, for her honest critique. Her encouragement gave me the resolution to open myself to these characters and tell their story. Her super-hero editing skills allowed me to turn a crappy first draft into an actual novel with a title that works. And her artistic ability is stunning. I would walk through fire for her. No. That's an exaggeration. I'd bring her a truck full of burly, tattooed firemen. Yes, she'd like that best.

A special thank you to Charlie Donlea, *USA Today* and international best-selling author of *Summit Lake*, *The Girl Who Was Taken*, and *Don't Believe It*, for his generosity of time and expertise in critiquing the first chapters of my novel, *The Urge*. I will forever be grateful for his encouragement and wise suggestions.

I wish to express my deep appreciation for the meticulous critique and spot-on edits of the first chapters of *The Urge* by award-winning novelist and journalist, John DeDakis, former editor on *CNN*'s "The Situation Room with Wolf Blitzer," and author of numerous mystery-suspense novels including, *Fast Track*, *Bluff*, and *Bullet in the Chamber*. John is a former White House Correspondent, taught journalism at American University in Washington, D.C., interviewed Alfred Hitchcock, and helped to make this book a great deal stronger.

"It were better for him that a millstone were hanged about his neck, and that he were drowned in the depth of the sea."

Matthew 18:6

The Urge

Chapter 1

2008

DATE OF BIRTH: 03/17/1988 SEX: F RACE: W WEIGHT: 167 HEIGHT: 508

Night pressed its black shadow into the alley, opened its mouth, and exhaled. Walls became sticky and wet with air too thick to breathe. Air that needed to be sucked through a straw and swallowed. Bloated gnats infested a nearby dumpster overflowing with rotting garbage, but it was the woman's stench that threatened to close his throat.

She reeked of cat urine—virtually jumped into a pool of it, touched bottom, and swam until her fingers got pruney. Holding his breath, he knelt down to get a closer look, and smiled.

Chalk-colored hair clung to her face like greasy clumps of pasta, and a worn-out rug of a coat hung from her bones. Her bedroom was a cardboard box, her bureau a shopping cart. Life was the thief that had picked her pockets bare, stole her youth, and left her invisible, unwanted, and never to be missed.

She was no one's mother, no one's daughter. She was no one. That's why he chose her. Decaying society had made her no better than a lab rat, but to him she was better. Shrouded in abject poverty and filth, she went unnoticed, and her anonymity made her priceless.

Mice, squirrels, and rabbits had been his test subjects. Most were trapped in parks, some from his back yard. Every so often an opossum, raccoon, or coyote ventured into his neighborhood. Consequently, he capitalized on his good fortune and the animal population decreased. But those studies had gone as far as they could. His research required that he prey upon big game now.

Duplicating zoologists' methods of monitoring large animals by attaching an electronic tag collar was implausible. Humans aren't easily tagged. He'd found her at the soup kitchen, where he'd purchased her medical history, age, and weight for the price of food, and tracked her to this place.

A week ago, she'd wolfed down the muffin he'd handed her in four gluttonous bites and was looking for more. Not today. Huddled into a corner of her box, all she wanted was water and a blanket.

He tucked the blanket around her, set two bottles of water near her, and began charting her symptoms: retinal hemorrhaging of the eyes, impaired vision, burning of the mouth and throat, nausea, vomiting, severe stomach pains, diarrhea, dizziness.

She wasn't much older than him, and she wasn't going to get any older. Judging from her rapid heartbeat, the convulsions would begin soon. Compiling her symptoms, he had deduced her internal organs were hemorrhaging, there was fluid buildup in her digestive tract and lungs, and her liver and kidneys were shutting down. She would die of kidney failure in approximately forty-eight hours.

All this from an innocuous, jelly-glazed oatmeal muffin. His last test subject's symptoms progressed too rapidly. The thirty-eight-year-old man dropped like a rock. He'd adjusted the recipe—fewer powdered seeds, a tad less toxic jelly—and voilà. Perfection.

The muffin's concealed ingredients attacked the body as a viral flu, but it was a poisonous glycoside that brought about death. The best part? It was undetectable.

This study was going well. Looking at his watch, he realized it was time to go. He hated to. The end was so gratifying. He'd be back to follow her demise, close out her chart, and conclude this experiment.

To stop the cycle of future victims, precise procedures had to be followed. There were more subjects on his growing list, so these results had to be exact.

He wasn't the priest that saw one of these people and passed by on the other side of the road. He wasn't a Levite, who did the same. He was the Good Samaritan who went to the infected person and made them right.

As he turned to leave, a fragile whisper slipped from the box.

"Thank you, sir. Thank you."

Chapter 2

Back - 1998

The old guy, first in line to the coffee counter, turned to his friend and said, "I bet if I ate a bottle of glitter, my shit would sparkle."

"Yeah and you'd fart rainbow unicorns," his elderly friend said, leaning hard on his four-pronged cane that sported a whimsical human skull design. Tucking the newspaper under his arm, he added, "Enough bullshit, grab the coffee and let's go."

Third in line stood Opal Futrell and her two children. Looking from one child to the other, she waited. Not to disappoint, Woody burst into loud guffaws as only a ten-year-old boy would. Vette, her twelve-year-old daughter, covered her giggles with her hand, while Opal's unapologetic belly laughter filled the coffee shop.

Trenton's, the trendy, yet purposefully vintage coffee shop, emulated a small town feel even though it was located at the heart of Third Street in wealthy Geneva, Illinois. Today Trenton's was packed, with a line stretching out the door. Opal's gaze followed the line and found Hugh Johnson at the end.

Opal waved to Hugh, but he didn't see her. His focus was fixed on her children.

4

Beside her, Woody was in perpetual motion, rocking on his heels to "Hit Me Baby One More Time" coming from the shop's speakers, bobbing his head side to side, his dark bangs swiping his forehead like windshield wipers. At ten years old, his face wore a little boy's softness with innocence in his eyes. Opal could guess what was happening inside Woody's head just by his movements. She knew he was envisioning MTV's video of Britney Spears alongside her classmates marching the school corridor with Britney in a gray school uniform and blonde pigtails bound by pink angora fluff. He did this every time that video came on the television.

To the right of Opal was her daughter, Vette, on the cusp of becoming a woman. Although as tall as her mother, Vette had no need of a bra, yet. She had the same long hair as Opal but unlike her mother's auburn hair, Vette's hair was buttery blonde. Waiting their turn, Vette's lips whispered softly to Britney's song, "Oh baby, baby how was I supposed to know." Opal believed Vette knew the lyrics to every song that played on the radio, and she was partially right. Vette knew the lyrics of every song that she liked.

As she stepped up to the counter, Opal automatically bit the tip of her tongue in a toothy grin that accentuated her deep dimples and made her appear more a school girl rather than a forty-two-year-young mother. Biting her tongue like that was a nervous habit she hated. Realizing she was doing it again, Opal sucked in her tongue and placed their order.

With drinks and treats in hand, Opal and the kids found a table. The room rumbled with the sound of moving furniture, of heavy lumber and metal legs scraping across the floor. Woody was rearranging the chairs to provide himself with the optimal seat incorporating the precise angle needed to reach his food. Once done, he plopped down.

Vette slipped daintily into a chair facing the window.

The aroma of newly ground beans anointed the air and intensified as he neared the counter. Hugh Johnson shuffled forward listening to the white noise of multiple conversations, whirling blenders, baristas asking for customer's names, metal utensils tapping cups, and the rustle of scones dropping into paper sacks. He glanced at Opal and her children. Having met Opal a number of times since being hired by her husband, Hugh felt he knew quite a bit about her. He knew she prided herself for having read the complete set of Encyclopedia Britannica and for still fitting into her 1974 Queen-of-the-Steam-Power-&-Threshing-Bee-Show gown.

Hugh's experience and age had taught him to listen. He knew she'd kept her slender shape by walking everywhere, including here most mornings with her kids. And he knew today was the last day for that walk.

With his coffee in hand he made his way to their table. "Are you causing all the ruckus?"

The neatly groomed man with close-cropped graying hair was recently hired to be Opal's husband's Used Cars Lot's manager. Max's new business, a used cars dealership, was currently a slab of open land with two trailers sitting on the corner of a busy intersection. This week the vehicles to sell were arriving and the doors would open.

"Oh Hugh, we're not the ones who started it," she said. With a head nod and a shoulder shrug, Opal indicated the two older gentlemen. She whispered, "It's those two in the booth over there that made us laugh."

"Ah, I see," Hugh said with a smile. "Can I join you?"

"Of course." Opal scooted over to give Hugh room to pull up a chair.

Hugh sat across the table from Opal between Vette and Woody. "So today's the big move," he said.

He saw Opal take a quick breath and he was sure she blinked back a tear.

"Yes, the movers are taking our things over to our new home right now. When we left to come here they had all of our belongings out of the house. Boxes and furniture from the kitchen, living rooms, and bedrooms, everything we have was covering the lawn, like a… like a death sale."

Opal looked down and sighed heavily. "Course we can't fit three-quarters of it in our new home. So some will be stored and the rest will be auctioned off. Max is supervising everything and today he told us to come here to relax. I think I won the husband lottery."

"Yes, I have to agree with you there." Hugh said. "Max is a good guy. Otherwise, I would never have left my job to come work for the both of you."

"Oh it's Max you're working for, not me. I'm the housewife, or as they say now, stay-at-home mom."

Ten-year-old Woody scoffed, "Home? Our new home is nothing but a single-wide trailer. Not double. Single. We're trailer trash."

Opal turned toward Woody so fast her knee hit the table's leg causing her coffee to tip. Like an athlete, she caught it mid-fall, not spilling a drop, while simultaneously rebuffing her son. "Woody Wynn Futrell."

Woody rolled his eyes and gave a playact shudder as he whispered, "Oooohhh, a full name warning."

Meanwhile, Vette had been ignoring all of them. She drank her chamomile organic tea with her eyes focused on the sheet music lying on the table before her. The tea was supposed to render a calming effect. It wasn't working. "*One Day More*" from Les Misérables had been playing off the paper and into her head, filling her soul, but the moment Woody said trailer trash, like a vinyl record, it scratched to a halt.

Woody slurped his double-chocolate hot chocolate with extra whipped cream. He'd already eaten one apple fritter and was about to devour the second.

"Well it's true," Woody said, with his mouth full of fritter. "We're moving from a magazine mansion with an indoor swimming pool, a movie theater room, four bedrooms, and six bathrooms." He pointed to the south, "that's just down the street on the Fox River. For globe's sake, it's next to a fricken Forest Preserve. We're not moving up, we're moving way down. It's worse than trailer trash. We'll be Naperville trailer trash."

"Four full bathrooms and two half-baths." Vette mumbled.

"What?" Woody asked, looking at his sister.

"It's not six bathrooms. And it's a Tudor-style home of brick, stucco, and stone, not a magazine mansion."

"Whatever," he sneered.

"I am going to miss the study, and the river," Vette said, staring at the sheet music. She began humming, then softly sang to herself, "One more day all on my own."

"Well, I'm going to miss my friends," Woody shot at her.

Vette cut short the song. "Me too, but it's done, it's over," she said slapping her sheet music closed. "That's it. We don't have a say."

"Yeah, we had to sell everything because Dad can't keep a job. Why didn't he sell his airplanes or those old cars instead of our house?"

Hugh saw Opal mouth the word, sorry.

She faced her son, and said: "Woody, selling the planes and the cars wouldn't have been enough to get the land and all. And you know that isn't true about Dad keeping a job," she lied. "Your father just doesn't work well for others. He needs to be his own boss."

Then Opal went to the fountain of encyclopedia facts she had gathered in her nightly reading to change the subject. "Did you know one of the very first American used cars lots opened in 1898?"

In unison, Vette and Woody rolled their eyes.

"Oh, don't do that. It's true," Opal said. "Okay. Okay. I'll admit living in a trailer behind a used cars lot is not a dream come true for any of us. But we have no choice. For now we have to be land-rich and cash-poor. We have to do this for your father because… because… we have to."

Because, Opal thought, *Max gets easily bored*. She adored the man. Truly adored him, but he was a job hopper. And with each job change, they lost money. He'd be out of work a month, making them once again suck on the teat of her trust fund. Next, it was two months, again draining her trust fund.

Hugh had gone invisible to her, sitting there between her children. Opal's memories and apprehensions erased all else. She didn't notice Hugh inching his chair closer to Woody.

Opal drifted with her thoughts.

Max and Opal had moved five times in two years before inheriting her parent's home. Back then. They'd lived in some roach-infested hell holes, so moving into a new, single-wide trailer would have been a blessing. But that was back before Woody, when Vette was only two.

Living in her inherited childhood home, they'd known stability and opulence for ten years. It didn't stop Max from changing jobs four times, but it did force him to do it within driving distance. Opal refused to move. Though with all the stops and starts, it was becoming obvious they would eventually lose the house, her trust fund, the planes, and the cars, if Max didn't stick to one job.

All of it was in jeopardy.

By selling her magnificent inherited home, Max and Opal Futrell were able to pay cash for twenty acres, split into five acres per corner. It paid for blacktopping the used cars lot on the Naperville corner, paid for their $13,000 trailer "home," and also bought a used job-site office trailer that they faced toward the busy, four-lane highway.

Max would only have two employees: Hugh Johnson, their Used Cars Manager, and Neil Parker, the F&I Business Manager. Opal was hoping the pressure to succeed and the urgency of being open from nine to nine, six days a week, would keep Max from being bored. He couldn't get pissed off at his boss, pack his "get-away" box, and quit, because he was the boss.

By agreeing to this, Opal was forcing Max to dig his heels into one spot and make it work. This sacrifice was unbreakable. She loved Max but they had children. Enough was enough. If Max quit this job, she'd quit him. At least that's what she told him.

Easy peasy, lemon squeezy, Max had said. The plan was that Max and Hugh would go to car auctions, buy the best used cars and trucks, factor in the cost of financing, and turn vehicles as quickly as possible. Before they knew it, they'd be able to buy a Ford franchise, then Toyota, then Honda. They'd have a new house and everything would be great.

Easy peasy, lemon squeezy, my ass, Opal thought. They were sitting on a live grenade. If they didn't pay on time, the bank would put them out of business, take their land, and their trailer-trash home. There was no plan B.

What was she doing? What if Max fucked this up? Where would she go? Opal swallowed the compulsion to vomit all over the coffee shop floor.

Closing her eyes, Opal could see the three-bedroom, single-wide gray trailer, propped up by concrete blocks and dropped on the lifeless five acre, northeast corner of the Naperville lot with four cement steps shoved up to a flat, nondescript front door. No landscaping. No trees, just tiny round spit-fulls of weeds separated by large patches of dull gravel. That was her children's new playground.

"Better for us? Really, Mom?" Woody asked sarcastically, snapping Opal back from her thoughts.

"Uh, yes. Dad won't have to work as a General Manager for someone else." Opal quickly turned to Hugh and added, "No offense, Hugh."

"None taken."

Opal turned back to Woody. "We will be the owners. No one can push Dad out of this job and one day the two of you can take over the businesses."

"I want to be a doctor, not a used car salesman," Woody said.

"I want to be a singer," Vette said, opening her choir's sheet music once more, which prompted her to begin humming.

Frustrated, Opal said, "Well, when I was ten I wanted to be a ballerina. You have plenty of time to figure out what you want to be when you grow up. This just gives you one more option. Keep in mind, dad and I will miss our house too. I'll miss my kitchen and the patio and everything, but we'll make do. All of us will make do. Okay?"

Vette's shoulders dropped. "Okay."

Opal raised her eyebrows at Woody. "Okay?"

"Yeah, okay." He mumbled.

Hugh turned to Woody, "Hey seeing as how you'll be so close to the sales trailer, maybe I can teach you how to make plastic model cars. It's a hobby of mine and I've gotten pretty good at it. Would you like that?"

Woody looked at the fifty-year-old man with the receding hairline. Hugh was five years older than Woody's dad, but those years sagged heavy on Hugh.

"Yeah. Maybe," Woody shrugged.

"Or better yet, you could come to my house to build them," Hugh said. "It's quieter there and I have a special room with all the equipment just for it. My wife calls it my toy room. Tammy, that's my wife."

Putting his arm around Woody's chair, Hugh's thumb almost touched the back of Woody's neck. "I'd really like to show it to you."

Chapter 3

Still 1998

He'd been here before. Sitting in the car. Watching through the rear-view mirror. The middle-school parking lot was a safe place for little ones to play, especially on weekends when school was out. Schools are always the safest place. The road in front of the school was black topped. The one behind was gravel. The girls were on the gravel side.

His hand slid up and down the right leg of his jeans. Watching. Studying.

Anticipation was part of the fun. He made himself wait. Prolonging the thrill of the hunt. The capture. The trophies.

His trophies were stored in the back of his closet inside a black duffel bag. Clear plastic boxes 2" x 2" x 2" with tiny hinged backs displayed ten souvenirs from each of his victims. He used needle-nosed pliers to rip them from his victim's fingers. Some were painted with polish, mostly from the older ones. The little ones usually didn't use nail polish. He needed a more secure storage location but the need for new victims was more urgent.

The last one was just a week ago Tuesday, before that he'd waited a month. He couldn't control it anymore. He needed. He needed. Older ones fought too hard. He focused on the little ones. Easier. So much easier.

Closing his eyes, he heard the sensual *ker-chink, ker-chink*, a mixture of scraping hubcaps, snapping fingers, and marbles dropping into a plastic tube that was the sound of the bicycle's rubber wheels rolling over gravel, announcing the arrival of the two little girls. They were coming ever so close to his car. They were coming to him.

He opened his eyes. They were coming.

Eight-year-old Betty Harte and her almost eight-year-old friend, Alice Rayburn, were riding bicycles on Old Mill Road, the gravel road just at the edge of Streator, when the man in his early twenties stepped out of a rusted-out white Ford Maverick and asked for directions.

Dirty-blond hair concealed half of his face as he walked closer, "Sorry, I can't hear you."

Alice whispered to Betty, "We have to go."

At that instant, the man grabbed Betty by the neck and threw her through the open window into the car like a ball through a goal.

Alice took off as fast as her seven-year-old legs could take her. Her strawberry-blond curls lifting in the wind and her necklace bouncing against her chest.

The man chased after Alice. In those frantic seconds, Betty scrambled to unlock the passenger door but the lock had been disabled. She lunged over to the driver's side window, jumped out, and fell to the gravel just in time to trip the man who had returned with Alice pinned under his arm.

Betty jumped up and ran. Alice could not.

Betty hid behind landscaping boulders at a nearby greenhouse that was closed for the day, and held perfectly still until she heard the car take off. Poking her head out, she saw Alice screaming through the car window. She couldn't hear her. The radio was pounding. Alice's big brown eyes round with terror. Her face plump, with baby-cheeks. Her tiny palms pressed against the window.

Betty stayed hidden, waiting until she couldn't hear or see the car anymore then took off running, ducking along the way, so if the man came back he wouldn't see her. She ran several blocks to the house of a teacher she knew.

She banged on the door until the teacher answered, Betty blurted, "Someone took my friend."

For the next two weeks, the police questioned Betty. It took fourteen nights and fifteen days before a deputy sheriff found Alice's ravaged naked little body face down in a drainage ditch, under three feet of water. She was found two days after her eighth birthday.

The only thing left on her body was the silver-beaded-word necklace spelling 'Lissy' that Alice had worn when she disappeared. Her two brothers, sixteen-year-old Carlton, and twelve-year-old Cody, had given it to her. Lissy was the name they called her, and from the moment they'd given it to her, she never took it off.

For those fifteen days before Alice was found, the entire community searched, covering an area ten miles in diameter. She was invisible until a deputy sheriff, who was training a rookie on hidden places local teenagers congregated, stepped up to the drainage ditch.

It was a place off the road where kids can get back behind the trees and not be seen from the road. It was impossible to see Alice's body unless one stood on the bank of the three-foot-wide ditch and looked directly down.

That day, for some unknown reason, the deputy looked down. The water was three-feet deep, and Alice's body was held beneath the surface by flat rocks. Some of her clothing was found in the ditch and the rest was scattered nearby.

Alice was identified through dental charts. When her body was found, she was only partially covered. It appeared she'd originally been completely covered, but those days in the water and the weather that had come and gone, unearthed her. The autopsy indicated she died within hours of her abduction. Seven-year-old Alice was alive when the man raped her, and raped her, and raped her again. She was alive when he ripped his ten trophies from her fingers. Alive when he secured them in the clean clear 2" x 2" x 2" plastic box. It was only after he held her head under water that her feet stopped kicking. Her cause of death was drowning.

Twenty-six-year-old Brad Denver was in his car again. His hand rubbing up and down his leg. He stared at Betty from his rear-view mirror. It had been five days since he'd raped and killed her friend. Brad couldn't care less about Alice, the dead one who was still hidden in the drainage ditch. No one would ever find her.

He wanted this one. Needed it. He was back for the one that got away. Eight-year-old Betty was walking along the edge of her lawn, not stepping over the line, not leaving her yard. Her mother guarded Betty from the stoop, helping her test the safety of being outside.

Brad, parked just a front yard away, ached for her to venture out. Needing her to come to him again. Come to him. This hunt was satisfying. Perfect. She was coming to him.

She was walking cautiously toward his car. He'd have her. Soon. So soon.

Brad knew he was taking a risk. He'd been picked up and questioned by authorities, just one day after he'd raped and killed the other one. He was stopped by authorities because of his car. Betty, this little one, had a good memory. She was smart and had described his car real good.

Brad was full of himself. If they had anything on him they would have locked him up right then and there. They had nothing. So he bragged a bit. He told investigators he was in Streator, near LaSalle Lake, the day Alice was abducted. He didn't worry. They didn't have anything on him. They didn't have a body.

Denver should have been less forthcoming. Less full of himself. He should have dumped the rusted-out white Ford Maverick that Alice's eight-year-old playmate, Betty, had escaped, but he kept it. He shouldn't have gone back for Betty, but he had to.

Betty's mother went into the house to answer the phone. Immediately Brad was out of the car, opened his trunk, and was moving fast toward Betty.

Betty's back was to the man.

He was an arm's length away from grabbing and dashing with her. He'd throw her in the trunk and take Betty to her dead friend. He'd lift the rocks so Betty could see what was to become of her in just a few hours. When he was done with Betty he'd bind the two little girls together and cover them with rocks. They'd be there forever and he'd be long gone. It was a sweet plan.

"Betty come in here now," her mother called from the house.

Brad jumped back into the shadows of a high cranberry bush.

Betty ran to the house, not seeing the man hiding, just at the edge of their lawn. Where she'd been standing a moment before.

Brad had a split second to chase after her. To throw her in the trunk. It was too late.

He'd come back. She would be his.

Slamming his trunk was the last thing he did with his freedom. Brad's arrogant obsession had led the police to him. Brad was watching Betty while the police watched him. They were waiting for him. He was arrested.

Ten days later, Alice's body was found near LaSalle Lake.

Forensics tied Alice to the inside of his car. Investigators searched his apartment, found his trophies. In custody, Brad watched as the authorities touched his boxes. In front of him. He didn't like that. Their fingerprints were all over the clear boxes. He didn't like that.

Fate is a mother-fucker. After the police discovered Alice's body, after learning of his daughter's rape and murder, Alice 'Lissy' Rayburn's father, Charles, laid down on the couch and died from a myocardial infarction. His heart gave up.

Opal Futrell sat across from her husband Max at their kitchen/dinner table, reading a section of the morning paper.

> *"Charles died when Alice died,"*
> *said Mrs. Rayburn as she cried. "It*
> *killed him. She was his pride and*
> *joy and they found her like that."*
>
> *Services for Alice, the only daughter*
> *of Charles and Alisha Rayburn,*

and for Alice's father and Alisha's husband, Charles Rayburn, were held at St. Paul's Lutheran Church of Streator Illinois. Alice and Charles are survived by Alice's mother and Charles' wife, Alisha Rayburn, Alice's brothers and Charles' sons, Carlton and Cody Rayburn…

The story went on.

They are buried side-by-side in St. Paul's Lutheran Cemetery, three miles south of Streator, Illinois.

Today Brad Denver pled guilty to Alice Rayburn's kidnapping, rape and murder. He took a plea in order to avoid the death penalty. Denver was sentenced to life in prison without parole.

Opal put down the newspaper and turned to her husband Max. "This just makes me sick.

"What's that?" Max asked as he got his morning coffee.

"This man raped and murdered this beautiful little girl. He'll live another sixty years and she's dead. It's not right."

Opal held up the paper showing a picture of Alice with her baby-teeth smile, curly pigtails, and bright eyes.

"He should have been charged with the father's death, too," Max said.

Another picture showed the mother, Alisha Rayburn, and her two sons, Carlton and Cody. Alisha looked broken with her sons sitting on either side of her.

Carlton and Cody didn't look broken. They looked enraged.

"That poor family." Opal shook her head. "How do you live through that? How do you go on?"

Max picked up the paper. "It says she's moving her sons away from there. It's probably the best thing for them."

Four miles east of Max and Opal's trailer home, a moving truck was unloading Alisha, Carlton, and Cody's things into a craftsman-style home in the heart of Naperville.

Chapter 4

Still - 1998

Hugh and Tammy Johnson were high school sweethearts who married right after graduation, and divorced a year later. No kids. No pets. No money. Nothing to divide made for an easy split.

Twenty-five years passed before they found each other again, and once again married. Still no children, but this time there was a pet and plenty of money.

Car salesmen are disrespected. Some are pathological liars, most are the butt of jokes, but a good car salesman can make a shitload of money. Hugh was a good car salesman. Hell, he made more than most lawyers and doctors. He'd been at Fox Valley Ford, Lincoln-Mercury for twenty-two years, and had built a huge customer base. The bulk of his commissions came from repeat and multigenerational sales. With his steady clients, and this year's new styling updates to the Lincoln Town Car and Ford's focus on higher MPG, Hugh's future appeared lucrative.

"So remind me again, why are you taking the risk of leaving a solid job at Fox Valley Ford for Futrell Used Cars?" Tammy asked, while lying on the couch.

Chunko, her cat, was sprawled face down like a bear-skin rug, covering Tammy from chest to waist. It was a wonder Tammy could talk at all with that cat on top of her. Chunko lived up to her name, at twenty pounds her belly was the size of a Pomeranian, though she sported the head of normal cat. Chunko resembled a cartoon-balloon cat that had eaten its adult twin.

Tammy sat up, and with a thud, Chunko dropped to the floor. "Remind me?" she repeated.

"It's an opportunity I can't pass up. If it works, I'll be the General Manager of four dealerships spanning twenty acres, making five times what I make now."

"And if it doesn't work?"

"Well then, I'll go back to Fox Valley Ford, or any one of the hundreds of dealerships in the Chicagoland area, and sell cars like I'm doing now. My customers will follow me no matter where I go. We'll be fine either way." Hugh smiled as he looked at Tammy.

In his eyes she was still a tiny firm-bodied seventeen-year-old cheerleader, but in truth Tammy, though still barely five-foot tall, was now a soft-bodied, plumper version of herself.

She was aging naturally as women of the Midwest do, proudly wearing lines across her forehead that fanned out from her eyes to her temples. There were parentheses lines from her nose surrounding her mouth. She wore a blonde bob with roots of gray rather than the long dark hair of her youth. The skin on her hands, neck, and arms, was no longer taut. It was sunk in to reveal blue veins, brown spots, and folds where there had been none. Her lips were thinner, but to Hugh, her smile was just as bright.

He was glad they found each other again. It was good to have a best friend, a companion from his youth to grow old with. A companion to see him as he was, not as he is.

Chapter 5

Still - 1998

Max and Hugh were hunting and gathering inventory at the auction for Futrell Used Cars. The auctioneer's velvet voice would have been perfect on the morning news, but a late night infomercial was better suited for his white Nike-collared shirt and the thick layer of Brylcreem that slicked his hair back.

"*Hup-Hup-Hup-Hup*." The man's fully-formed moustache moved to the rhythm as his hands jerked and grabbed air.

"*Yup-Yup-Yup.*" The pace of his voice raced as if to the *thrump, thrump, thrump, pha, pha* of the Lone Ranger's theme song.

A sudden bang to the car's hood prompted, *"Go-Go-Go!"*

We need to check for dents after buying a car from this guy, Max thought.

Max was finally in his element and felt alive. Having already set up his line of credit at auction houses from Indianapolis to Chicago, Max was filling his used cars lot. His used cars lot. No more unethical owners breathing down his neck and sucking his soul. No more having to bend principles, and in some cases laws, to feed the greed of a boss.

Max vowed his dealership would be a clean business where standards actually meant something. His lot, his rules. No more back-room compromises. No more feeling the oil of deceit cover his skin. He was bringing respect back to the industry, or at least to his car lot. Standing in the auction house heavy with exhaust fumes, it was as if for the first time in years, Max could breathe.

Max was an ordinary, family man who had worked for the devil, or several devil's helpers who happened to own car dealerships. Not all were bad, but the bulk of owners Max dealt with fit that bill. Those owners didn't whip out their forked tongues or spikey tails, they simply nurtured an environment that lowered Max's standards drop-by-drop until there wouldn't be any left to uphold. That's when the hairs went up on the back of Max's neck, that's why he'd grab his get-away box every few years, and that's why he'd run. Thank goodness he didn't have to run anymore.

Commercial car carrier trailers, hauling up to nine cars at a time, delivered Max's purchases to his dealership. The doors were open to Futrell Aurora/Naperville Used Cars, and today Neil was watching over the dealership while Max and Hugh purchased ten more vehicles.

"Heeeeeep." The ringman banged the hood to stop a car. Bidding ensued and, *"Heeeeeep."* Another slam to the hood made it go.

There were eight lanes running at the auction house. It took less than a minute per vehicle to enter, drive through, and sell. The only people looking like they were having any fun were the ringmen; they were the New York Street Cops of the auction.

"Testify–Let's go-Let's go." The auctioneer in lane six called to a wholesaler, prompting him to get up or block.

Max was building his inventory securely by selling clean cars he'd gotten from the auction houses, and adding trade-ins to his inventory. Going forward there would be no more than one car carrier trailer delivery a week. Max was going for the slow and steady build.

He was a lucky man who had married up. Opal, with her long legs and deep-dimpled smile still made his heart ache. He made the sun rise if he made her smile. Max swore he would make a success out of this dealership or die trying. With Opal's faith, her love, her inheritance and her trust fund, it was going to be a triumph. It had to be.

A blinding spotlight flashed on Max's face as the sun shot off chrome in lane seven. It brought him back to the shirtless men in long, baggy shorts that were washing and polishing cars. Between lane five and six, a man in a wheelchair was selling popcorn for a dollar a bag. Hugh was there buying two bags. It was good popcorn.

A new auctioneer was exercising his mouth. Eight lanes moving with vehicles created a constant rumble of thunder. At 2:45 p.m. Max's eyes burned from the steady breeze of exhaust fumes.

Max and Hugh took a break on the bleachers where heat reached under Max's shirt and a '97 Range Rover passed behind them. They were surrounded by white t-shirts pushed to the limit by beer guts, and men wearing diamonds and gold on every finger, gold nugget bracelets and thick gold chain necklaces. Cellphones were clipped to the men's belts along with self-important beepers.

Many of these men studied people for weaknesses to take advantage of them. Some were experienced liars appearing relaxed when they made direct eye contact that tickled the edge of piercing. Max wasn't like that.

There were honest, good car-guys. There were. Max believed he found one in Hugh. Max had known Hugh for over five years and had worked several deals with him. Hugh came highly recommended as a trustworthy business man, he had extensive experience, was loyal to his employer, and most importantly had a large client base. Max felt lucky to have him on his team.

"*Hey-Hey-Yo.* What's wrong with you man? Hey," the ringman yelled directly at Hugh.

"Hey Virgil," Hugh greeted.

Virgil Stewart was the perfect age for a man, not young, not old, spot-on his prime at thirty-six years old. He wore the look of a leading man with his receding hairline and cleft chin. Hugh had both the hairline and chin too, but Hugh was past-prime and taking steps toward timeworn. Max was only five years behind Hugh, but didn't color the gray out of his hair. Max was wearing his graying hairs with honor.

Hugh knew Virgil liked being called a ringman. It made Virgil think of himself working in a circus, and a car auction was definitely the freak show in the auto industry circus. Virgil loved it. Besides being a ringman, Virgil picked up shifts as a car transport driver.

Hugh also knew Virgil's long-term goal was to become a licensed auctioneer, and was working his way up by learning all aspects of the auction house. Hugh knew a great deal about Virgil. They'd met at a club of like-minded men many years ago. They had a lot in common. A lot that people didn't usually talk about.

"Hey that maroon '97 Ford Taurus LX four door sedan is about to come through," Virgil said.

"The one with 4,221 miles?" Max asked.

"The very same."

"Great. That's the last one I want."

Virgil went into ringman mode, bouncing Max's bid back at his auctioneer, "*Yup-Yup-Yup.*"

A few circles back and forth, the gavel smacked at the sound block, a hand hit the hood then, *"Go-Go-Go."*

Hugh asked, "So, Virgil, are you going to be driving these cars out to us again?"

"Sure, if you want me to. Just let the-powers-that-be know and I'll do it."

"Sounds good," Hugh nodded. Turning to Max, Hugh added: "Whenever Virgil brings the cars out, he wipes them down clean. Makes life easier."

"Works for me," Max agreed. "I'll put in a standing request for him."

Walking toward his car, Hugh watched Virgil lean against the building, inhale a deep drag of a cigarette, and like a chimney on a winter's day blow precise white rings.

As if passing a secret, the two men nodded to each other.

Chapter 6

Forward - 2008

"Yeah. I'm a psychopath. I have rage. I'm dangerous," Brad Denver admitted to the empty chair. Alice Rayburn's killer continued, "What the hell else do you want me to say?"

How much psychotherapy have you had?

"Enough to know that I rank high on the crazy graph."

What do you mean, crazy graph?

Brad fluffed his pillow on the single bed and tucked his thread-bare blanket tightly in place as he spoke.

"I'd been in here about three years when they sent in some researcher who did a brain scan on a bunch of us. I apparently have a defect and don't process emotion, self-control, or judgement. But seeing how I pled guilty, the prosecutors argued that I chose not to control my savagery. Savagery really? Was it savage? I don't see it. Anyway they sent me here rather than a nuthouse. Win-win for me."

Brad sat on the bed facing his tiny desk and the empty chair that was pulled out. "As far as the researcher's results, on a scale of zero to forty, with forty being the highest level of psychopathy, I rank thirty-nine. If you're normal, you probably rank three or four."

I have a question. The jury would have sentenced you to death but instead you admitted to abducting, raping and killing that third little girl so you could get life without parole. Now that Illinois abolished capital punishment and there is no death row, shouldn't you have been moved to double celled housing rather than stay in this single cell?

"Probably should be there but after the last two attempts on my life they decided to keep me in isolation. I'm always by myself. Eat alone. Get one hour of recreation outside of my cell alone. And I get three non-contact visits a week."

Sorry to interrupt, but do you get many visitors?

"I send letters to my known victims' families, but oddly enough, no one wants to come. They're too afraid. Whatever."

Brad cleared his throat and shrugged. "The first year I was here my mother came to visit me twice, but she stopped coming and hasn't answered my calls in nine years. Maybe she's dead. I don't know. Just found out my brother's dead. She could be, too."

What do you mean by known victims? Are there more than the three murders and five rape victims you confessed to?

"Seriously?" Brad smirked. "Think about it. I was born this way. I've always been like this. I was twenty-six years old when they caught me for five rape victims that are still alive and the three dead ones they could prove. But they could only prove them because I told them. Yeah, there are a lot more. A lot. But confessing to any of them isn't going to get me out of here so why the hell would I give them the satisfaction of knowing?"

Could any of your victims have done anything differently to survive?

"Nah, once I had them, they were… just things. Things to play with, to use. When I was done, I was done. Just threw 'em away. No big deal."

He spun the empty chair. "The ones I raped and let go? I knew I wouldn't get caught for those. I was safe. Hell, I was even stopped by a cop an hour after killing that last one in LaSalle County. Should have been two, but the one little shit got away. Anyway, cops are stupid. That cop stopped me, took my information, looked in my car and let me go."

Brad leaned forward, "Ya' know, five days later I was just about to get that little shit again. She was so close, almost in reach when the real surprise came. Cops arrested me right there, just outside her yard, for one of the sex attacks, not the murder. Dumb bitch talked. Women aren't supposed to talk about that kind of shit. They're supposed to shut-up and take it. Bitches. You can't trust them. Especially the older ones. "

Can we go back to the attempts on your life? What happened?

"Some guys jumped me and stabbed me. Once in the shower. Once in the hall. But I'm still here. Fuck 'em. Apparently it's frowned upon in here that I go after little girls. Women they don't care about. It's the little girls. These guys don't like that shit. So, I spend my time alone. Luckily, with the turnover of inmates, the new guys in here don't know what I'm in for. I'll keep it that way and stay alive. I figure I got another fifty years of free food. Free medical. Free time. It's all good."

The cell was stark. A small shelf above the desk held two books, *Thinking, Fast and Slow* by Daniel Kahneman, and T*he Complete Folk & Fairy Tales of the Brothers Grimm* by Wilhelm Grimm and Jacob Grimm. Nothing hung on the walls. A few toiletries sat on the sink. The room was faceless. Empty, except for Brad Denver and the empty chair.

A guard paused outside Brad Denver's cell to listen and watch Denver play-act at being interviewed by the empty chair that sat across from him.

Do you have any regrets?

"Yeah," Brad said to the chair. "That dark-haired one that got away. I'd like a chance at her. Maybe I'll write her another letter. Dear Betty… come back."

"HEY ASS-WIPE, SHUT THE FUCK UP!" came from the next cell.

Brad Denver scanned his empty cell. Lately, the best conversations he had were the ones he had with himself.

The guard shook his head in disgust and moved on down the block.

Chapter 7

Back - 1998

Futrell Aurora/Naperville Used Cars was up and running with Max as the Dealer, Hugh as the Used Car Manager, and their business manager, Neil Parker. Neil started in the car business straight out of high school and was an F&I manager by the age of twenty-five. At thirty-two, Neil came to Futrell Aurora/Naperville Used Cars from the Norwick Buick/Olds dealership in DeKalb, where he was making a quarter-million a year. He was a hell of an F&I man, but he'd gone as far as he could in that small college town. Neil wanted to move closer to the city, not in Chicago, but closer to it, mostly because his partner, Kent, wanted to live in Oak Park.

Neil was gay, though no one knew, at least no one said anything about it. Kent and Neil had been together for four years, sharing a better marriage than any couple they knew. Same-sex marriage wasn't legal and probably wouldn't be in their lifetime, but to Neil and Kent their commitment to each other was stronger than steel.

Neil would do anything for Kent, who to Neil looked like a stylish, young Liberace that could pull off a bow tie. Neil was no slouch either. He wore impeccably tailored suits made in Italy, medium-starched shirts and silk ties. His blond hair was perfectly tousled, his face clean shaven, and his nails manicured.

Max and Opal met Neil and Kent at a dealer show in Las Vegas a few years back and knew they were a couple. It made no difference to Max and Opal. They liked them. So when Max offered Neil the job starting as F&I business manager at the used car lot along with the promise of all of Max's dealerships to come, Neil grabbed it. He knew this type of opportunity didn't come along often, or at all, for a gay man working in a testosterone infused, homophobic business. With Max and Opal on his side, Neil felt protected, almost safe. He and Kent would continue to mask their sexuality and stay in the closet for the rest of their lives, but with this job, they'd be able to afford a private closet in an exclusive neighborhood.

As Futrell's F&I manager, Neil controlled every sale and generated profit, lots of it. He knew the best bank buy-rates, how to get a customer approved even with bad or no credit. He could sell GAP coverage, credit insurance, service contracts, maintenance plans, and all the after-market products their customers could ever want, and made each piece go down like cream pie.

He was a master of paperwork and trained both Hugh and Max on gathering information accurately and quickly, not that Max needed any training on it, but Hugh, although a crackerjack of stock and an adept salesman, he was not comfortable with legal forms of any kind. Hugh liked to knock 'em in the creek and dump 'em at Neil's door.

With only the three of them in the sales trailer, there were days Hugh had to know where to have the customer sign and on which forms. Some days, depending on a rare day off or auctions, there would only be two in the office and at times only one person for lunch time or emergencies. Those were the times Hugh hated. Hugh, the oldest of the three, was a two-fingered typist who despised computers. Neil recognized this about Hugh and was an understanding trainer.

Two months had passed since they opened Futrell Aurora/Naperville Used Cars, and in that short time Max had netted over sixty-thousand dollars. Of course he couldn't bank on that amount every two months, but at this rate, conservatively, he and Opal would have an annual net income of over $300,000 this first year, which meant they would be able to finance, buy, and build the Ford/Lincoln-Mercury dealership on the northwest corner. Next up would be getting the Toyota dealership built on the southwest corner. After that they'd put the Honda dealership across the street on the southeast corner. And somewhere in that time frame, Max would move his family out of the trailer and into a real house.

For now at least the commute home is quick, Max thought as he walked across the back lot to their trailer home.

Chapter 8

Still - 1998

"Bus is coming. Get your backpacks and lunch," Opal called. End of August and thanks to their dad the school bus drove straight through the used cars lot to park in front of their trailer home.

It was the most embarrassing experience to date in the lives of both Vette and Woody. Grabbing their things, both ran to the bus just outside their front door. They thanked God with every step that they were the second group to board the bus in the morning, and the second to last, who got off in the afternoon.

Randy Wheel, a mean high schooler, sat in the very back. Nobody messed with Randy because he would hurt you bad. Randy didn't bother with Vette or Woody. They lived in a trailer. He lived in an apartment behind his mother's nail salon. So what if he had to clean out the pedicure bowls, at least he wasn't trailer trash.

Vette went to the left side of the bus, third row back, and Woody took the right side, one row up. School buses are segregated by age and class. Woody was beginning fifth grade at the elementary school, and Vette seventh grade at the junior high school, but they sat close on the bus just in case one needed the other.

Making a great impression on the first day of school was crucial. They both wore their interpretation of the best version of themselves. Dressing as a character from TV's Stargate SG-1, Woody wore a black-collared Polo shirt, black jeans, and a military-green bomber-windbreaker. All he was missing was a rifle strapped to his leg.

Vette, influenced by Beverly Hills 90210, was in white jeans, a white tank, and a worn blue-jean jacket with the sleeves rolled up. The moment they were about to sit, the bus driver stepped on the gas sending their butts into the seats.

Across the empty lots north of the car lot was the West Jefferson Estates subdivision where Shelley KerPatrick held the binoculars against her second floor bedroom window, watching the yellow bus move.

"Bus," she screamed, dropped the binoculars, ran down the stairs, grabbed her backpack, kissed her mother and ran out the door.

"Have a good day Sweet-Swirl," her mother called and blew her a kiss.

Shelley grabbed the air to her right and put the air kiss to her lips. Her dad had given her the nickname Sweet-Swirl when she was in diapers. Her skin tone was a blend of honey, vanilla, and chocolate, so Sweet-Swirl fit. Her mom was mostly French with a smidge of Norwegian, and her dad was a combo-platter of African, Scottish, Jamaican, and Native American.

Shelley's jet black hair from her African side, was lighter than air and softer than water. It could span the width of her shoulders to cascade down to her chest when natural, but today was a cornucopia of box braids thanks to her mother's help. Shelley's sumptuous lips sported Carmex and her slim nose and high cheekbones showed clean. She wore bib-overall jean shorts with a white tank underneath, and a white blazer was thrown over her arm in case she got cold. But the blazer would stay in her locker for the day. She rarely got cold.

The bus drove through the car lot on the edge of Naperville, turned north onto the four-lane highway, and went to the next light to turn right on West Jefferson Avenue where it stopped just before Ambassador Drive to pick up the hordes of kids from the subdivision.

Shelley's best friend, Sarah Wilson, had moved over the summer. Her family was following their pastor to California, which seemed weird to Shelley but it was also very sad. She was lonely for Sarah. Climbing on the bus, Shelley saw a new girl with long blonde hair who looked just like a young Princess Bride.

"Can I sit with you?" Shelley asked.

"Sure," Vette said scooting over toward the window.

"You look just like Buttercup in The Princess Bride." Shelley said.

"The Princess Bride?"

"Don't tell me you've never seen it," Shelley said.

"Inconceivable," Vette said then firmly added, "Farm boy, polish my horse's saddle. I want to see my face shining in it by morning."

"As you wish," Shelley replied. They both burst into giggles. "It's my favorite movie."

"Mine too. I think I've watched it a hundred times."

"Me too." Vette smiled.

"I'm Shelley KerPatrick, and I'm in Mrs. Swanson's seventh grade."

"Me too!" Vette couldn't believe her luck. "I'm Vette."

"Say your last name too. Girls usually only say their first name, whereas boys give both first and last names. Girls need to be as strong as boys."

"Are you a feminist?" Vette asked.

"Yes," Shelley cocked her head. "At least I think so, if you mean by feminist that I stand up for myself and won't take less than a boy."

"That's what I mean."

"Are you a feminist too?"

"Truly you have a dizzying intellect." Vette smiled quoting from The Princess Bride. "I am no one to be trifled with, and yes I am a feminist."

They were instant friends.

"Is your full name Yvette with a Y or E?"

"If I tell you the truth of my name, you have to promise not to speak of it to anyone," with a wink Vette added, "or prepare to die."

Shelley snorted and laughed.

"My name is Corvette Honey Futrell. My mother allowed my dad to name me and my brother, so being the dork that my dad is, he named us after cars."

"No."

"Yes. My brother's name is Woody Wynn Futrell. But it could have been worse. Dad loves airplanes too, so we could have been Piper and Cub."

"Shelley was my grandmother's name. Nothing as cool as your names." Shelley cocked her head in question. "I get Corvette but why Woody? Is that a car?"

"Yeah, it's like an old Ford station-wagon only taller with wood on the outside."

Woody heard his name and turned to them. Looking directly at Shelley, he asked, "What are you?"

Shelley asked, "What?"

"Are you black or white or what?" Just then the bus pulled up to the elementary school. Not caring about an answer, Woody jumped up and ran off the bus.

Vette rolled her eyes. "Don't pay any attention to him. Siblings suck. Woody is a disorder with no filter. Sorry."

Chapter 9

Forward – 2008

DATE OF BIRTH: 04/06/1969 SEX: F RACE: W WEIGHT: 167 HEIGHT: 503

He went back to the alley to see if she was dead and she was. He found a man with the blanket he'd left for her wrapped around his shoulders.

"What happened to the woman who lived in that box?" he asked, pointing to the recently inhabited box.

The man pulled the blanket tightly around his shoulders, and said: "She died a few hours after you left."

"I've never been here before," he said pointedly.

The man took a step back. "Okay. Sure. Can you give me some money? I'm hungry."

"No money, but I can give you this." He handed him a paper bag that held one muffin. He thought, no witnesses.

The homeless man looked into the bag, grabbed it, and walked away. The Good Samaritan saw him throw the paper bag and muffin into a burning barrel.

Once in his car, the Good Samaritan opened his Criminal Watchdog List. He pulled up eighty-seven registered sex offenders within twenty miles of his home, where he'd grown up. Their old home neighborhood was infested with them. It seemed to be a breeding ground for sex offenders.

How could his parents have not known that? How could they have put their own children in such grave danger? Back then his parents didn't have the Internet. They couldn't look up who was a sex offender or where they lived or what ages of children they attacked. He couldn't blame his parents. They'd had no clue. But he knew and now he was doing something about it.

Having expanded his offender's list to Chicagoland, he found thousands of convicted sex offenders. He narrowed his search to contain only a select target market. His targets, including this last woman, had all committed aggravated criminal sexual abuse on victims from infants up to the age of twelve-years-old.

Flipping through his listings, he found Janice Stanley Knight who was the woman from the alley who, together with her boyfriend, had raped a five-year-old boy, beat him unconscious, slit his throat, and left him for dead. Miraculously the boy had survived, and now Janice was dead.

Janice had only served a third of her twenty-year sentence due to prison overcrowding. Her boyfriend was still in prison, unfortunately.

A red X marked Janice's record and the page was moved to the completed folder. The Good Samaritan then pulled out Amy Miller's sheet, the only other female in his thick file. Amy had sold her three-year-old daughter for sex since the girl was two years old to pay for Amy's opioid drug habit. Amy had been prosecuted, served her time, and was living alone just ten miles away. Her daughter was lost in the foster-care system.

Closing the plastic container of toxic muffins, he laid her sheet on the passenger seat. "Down. Settle," he said to his massive dog in the backseat.

He parked in front of her apartment, put a muffin in a paper bag, and went to her door. His beloved dog lifted his head just enough to watch his person go into the building.

"Hello?" came from the peep hole. He knew it was Amy.

"Hi. I'm Thomas Hill. I live on the fourth floor and wanted to welcome you to the building."

He watched the door open three inches; just wide enough for Amy to peek out, and if need be, narrow enough to leverage her hefty weight to slam it shut.

"Hi," he said again with a big smile and took a step back to make Amy feel safer.

As the door opened wider, he saw Amy's chest drop as if she'd been holding her breath. He extended the paper bag to her.

"This is one of my famous welcome muffins," he said. "Let me know if you like it. I'm in 402, but I'm just heading out now." He turned to leave, adding "It's actually best if you eat it while it's fresh tonight."

Amy smiled. "Thank you I will." She took a bite out of the muffin. "Yum. That is good. I appreciate it."

"You're welcome. Have a great night."

Back in the car, he reached into the back and stroked his dog's fur. "Good boy," he said, as he wrote the date and time on Amy's sheet. He added the type of muffin and re-filed her sheet in the progress file. He would have to chart her departure through the local obituaries and news.

He'd finally reached the precipice. He was the welcoming committee, hoping to bring hundreds of pedophiles a painful one-time-only death experience. It would never match the wreckage they had left behind with their actions, but it did give him a fleeting sense of peace as he thinned the herd.

That was a good thing, but it didn't last. It didn't remove it. The mask was too strong.

Chapter 10

Still - 2008

"We have to go." Ten years had passed since Betty Harte first heard her best friend, seven-year-old Alice Rayburn say those words to her as they stood on the side of the gravel road. Every night for ten years that scene replayed in Betty's head.

Betty was eighteen, though in her recurring dream, Alice was still seven each time she repeated her plea to leave.

They'd been riding bikes, but their bikes were dropped on their sides in the ditch. Betty felt the man's fingers latch onto her neck. His sweaty hand clutching the back of her neck. She flew through the open window. A ball through a goal.

She was in the car jerking the handle, willing the door open. He wasn't there. He was chasing Alice. Betty's heart raced, banging against her chest. The locking knobs that go up and down were jammed deep down into the door. No locks to unlock. The driver's side window was wide open. She lunged over, just about to jump out and fall to the gravel, when she looked in the backseat.

"Come back here with me," Alice said to her. She was smiling.

Betty was in the back with Alice. They beamed at each other. There was no fear. No urgency.

A man in the front seat was waving at a little girl running toward the car. He wasn't their abductor, he was different. He was their rescuer.

"The bad man can't hurt us anymore," Alice said. "He's gone. Gone far away."

"Who is that?" Betty pointed to the man now out of the car hugging the little girl.

"Oh, that's Jack. He saved us."

"But Alice, you weren't saved. We weren't saved," Betty said.

"Oh yes we were. You'll see," Alice said. She calmly opened the back door and took Betty by the hand. "Come on."

They walked away from the car. Alice handed Betty an original rainbow ice cream cone and started to skip. Betty matched her steps, while licking her cone.

It was a delicious dream that always ended with the car out of sight, ice cream on their chins, and the sound of the two little girls giggling.

Waking brought the nightmare of memory.

Alice pinned under the man's arm. Betty cowering, not helping Alice. Watching the car drive away, Alice's terrified expression. Police interrogating Betty. It was her fault. If she had listened to Alice. If they'd left. But Betty didn't and Alice was dead.

It was a month after Alice's murder that eight-year-old Betty learned the gruesome details. Small towns are like that. No secret is ever left unsaid.

Alice's ravaged body was found face down in a drainage ditch held down by flat rocks, under water, two days after her eighth birthday. Naked except for the beaded-word necklace spelling her nickname, Lissy. Alice was abducted, raped, and drowned in a creek. She died within hours of being taken.

Betty's memory took her back with her parents to St. Paul's Lutheran Cemetery three miles south of town. She'd watched the two caskets, Alice's and her father's, both being lowered into the deep holes.

Alice's mom crumbling to the ground, howling like an animal. Sixteen-year-old Carlton, her oldest, on his knees next to her, holding her in his arms. Twelve-year-old Cody standing ram-rod straight, his head bowed slightly, with his angry eyes looking up at the crowd.

The man, Brad Denver, was in jail never to be killed, never to be let out. His medical needs, food, housing, and education paid for by the government for all the days of his life.

It was years after that awful day when Betty overheard her own mother and Alice's mother talking about Brad Denver. Telling how two years after being imprisoned at the Collinsville Correctional Center, the convicted killer was stabbed with a homemade knife nine times in the chest and arm by another inmate. But destiny is capricious and he lived. They talked about how inmates convicted of killing or molesting children were the targets of other prisoners.

Today, Betty's hope was the same as it was then, that the man would be raped then stabbed at least five times a week for the rest of his life. She realized early on that time doesn't heal shit. The nightmare continues because life goes on.

Betty's body blossomed early into a Mae West 36DD with a 27-inch-waist and 37-inch hips. Her curvy five-foot, four-inch frame compacted one-hundred-forty pounds perfectly into a form-fitting size eight, and because of that she wore a size fourteen. It was either camouflage or gain an extra fifty pounds. Whatever it took to hide her body, she would have done it. At eighteen, the extra weight wouldn't come, so loose clothing became her shield.

She couldn't remember a time when she wasn't terrified of everything. From the night of the abduction, Betty had slept with her parents, and continued to until she started developing at age twelve. One, or both of her parents, had to accompany her everywhere. She was home-schooled because she couldn't deal with the fear of living.

Bit by bit, with the help of numerous psychiatrists, psychologists, and her parents, Betty was able to pretend to be a human in the world. After years and years of pretending, she started to believe just enough to go out on her own, to drive, and finally to go to college.

Betty's parents remained close friends with Alisha, Alice's mom. So to help Betty with the transition into the world, Alisha suggested Betty live with her through the college years. It was a godsend.

The only way Betty got through that first year of college was by living at Alice's mom's house which was mere blocks from the campus in Naperville. Alisha welcomed Betty with open arms. But it wasn't Betty being hugged. Betty knew she was a conduit to Alice, and all that did for Betty was to trigger guilt. I'm alive and Alice is dead guilt.

Even so, Betty was grateful to Alisha, Carlton, and Cody for opening their home to her and keeping her safe in the terrifying world that was her life. Carlton and Cody weren't there much. At least Carlton wasn't.

Cody had graduated from University of Illinois and stayed on to learn more about molecular biology, environmental sciences, ecology, and agronomy, but mostly he stayed to get his PhD in Plant Sciences. He had three years left to go. So about the same time Betty would graduate with a Bachelors in Elementary Education, Cody would have his PhD.

Like Betty, Cody wanted to teach, but he preferred college-aged students rather than first graders. Besides having the love of teaching in common, they had gin, poker, 500, Crazy Eights, and their favorite card game, euchre. But they only got to play that when both Carlton and Alisha completed the foursome.

"Well, look who's here," Alisha said and opened her arms to welcome Cody with a warm hug. Although the drive from Urbana-Champaign was two-and-a-half hours one way, Alisha noticed over the last year Cody had been coming home more and more weekends. He was coming to be with Betty, but neither Cody, nor Betty, admitted it.

But a mother knows.

"Hey ma," Cody said, as he lifted her off the floor in a tight hug. Seeing Betty come down the staircase, Cody set his mother down and went to Betty with outstretched arms.

"Cody," Betty mock-protested as he lifted and swung her once around. "Put me down."

"Why, you got a hot date?" he asked, as he gently set her down.

She said, "No." Looking up at him she asked, "Do you?"

"You bet I do."

Her smile dropped. "Really. With who?" she asked, with a slight edge.

Cody walked to the record player, put on the Bob Seger album, chose the song and cranked up the volume.

He leaned down to look directly into Betty's honey-brown eyes. "With you and a deck of cards. So grab a hold of something and hold on tight "Betty Lou's gettin' out tonight.""

With the bass pumping against the walls, Cody took Betty in his arms and led her in their perfectly practiced welcome-home ritual dance: the jitterbug.

Alisha stood by the kitchen entrance beaming as the two laughed and twirled around the room.

They were a beautiful couple. Her long coal-black hair swinging with each spin, he with his dark hair, thick moustache, and lean build. He flawlessly guided her around the room. There was a full foot-and-a-half difference in their height, but they fit together perfectly.

Alisha wondered when they would see it too.

Chapter 11

Back - 1998

Vette and Shelley wore a path from Vette's trailer home to Shelley's back door and vice versa. Opal stood outside and watched across the vacant lots as Vette walked to Shelley's home to make sure she got there safe. And Shelley's mom, Diane, did the same.

If the girls went anywhere else they first had to notify both mothers and then call them both once they arrived at the new destination. No exceptions. If they didn't call, and God forbid either mother called them, the girls knew there was hell to pay and they would have to go home immediately. They always kept their mothers informed. Always.

Today, Vette had to bring Woody with her to Shelley's house because Opal and Max were off together at an auction or running some errands, Vette wasn't sure what they were doing but did know they wouldn't be back until after 6:00 p.m. They would pick up Vette and Woody from Shelley's when they got back.

Virgil Stewart, the ringman and part-time car transport driver, pulled into the lot with a new delivery of cars from the auction house. He parked in the back and started off-loading. Once unloaded and the cars wiped down, he took the paperwork in to Neil, Hugh, or Max, whoever was handy. Neil was alone in the sales trailer when Virgil walked in.

"Hey Neil, here's the bill of sales for the batch I just off-loaded and put out back."

"Thanks Virgil," Neil said. "How's it going for you today?"

"It's been crazy, crazy, crazy. I just realized it's 3:30 and I haven't even had time for lunch." Virgil pointed his thumb towards his truck transport and asked, "Is it okay if I leave the truck here while I walk over to Hooter's for a burger and fries? They get pissed if I park over there."

"Can the school bus get around you?" Neil asked.

"Yeah, I pulled over close to the trailer, so the bus can drop off Vette and Woody no problem."

"Then sure." Neil answered, wondering how Virgil knew the kid's names. Max of course, he thought.

"Where's Hugh today?"

"You just missed him. He ran out a minute ago to get something to eat. Not sure where he went; maybe you'll see him at Hooter's." Neil said.

"You hungry? I can bring you something back if you want." Virgil offered.

"Oh, I'm good. I brought lunch today, and anyway it's my short day. I'm out of here at seven."

Virgil mock-saluted and headed out. Neil watched from the window as Virgil cut across the busy, four-lane highway and disappeared from sight.

Chapter 12

Still - 1998

He had draped a white extra-large bath sheet across their navy down comforter. An open jar of petroleum jelly was to the right of the towel, its blue lid on the end table. The room was dark with the drapes pulled tight.

In his hand he held the white, full face unpainted mask. It was expressionless. He could have gotten the Venetian, Comedy, Tragedy, or even a bunny mask. All were unpainted. All basic white. But this was the one he'd used for over thirty years. He had a spare mask at home just in case, but this was the one that made it all work. Whenever he put it on, they became objects, play things to be used and tossed.

He didn't know why he did it. It might have been for the sex, but he didn't really understand why. He wished he understood.

The bus pulled up. Taking a deep breath, he put the mask on and took his place behind the front door. The two got off the bus. He had hoped for just the boy, but would deal with the girl.

Vette and Woody were out of the bus, and ran around Virgil's car carrier. They promised their mom that morning they would do their homework before walking over to Shelley's house. Once done with their homework they had to call Shelley to let her, and more importantly, her mom, know they were on their way. Diane would watch them walk over and call their mom to let her know the moment they arrived.

Both Vette and Shelley had done their homework, partly in study hall, and finished the rest on the bus so that they could have more time together. Vette had instructed Woody he had to do his homework on the bus so they could dump their stuff and run over to Shelley's. Luckily Woody didn't have any homework.

The trailer door was never locked. They burst through the door, Vette first with Woody an inch behind. The door slammed shut behind them. They were grabbed by the back of their hair, strategically aimed away from the intruder.

Book bags fell to the floor as they were pulled back against their captor.

Behind them, the voice said, "If either of you scream or look at me, I will slit the other's throat in front of you, then I'll slit yours." A whispered hum through the mask. His breath confined within the mask warmed his face. "If either of you ever talk about this to anyone, ever, I will come back, cut your parents throats then do the same to you. Then I'll burn this fucking trailer to the ground with all of you in it."

Vette took Woody's hand, squeezed and held tight as they were thrust into their parents' bedroom. The door banged shut behind them.

He grabbed each by the shoulders. First Vette. Next Woody. Shoving them face first against the wall. He ordered, "Take off your clothes. Now."

Tears fell silently from Woody's eyes and Vette saw that he had wet himself. She squeezed his hand and with a slight nod began taking off her clothes.

Vette knew as the man took pictures of their naked bodies that she would be raped. Woody just needed to face the wall, not say a word and he would be saved. No memories. No pictures in his head. No pain.

But when the man pulled Woody back to the bed Vette screamed, "Noooo. Take me, not him."

"Shut up girl or I'll slit his throat."

Vette and Woody were silent. When Vette vomited on the floor, she did so silently. When blood trickled from Woody's lip from biting down, he did it silently.

On and on and on it went until the man flung Woody next to Vette, their faces to the wall. Woody's body now cowered, his stature shrunken. Blood was running from his lip down his chin. Directly behind them both, the man took scissors and cut a section of Woody's hair, next he lifted Vette's long hair and cut a section of her hair from underneath. Both hair samples went into a baggy.

"Don't move." The man wiped himself with the towel, put the lid on the petroleum jelly and threw both at their feet. The baggy and their picture were in his pocket as he turned to leave.

Expecting to be pulled to the bed for her turn, Vette jerked slightly when the petroleum jar rolled over to hit her foot. She saw the man open the bedroom door. He was dressed in black, was taller than their dad, and wore a white mask that wiped his face away exposing only small sections of a balding scalp.

"Vette." The man's muffled reprimand snapped her back in position. He fucked up. He said her name. "Stay where you are for the count of five hundred or I'll come back, kill you both and your parents. Don't ever tell anyone, anyone about this. Ever."

Vette and Woody started counting.

From the moment they ran from the bus to this counting, only thirty minutes had passed. Thirty minutes. Less than an episode of Murphy Brown.

At the count of five, Vette ran to the back and front doors, locked them, then ran back to their parents' room. Woody hadn't moved. He stood facing the wall, counting. Vette rushed into the bathroom grabbed a towel and wrapped Woody tight. Holding him snug against her she took him into the bathroom where she filled a bubble bath and eased him into it. Woody hadn't said a word. He stared forward as if he'd gone away, left his withered shell of a body behind.

Vette gathered Woody's soiled underwear and jeans, along with the rest of her clothes and the petroleum jelly, and wrapped it all in the wretched bath sheet. Cleaning the vomit off the floor she glanced at Woody. He hadn't moved.

Wearing clean clothes, Vette brought in fresh clothes for Woody. He still hadn't moved, but… ever so softly she heard him counting, "100… 101… 102… 103…" On he counted.

"Okay. Okay. That's enough. We're done with this. After now, we'll never talk about this to anyone, ever," Vette said as she knelt next to the bathtub and gently washed her brother clean. All Vette wanted to do was run to her mother. Tell her everything. She couldn't. The man knows where we live. He knows my name. He'll come back for Woody. He'll come back.

Vette had to protect Woody. They couldn't talk about this to anyone. She spoke softly, "It's my fault. I should have stopped him. I should have… it's my fault. I'm sorry. I'm sorry. He was a bad, bad, bad man. He will never, ever come back here again. I'll keep you safe. I'll never let him come back." Tears rolled down her cheeks. "I'll kill him. I'll kill him myself. I promise you that. I'll kill him. No one will ever hurt you again, Woody. Woody, I promise you that."

Vette began singing through her tears to Woody. "Taint Nobody's Biz-ness If I Do" was one of his favorites and it was the only song her staggered mind could attach to at that moment.

The verses and refrain flowed randomly. The un-orderliness of it, made it almost bearable, but not quite.

> *"If I should take a notion*
> *To jump into the ocean,*
> *'TAIN'T NOBODY'S BIZ-NESS IF I DO.*
>
> *If I go to church on Sunday,*
> *Then cabaret on Monday,*
> *'TAIN'T NOBODY'S BIZ-NESS IF I DO.*
>
> *If I kill him with a knife,*
> *And we live a happy life,*
> *'TAIN'T NOBODY'S BIZ-NESS IF WE DO.*

She changed the last line for him and for her. As she tenderly washed him, and sang to him, tears began rolling down Woody's plump ten-year-old cheeks.

Woody's mind began his process of building blocks to bind this thing, this memory, behind a mask of a wall. Before the self-imposed blocking silence fucked up his childhood, his adolescence, his entire life, his ten-year-old confused mind pondered what had just happened.

Why didn't I fight? Why did I have an erection while he raped me? Am I ruined? Boys aren't raped. What if I'm found out? Am I not going to be a man now? What will I be? What am I?

His blocking mask of silence slammed shut. There would be no answers.

Chapter 13

Still – 1998

It had been over an hour and Vette and Woody still hadn't come. Shelley watched through the binoculars as the car hauler drove off the lot, and a man in black carried something white around to the front of the trailer, but that all happened over thirty minutes ago. Neither Vette nor Woody had any homework. She knew that for a fact. What was taking them so long?

Enough is enough, Shelley thought. "Mom, I'm going to walk over to Vette's house to get them. I'll be right back." She ran out the back door.

Shelley's mom called after her, "You come right back. No lollygagging."

"Okay," Shelley called back thinking, *what the heck is lollygagging?*

She turned the knob on the trailer's back door. It was locked. Banging on the door she called, "Vette. What are you doing?"

The battering of the door sent Woody, now fully dressed, racing into Vette's arms. When they heard Shelley's voice, both their bodies relaxed.

"Coming," Vette yelled. Holding Woody close to her, Vette went to the junk drawer in the kitchen, pulled out two vintage pocket knives and offered one to Woody saying, "Keep this in your pocket and never tell anyone you have it. I'll do the same. We'll learn how to open them with one hand. Promise you'll never tell anyone and you won't cut yourself, okay?"

Woody nodded and put the two-inch closed knife in his pocket as Vette answered the door.

"What the hell happened to your beautiful hair?" Shelley exclaimed.

"I cut it off. Will you help me shave the back?" Vette asked. "I can't reach it."

Shelley looked from Vette to Woody and back. Something was off. "Sure, I'm good with a razor. My dad lets me trim his hair."

Fifteen minutes later, Vette's new boy-haircut was complete. "Good," Vette said staring into the mirror. Looking at Woody, she added, "Ready?" He nodded. "Good. Let's go."

Shelley went to pick up the bath sheet bundle. "Want me to throw all this in the laundry room?"

"No." Vette grabbed the wretched bundle out from under her. "I'll take it. Give me a minute." Nodding toward Woody, Vette added, "Stay with him and I'll meet you both at the back door."

"Uh. K." Shelley said softly.

Vette shoved the wadded sheet to the very back corner of her closet and covered it with an old blanket.

Watching out the back window of the sales trailer, Neil said to Hugh, "Looks like the kids are heading to their friend's house now."

Hugh, back from his errands, followed Neil's gaze and saw the three children heading north through the empty backlot. "That's good. Do you want to call Max to let him know, or do you want me to?"

"I will," Neil said heading to his office. Neil liked watching out for the kids. Vette and Woody were smart and funny. They'd hang out in the sales trailer when it was slow, and vanish when it was busy. *It'll be lonely once they move into a new house,* he thought reaching for the phone.

Vette and Woody heard their Mom's voice at Shelley's front door and raced down the stairs toward her. Woody reached her first, grabbing her around the waist, Opal's arm automatically wrapped around him. Vette latched onto her other side, Opal smiled at Diane and said, "Well, it sure is nice to be welcomed."

Looking at Vette, then at Diane and back to Vette's lack of hair, Opal said, "Did you go get a haircut?"

Diane answered for her, "No, *we* did not."

"I cut it," Vette announced.

Shelley stepped forward, "And I helped with the back."

Opal smiled at Diane, then looking in Vette's eyes she said, "I really like it. You two did a great job."

Diane smiled, "I'm so glad you'll be staying close. We love having Vette and Woody here."

"I'm thrilled too. We love Shelley and I cannot wait to move in."

Vette looked up at her mother, "Move?"

"We'll talk in a minute. Dad's waiting. You two grab your stuff and go get in the car now."

"Bye Shelley and thanks!" Vette called to her friend. Having no stuff to grab, the two ran to the car and jumped into the back seat.

After backing out of Shelley's driveway and pulling into another driveway, just four houses up, Max asked, "Well what do you two think?"

Vette and Woody looked up at the two-story beige house with the big front porch, gray trim, and red roof. Lush century-old trees surrounded the house and the detached garage, and gave privacy to the big backyard encompassed by five-foot black chain-link fencing.

"It's nice," Vette said. "I can see Shelley's house."

"It's across the street and only four houses down," Max said.

"So you'll always have to look both ways for cars when you cross the street," Opal added.

"What do you mean?" Vette asked, looking puzzled. "Are we moving here?"

"Yes, we are," Max smiled. "You'll be on the same bus route and same schools, too."

Opal wore a Christmas-morning smile as they delivered this great present to their children. "It's not as fancy as our other house, but it already feels like home. It was built in 1916. Think of it, this home was built in the middle of World War One. Isn't that something?"

Opal always attached history lessons to things, Vette half expected to see a landmark boulder slapped with a plaque out front of the house.

Inside the three bedroom, two-and-a-half bath home, there were hardwood floors and wood trim surrounding all the windows and wide-open doorways. The house pulled in so much light through its many windows, it belonged on a farm, not in town.

"Can we move in tonight?" It was the first words Woody had spoken.

"Can we?" Vette echoed.

Max and Opal laughed, relieved that the children were onboard. They had worried the children would think it was not enough. Not grand enough. Not pretty enough. They didn't realize this new home was to be their children's place of refuge and security, or that it came at a time that might actually salvage their children's sanity.

"We closed on the house today," Max said.

"The movers are coming this week," Opal added.

Hand in his pocket, Woody clutched the knife and asked, "Can we get a dog? A big dog?"

Piling out of the car next to their trailer home, Max wrapped Opal in his arms and bent her back with a kiss. "Got to go back to work now," he said.

Vette took Woody's hand in hers. Looking from the trailer to her dad, she asked, "Can we come with you?"

"It's getting kind of late," Opal cautioned.

"Oh, it's just quarter-to-seven," Max said with a plea in his eyes. "Please?"

"Okay," Opal rolled her eyes. "But you have to walk them back here in a half hour, Max."

"Will do!" He blew Opal a kiss. "Come on you two, let's go!"

Vette and Woody automatically walked into Neil's office as he was packing up for the night.

"Hey you guys. So I understand you won't be living here much longer."

"No," Vette said. "We have a new house."

"That's so cool," Neil said. "But we'll miss not having you both here." Turning to Woody, he asked, "What do you think about it?"

Woody stared at the floor and held Vette's hand tight.

"He likes it," Vette answered. "Both our rooms have skylights."

Max called from the far end office, "You two let Neil pack up for the night and come down here."

"Bye Neil," Vette said for both Woody and herself. They walked the narrow hall to their dad. At the door of Hugh's office, she heard him.

"Vette," Hugh called.

She smelled it, and tasted it, before it came. A roller coaster ride of walls shifting up and down, her stomach seized in a cramp as she turned toward Hugh. Vomit exploded out of Vette's mouth, spraying Hugh's pants, outlining his form on the wall behind.

That's not possible. The thought flicked across Vette's mind. It was gone.

Chapter 14

Still – 1998

"She doesn't have a fever and says she feels fine. Do you think it was something she ate?" Opal asked Max.

"Could be, but whatever she ate we can't have her eating that again, that's for sure."

Opal pulled the navy down comforter up to her neck and snuggled closer to Max. "Poor Hugh, I felt so bad for him."

"Yeah, he got the worst of it. He had to go home and Neil ended up staying tonight." Max said. "Thanks for coming and cleaning that up. You know I couldn't do it."

"Yeah, I saw you gagging in your office," Opal said. "Vette wants to go to school tomorrow. I'm going to let her and hope it was a quick bug."

Tucking the comforter around his wife, Max agreed, "I hope you're right. We don't want to be fighting the flu with the movers coming."

At the other end of the trailer, Woody crept across the hall and climbed into bed with Vette. Vette's tears soaked her pillow as she held her brother.

Woody whispered, "Maybe I deserved it."

"Never…, ever say or think that," Vette whispered firmly. "We didn't deserve that. That was a sick, bad, bad man. We're leaving this here, in this trailer and we'll never come back. We're never going to talk about it or think about it. It's over. It's done."

Vette held Woody tight as he sobbed himself to sleep.

This is all my fault, she thought. Vette vigilantly watched the door, opening insomnia into her life.

Chapter 15

Still – 1998

Hugh showered and changed the minute he got home. Luckily he had a pair of jeans in his trunk to change into for the drive home. He put his dress pants in the two-gallon plastic zip bag that Opal had given him.

Once cleaned up, Hugh took his briefcase into his toy room, as Tammy called it. There was a big screen TV, a large hobby table with all of the tools meticulously organized for building his plastic model cars, and a shelf that ran around the entire room displaying his completed models. Thirty-one models sat on the shelf.

Opening his storage closet, he pulled out the new 1941 Ford Custom Woody Car 1/25-scale assembly kit. His briefcase was open on the table and inside was a baggie with hair, a Polaroid picture of two bodies facing a wall, and his white full face unpainted mask. On the baggie in thick black marker was written, *Woody & Vette 1998*.

Hugh looked up at each of the finished models, each model camouflaged one picture and one baggie of hair with a name and date. Each represented another little life he'd ruined.

At the time each happened, he didn't see it that way. He was nicer to the child than any father could be. He loved them. Then somehow it all got twisted in his head and they became nothing to him, just things. Nothing.

It was always now, after… that he saw what he was, who he was. It made him physically sick each time. How could he do this? How could he do it? He vowed he'd never do it again.

But he knew he wouldn't be able to keep that vow. He had never been able to keep it. Never made it over a year. Not since he was eighteen. Never over a year.

He didn't know why he did it. He wished he did, so he could stop. Stop being this person.

Thirty-one models sat on the shelf above him. Holding the thirty-second kit in his hands, Hugh's shoulders shook as he wept.

Chapter 16

Forward – 1999

Max and Opal had been in their new home for three seasons and now the summer garden was blooming. Opal was glad the school year was done. It had been a rough one.

Maybe it was all the changes, the move, their growing hormones, whatever, but Vette and Woody did not have a good year. Woody had turned morose and was like an exposed nerve acting out at the slightest touch, getting into fist fights. Getting into trouble at school. Getting into trouble at home. The only thing that calmed him was his puppy, Sergeant Pepper. Sergeant was attached to Woody like Velcro.

At the same time Vette was sullen one moment, then anxious the next. Thank God for Shelley and her vivacious personality. She was the only one who could pull Vette out of her self-imposed stupor.

Opal stumbled upon a project for Woody when she took him on the Acorn Express tram tour at the Morton Arboretum, a place dedicated to the planting and conservation of trees. For the first time in a year he was actually paying attention. Jumping on

Woody's glimmer of interest, Opal quickly organized a trip to the University of Illinois, College of Veterinary Medicine Poisonous Plant Garden. A perfectly timed trip for just the two of them.

Max was working and Vette was sleeping over at Shelley's, so a mother-son trip to the campus was just right. The student-run garden, of poisonous plants, was a bit ghoulish, but Opal and Max both thought it was just the thing for an adolescent boy. Opal booked the personalized student guided tour. Most of the plants on the tour were native to Illinois, which made it more attention grabbing and gave Woody specific direction to plan his own garden at home.

Janice Keptner, their young guide, handed Woody his own brochure that mapped out the garden and what plants were in each plot. The brochure named the plant, the toxic parts, the toxic principles and the signs of poisoning for animals and humans. They passed through the tall arched iron gates with a large skull and crossbones on top with the words, "These plants can kill."

"Oh my," Opal gasped, as they entered the garden. "It's so beautiful." Each plant had a marker giving the name, description, and of course each was stamped with the skull and crossbones. There were black-eyed Susan plants, hyacinth, azalea bushes, Ohio buckeye trees, lily of the valley, buttercups, and hydrangea bushes. Opal had no idea any of those were poisonous.

Janice smiled, "Yes that is the surprising factor. You expect poisonous plants to be gnarly and unattractive, but as you can see, they're magnificent."

Janice pointed out each plant, what made it poisonous and which were the deadliest.

"Do you want to be a veterinarian?" Janice asked Woody.

"I don't know," he answered. "I have a new puppy. I don't like cats much. I think a veterinarian has to like both. A friend of mine has a cat that flops its big butt down in front of me, yowling to be petted and when I do, she bites me. Cats are mean."

"Well, not all cats are like that, but I've met a few like that, too. In any case, it's good for you to know which plants to keep your dog from eating. What's your puppy's name?"

"Sergeant Pepper, but we call him Sergeant. He's an Akita and he's attached to me."

Opal was thrilled Janice was drawing Woody out. He'd become standoffish this year. Opal and Max were trying everything to bring him back to the boy he had been. He had been outgoing in a reserved, academic sort of way. He ran with a pack of friends who would create their own games with inventive rules using buckets, brooms, and original goals. They were serious, gregarious, smart boys. But Woody had left the group. His mood swings were explosive. His puppy, Sergeant, soothed him, but when they were apart, Woody was volatile. Watching him take an interest in anything gave Opal hope.

Their guide, Janice, said, "Akita's love the entire family, but you're right, they do attach to one person in particular, and they become their person for life. You're lucky to be that person. Have you taken him to puppy classes?" She asked, as they moved on to the next plot of plants.

"Yes, he's passed Puppy Kindergarten, Advanced Puppy, and we're about to start Canine Good Citizen classes so he can get his CGC. I'm the one doing all the classes with him," Woody said proudly. "My mom and dad sit on the sidelines and watch."

"It should be you. You protect him and he will protect you."

Taking a deep breath, Woody smiled. "Yep, that's the plan."

Opal jumped into their conversation. "The Akita came from the mountainous northern regions of Japan, and they say an Akita in a home is a symbol of good health, prosperity and good fortune." Then quickly added, "Oh, and Helen Keller brought the first Akita to the United States in 1937."

Woody looked down and shook his head. He turned to their guide and said, "Sorry, she's a walking encyclopedia. She actually reads them."

"I have a complete set," Opal said, beaming.

In the following weeks, Woody began to design their backyard. Max and Opal hoped by putting him in charge of the landscape design and the plantings, it would build his self-confidence. Giving him more power would help him re-blossom along with his plants. Woody's first order of business was to get a fenced-in area for his poisonous plant garden so that Sergeant couldn't be harmed.

Vette wasn't interested in gardening of any type but was relieved to see Woody come alive again. Her parents were attaching an enclosed greenhouse to the back of the house to keep Woody's interest up throughout the winter months.

With Woody occupied, Opal moved her focus to Vette. Opal recognized her daughter was anxious, probably due to her changing hormones. Vette started her period a few months back, but Opal knew that didn't account for Vette's sleepless nights, poor concentration, and excessive worrying. Opal was concerned. At times Vette's anxiety level was so high that the slightest noise made her jump, made her scream, then there would be the heart palpitations, sweating, and the shortness of breath that followed.

"I think she needs to see a child psychologist," Opal said to Max.

"Oh, she's not that bad," Max answered. "She's like every other girl who just turned thirteen. And now that she and Shelley have started that garage band, she'll be focusing more on music. She's smart as a whip." He hesitated for a second. "Nah, she doesn't need a psychologist. She needs time to get through middle school and find her footing."

"Maybe you're right," Opal agreed.

"Just be thankful the band practices in Shelley's garage," Max said.

"About that, they'll be practicing here every other week. Starting tonight."

Vette and Shelley's band wasn't your average junior high or high school head-banging group. Shelley was on the keyboard, and sometimes on the flute. Vette sang, and their friend, Pete, played the double bass, cello, guitar, and violin. Another guy from their class did the percussion instruments. Their concentration was a vintage soul sound. Somehow they worked together to take songs by Aerosmith like "*Dream On*," and "*I Don't Want to Miss a Thing*," and flipped the songs on their backs to become 1940's ballads. They did the same to songs by artists like the Rolling Stones, The Beatles, Backstreet Boys, and NSYNC.

Once the music began, Max and Opal were stunned, especially with their daughter. Vette sang as if her soul was the composer and her voice the symphony. Her range from alto to soprano fell full in round hues, warmed with a whisper that grew bold and belted out goosebump Aretha Franklin wails that could explode to fill an auditorium. It was as if she'd been performing a lifetime. She knew all the lyrics and her notes hit sound, never pitchy. She sang with her eyes closed until the very last note when she would stare her audience in the eye, as if to say: "There. Take that."

It was hypnotizing watching her. Sitting in their driveway, Max and Opal were under the stars in folding chairs listening to the band play inside their garage. Even though Woody was up in his room, and probably not coming down, Max had an extra chair waiting for him next to Opal.

"Damn," Max said under his breath.

"I told you," Opal answered.

"I know you did, but how does all that sound come out of that tall, skinny little girl?"

"Right?" Opal agreed. "Neither one of us can sing. I don't know where she gets it."

Opal and Max looked at the surrounding houses and noticed their neighbors out on their porches. When each song ended, Vette and Shelley would giggle at the applause coming from the neighborhood.

Shelley backed away from her portable keyboard. Pete picked up his guitar and Vette stepped up to the microphone to sing her version of "The House of the Rising Sun." Vette's voice echoed in the night. From her lips it became a version of Sinead O'Connor's melancholy ballad. As she sang, tears slipped down Opal's cheeks.

Max leaned over and wiped away Opal's tears with his thumbs. "Proud mama."

Opal sniffed. "Of course."

Max whispered, "When I fly back from Detroit we're going to have to figure out how to help her with this gift."

Vette's voice haunted the night.

> *"Oh mother, tell your children*
> *Not to do what I have done*
> *Spend your lives in sin and misery*
> *In the House of the Rising Sun*
>
> *Well, I got one foot on the platform*
> *The other foot on the train*
> *I'm goin' back to New Orleans*
> *To wear that ball and chain*
>
> *Well, there is a house in New Orleans*
> *They call the Rising Sun*
> *And it's been the ruin of many a poor girl*
> *And God I know I'm one"*

Exactly as the song began, Vette ended by singing the final verse alone. Pete quieted his guitar as Vette held the last notes to hang in the air. Silence held cricket's wings and the neighbor's breath. Applause erupted just as Carlton Rayburn pulled up to the house. He was there to pick up his younger brother, Cody, the percussionist.

Chapter 17

Still – 1999

Max's father taught him to fly at fourteen. He soloed at sixteen and was issued his pilot certificate at seventeen. When they sold everything to buy the land and cars, the one thing Opal insisted on was that they not sell Max's planes.

Max's passions, after Opal and the kids, were cars and planes. Long before their two babies arrived, Max had decided on names. Luckily the children were named after cars. It could have been worse. They could have been named Texan Warbird, Piper Cub, or Cessna.

Max was the proud owner of a T6 Texan Warbird two-seat tail-dragger, and a 1937 Piper Cub which had been his grandfather's plane that passed to his father, then to Max. These two planes Max kept polished in the hanger. For actual trips, he chose the Cessna 421 equipped with leather, a serving bar, and restroom.

As the dealership grew more successful and more employees came on board, Max and Opal were able to afford to take the Cessna out and fly off with the kids, and their four-legged, fur-child Sergeant, for weekend trips. Max did his preflight, got everyone strapped in, received clearance, and with the blast-off card filled in, off they went. The DME clicked the silent miles away as they raced the sun through a thousand counties to watch mountains approach, then recede. Before they knew it, it would be time to start down. Max would check the minimum sector altitude in the quadrant, get in the traffic pattern, and plant one right on the numbers. Then he smoothly pulled the speed brake lever.

Those trips took Vette and Woody away geographically, but their problem was deeply rooted. They could never leave the horror of their attack or their masked attacker, but for Vette, having her dad fly them away released a hint of pressure.

For Woody there was no release no matter the geography. He was locked and loaded behind his mask of silence both in the daylight and the night.

But the night was worse. Nightmares saw him raped by strangers, by teachers, by kids. He'd wake to split lips that he'd bitten open in the night. Flying away for the weekend merely took his nightmare to a new location. Only Sergeant could save him from the nightmares by laying his massive head on Woody's chest. Sergeant was Woody's therapist.

No matter how many vacations were taken, that one scarring afternoon with their attacker stayed with Vette and Woody throughout their childhood, adolescence, and into adulthood.

Ignorant of their trauma, Max and Opal opened their hearts to their children and gave laughter, hugs, singing lessons, horticulture lessons, and dog training classes, and love.

But there was no therapy, no psychiatrists, and no psychologists. Max and Opal had no idea of the parasitic damage that feasted under their children's skin. Regardless how much love Max and Opal poured onto them, their trauma could never be flown away.

Chapter 18

Still – 1999

Their flight time today would be one hour, eleven minutes. Max was taking the Cessna to Detroit, Michigan for his final meeting with Ford prior to breaking ground on the new Ford dealership. Hugh was going with him. They'd rent a car at the airport, go to the meeting, and be home later that afternoon. That was the joy of flying.

Hugh was a bit twitchy when it came to flying. A twin-engine plane that seated thirty-four, with a crew of two pilots and one flight attendant made him sweat bullets. Hugh was sure, having one man flying him in a cartridge tin was going to give him tremors.

With Hugh's briefcase and Max's backpack stowed in the nose of the Cessna 421, Hugh strapped into one of the seats behind Max, far from all the gauges and gadgets.

The Cessna seated six passengers sweetly, though originally it was set up for eight. That configuration only gave them an emergency toilet that had no doors, just a removable privacy curtain. Unacceptable. Max took out two seats and upgraded to a lavatory with a door that was located at the rear of the cabin. It featured a lighted vanity mirror, sink, and a coat rod.

Hugh was thankful for the private restroom in case he felt the need to throw up, which was a distinct possibility. Hugh was not talkative while he worked to tamp down his nerves.

"How you doing back there Hugh?" Max asked. It was a beautiful clear day for the flight.

Hugh's fingers dug into the leather arm rests. "Just good. I'm ah. I'm good."

"Take a breath Hugh," Max laughed. "You'll be fine. And when we get back we'll break ground for the Ford store."

As they taxied to the runway, Hugh swallowed hard. "Yep. All good."

Max chuckled and shook his head slightly. He loved screwing with Hugh's fear of flying.

The used cars lot no longer held the two parked trailers, only the trailer home remained hidden at the far backend of the lot. Erected in the middle of the lot was a modern curved-glass-front showroom with industrial-steel beams where bright lights glistened off the high-wax finishes of the vehicles. Connected to the north side of the building was a seven car service station with an office for the new service manager.

Inside the main showroom were offices for Neil, Max, and Hugh, along with a Sales Manager's office, and one salesman's office. Out on the showroom floor were two sales desks, and just inside the front door was the receptionist's desk.

Jutting out of the south side of the showroom was a framed-out alcove that housed Max's prized 1965 Goldwood Corvette convertible and his 1941 Ford Woody Wagon, Vette and Woody's namesakes.

The gray trailer home had finally sold and was scheduled to be moved that very day. As Max and Hugh flew to Michigan, Neil and Gary, a salesman, looked out the back window of the showroom and saw a small figure running from the trailer home just as a burst of flame ignited below the trailer's master bedroom. They grabbed fire extinguishers and raced outside to squelch the fire before it caught the trailer completely on fire.

While inside snatching up the gear, Neil and Gary missed seeing a second figure scramble under the trailer, pull the burning pile out from under the trailer, and stamp it out before running away.

"Did you see who set the fire?" Gary asked Neil.

"Just barely, but he was so far away I couldn't describe him. Or it could have been a girl for all I know. Sorry." Neil said.

"Thank God you saw it. Didn't you say the fire was *under* the trailer?"

"Yes, but apparently I was mistaken. I could have sworn it was blazing. Anyway, thank goodness it didn't catch," Neil said.

"I'll be glad when that thing is gone. They're taking the trailer today, right?" Gary asked.

Neil nodded as they headed back to the showroom.

Vette hid with Woody at a construction site just north of the dealership until Neil and Gary were out of site.

"*What* were you thinking?" Vette said angrily.

"I wanted it gone. I can't look at it anymore. That's what I was thinking," Woody said.

"Well you got your wish. I heard Dad say it was going today,"

Vette said. "So you didn't have to set fire to it. What if dad or mom, or if I had been inside checking it before it got hauled away? What if you killed an innocent person? Could you live with that?"

"No. No I couldn't," Woody admitted. "But no one died."

"Well, they could have," Vette scolded. "Thank God I saw you with your matches coming over here. Thank God I followed you. You could have been caught. Did you ever think of that? That's arson, the police would take you away. I won't, I can't let that happen."

"Yeah. Yeah. Yeah. You saved me again," Woody said.

"Well, I did. Woody, please be more careful. Please think about what you're doing. About right and wrong. About consequences."

"I will. I promise," Woody said. "You sound like mom."

"No I don't."

"Yes you do."

"No I don't."

"Yes you do."

As they walked away, Vette put her arm around Woody's shoulders. "I love you, you little poop."

"I love you too, you big poop."

The trailer home was moved a few hours later, headed for a trailer-park out west near Iowa. From Shelley's bedroom window, Vette and Woody watched and listened to the monstrosity creak and groan as it was towed away.

The meeting went well for Max and Hugh and the flight was uneventful, for which Hugh was most thankful.

Not long after that meeting, the Ford store grew from the ground up.

Everything was going better than Max and Opal could hope for. The Ford store was close to completion. They had a real home. The used cars lot was breaking records in profitability. If all kept going as it was, the Toyota and Honda dealerships wouldn't be far off. Life couldn't be better.

Just after midnight, eleven-year-old Woody crept out to the backyard, reached behind the evergreen Juniper shrub and moved aside the large box of matches kept dry in a plastic baggy. He found the bottle of Kentucky Straight Bourbon Whiskey. After two big swallows, the bottle was tucked back into the shrub.

Vette's bedroom was dark when she lifted the window's screen, lit her cigarette and watched him from above. Tonight he leaned against the fence with Sergeant standing guard next to him. Woody reached for the bottle once more and lost count of how many swallows he took. It helped him sleep. It didn't stop him from wetting the bed.

Woody took another sip and felt the familiar heat ease on down as he gazed at his neatly landscaped back yard thinking, *I'll have to research my plants to see if any of these can make me stop pissing the bed.*

After Woody stumbled to his room in the dark and dropped into bed with Sergeant resting next to him, Vette went outside, as she did many a night, and tucked the whiskey bottle back behind the Juniper bush.

Chapter 19

Forward – 2009

Date of Birth: 10/15/1960 Sex: M Race: W Weight: 130 Height: 509

The Good Samaritan was outside Wendell Jack's house at 159 North Jumper Avenue in Fox Lake. Wendell had committed aggravated child molestation to a four-year-old boy. He'd sodomized the boy and threw him out of his speeding car going 60 mph. The boy, though paralyzed from the waist down, lived.

Wendell was just released from jail after serving twenty-five years. He had moved into the studio apartment two days ago and was starting work tomorrow at a restaurant within walking distance.

Janice Stanley Knight and Amy Miller were both in the completed file, along with two other dead offenders. The Watch-Dog-List file was an inch thick with *Dogs,* as he liked to call the pedophiles. His In-Progress file currently held one sheet and with Wendell, there would now be two. Two kills a year during flu season, kept him under the radar.

He was extremely meticulous and random at the same time. He chose various aged *Dogs*, from haphazard locations, never close in vicinity. He only focused on the molesters of children aged twelve and under. Yes, Amy had been an exception as she hadn't done the molesting herself, but seriously… selling her own three-year-old daughter for sex for over a year before she got caught? Amy had to go.

He closed the plastic container of toxic muffins, and laid Wendell's sheet on the passenger seat.

"Down. Settle," he said to his dog in the backseat. He parked in front of Wendell's apartment, put a muffin in a paper bag, and walked toward the apartment's glass-front double doors. The Good Samaritan cocked his head to the left and stared at his reflection to see a dark haired man with a 1970's porn-star moustache staring back.

He went down the hall to find Wendell's apartment.

"Hello?" Wendell said.

"Hi. I'm Chet Farmer." The Good Samaritan always used another pedophile's name, just in case this one told someone about the meeting. He enjoyed the irony of it. "I live on the third floor and wanted to welcome you to the building."

The door opened tentatively.

"Hi," he said again with a smile and took a step back to make Wendell feel safer. He extended the paper bag to him. "This is one of my famous welcome muffins. Let me know if you like it. I'm in 302, but I'm just heading out now." He turned to leave, adding, "It's best if you eat it while it's fresh tonight."

Wendell smiled. "Thank you I will." He took the muffin out of the bag and bit into it. "That's good. Thanks."

"You're welcome. Have a great night."

Back in the car, the Good Samaritan wrote the date and time on Wendell's sheet, added the type of muffin and re-filed his sheet in the progress file. He would never come back. Again he would chart this one's departure through the local obituaries and news.

Chapter 20

Back – 2008

Lissy's Bakery was named for seven-year-old Alice Rayburn who had been taken, raped, and killed ten years prior. Her mother, Alisha, had bought the building and opened Lissy's Bakery when she moved her two boys, Carlton and Cody to Naperville. That was just after Alice, and Alisha's husband, died.

Alisha and the boys worked together to make a go of their new life. Alisha vowed to herself that the boys wouldn't be marked with the stain of their sister's murder or the death of their father, forever. Alisha worked hard so that Carlton and Cody didn't feel the need to be the "men of the house." She was the head of the house and made sure they knew it.

Bakers typically don't get to watch the sun rise. They rise before it and are deep in dough when it comes. Alisha produced pastries, breads, and cakes in the wee hours of the morning, every morning. She stored her recipes in her head, and those recipes secured daily orders with local restaurants, delis, and retail stores. Her baking day was filled with lifting seventy-five-pound bags of flour. Alisha had a strong back.

The boys stood by their mother and helped when she let them. They learned early the meaning of a strong work ethic and the value of a dollar. Soon business started growing and so did the staff.

Carlton helped bring in new accounts. He was a born salesman. Both boys enjoyed creating and finding new recipes. Not all of their creations made it to the counter. Although Carlton's lima bean and broccoli muffins had the consistency of concrete, it meant the world to Alisha that both Cody and Carlton wanted to help.

In truth, Carlton and Cody would walk through fire for their mother. No one was ever going to hurt her or their family again. Ever.

And when Betty came to live with Alisha, they felt the same for her too. Betty had escaped Lissy's killer. To Carlton, Betty was his lost sister that had come back. To Cody, even if he didn't admit it yet, Alisha and Carlton knew Betty and Cody were soulmates.

Lissy's bakery business was steady at the beginning. It was hard long hours for Alisha but then heaven opened its window and out poured an abundance of blessings. The bakery was voted one of the top ten bakeries of Chicagoland in 2002 and stayed on that list to this day.

Carlton Rayburn finished his early-morning jog outside his mother's bakery. The bakery appeared to be plucked from 8 rue

Monge in Paris and dropped on the corner of Jefferson and Webster just nine short blocks from the family's home. The shop's face had a green-trimmed glass front door tucked deep in the center of two large window displays. Inside the windows were sweets, cakes, breads, and bagels.

Bistro tables and chairs sat in front of each window under the green awning. Perfect for morning coffee and conversation. Just inside the door, free for the taking, was the morning's newspaper. All the chairs outside and in were filled today.

Carlton looked around the corner and saw Betty's old-school pink Schwinn bicycle with its upright riding position, wide pink and white seat, large front basket, and silver fenders. Next to the iPhone DryBag holder was her signature green frog squeeze horn. It had a headlight, taillight, and a custom back-rack with dual metal saddle bags. It was a majorly tricked-out old-lady's bike, and Betty's pride and joy, which was why she had it locked up tight in the bike rack.

Carlton's brother, Cody, had given her the green frog horn on her eighteenth birthday along with a pastel pink helmet. Cody pointed out that the helmet's ventilation holes were meant to keep her cool as she cycled, but he liked it because the holes looked like the frog's eyes and the visor would keep the sun and rain out of her eyes.

Upon opening her present, Betty squealed with joy.

"Well, that's the best present I've ever gotten," Cody said at the time.

Thinking back to that day, Carlton shook his head. *When are those two going to figure out they're in love?*

Nearing the bakery's front door, the scent of yeast and burned sugar, of cinnamon and hot apples, warmed him like a hug from home. The vintage bell jingled above his head. Early morning light slanted through the windows to slide off the white subway tiled walls, touched the exposed brick, and fell to the hardwood floors. Sugar sparkled like snow in the glass cases as employees bustled to fill the morning orders.

"Hey Ma," Carlton called. "That old guy's French bulldog is licking the front window again."

Three dozen people turned in unison to look out the window.

"Well, what better compliment is that?" Alisha said, as she walked from the back room.

"What?"

"If a dog is licking your front display window, you know the food must be good." Looking to her customers, Alisha asked, "Am I right or am I right?"

"You're right." The crowd agreed as one, and went back to their private conversations.

Unfazed, Carlton turned to Betty behind the counter: "Morning. What time do your classes start today?"

"Nine. How was your morning workout?" Betty asked as she put an oatmeal muffin in the paper bag. "You're looking pretty ripped, maybe it's time for a cupcake and some glazed donuts."

"I'll stick with the oatmeal muffin and coffee, thanks."

"Your mom tells me, you're creating new muffin recipes for us again." Betty handed Carlton the paper bag.

"Yep. Working on sugar-free, gluten-free recipes. It's time Lissy's stepped into the twenty-first century."

"Argh," Betty mock gagged. "I'd rather slurp mud."

"Healthy food is the way to go." Carlton called back at her from the coffee pot. "And with this great recession we're in, we have to be ahead of the times."

Betty spoke to the customers at large, "Hey everybody. Should Lissy's be a bakery or a health food store?"

The room called back as one, "Bakery." Once again the crowd went back to their private conversations.

"We are already ahead of the times," Betty said to Carlton.

"Whatever," Carlton answered. "By the way, I saw your bike is missing something."

Betty jumped to look out the window at her beloved bike. "What? Where? What?"

"A hair net for the old lady who rides it."

"Ha. Ha."

Alisha scolded Carlton, "You nasty child. Don't scare Betty like that. She's been up and working since 3:00 a.m. and has to leave for her classes in a half hour. You remember these hours when you used to work them. It's not easy." She added, "And we love her bike."

"I wouldn't go that far." Carlton grinned and rolled his eyes. Then said to Betty, "Don't forget your hairnet when you leave for class."

"Shut up." Betty answered.

"Okay you two. Stop your bickering." Alisha said.

In unison, Betty and Carlton sing-songed, "O-kay."

Carlton snapped the coffee cap on his travel mug and looked over at the antique five-gallon glass jug with its wooden lid. Coffee ran plentiful and was always free at Lissy's. The five gallon donation jar sat next to the one-hundred-cup commercial coffee maker.

The note on the jug read:

FREE COFFEE

All donations for FREE COFFEE goes to
The Illinois AMBER Alert Program.
"Seventy-four percent of children who are kidnapped and later
found murdered are killed within the first three hours after
being taken." — University of Washington Study
In memory of our sweet Lissy.
Alice Elizabeth Rayburn 1991-1998

Below her name, with her beginning and end date, was Lissy's picture with her strawberry-blond curls, sparkling honey-colored eyes, full baby lips, and her sweetheart-shaped face. It was a baby's face at the door of becoming a young girl. She was wearing her favorite blue sweatshirt with the rhinestone heart, over a sunny t-shirt, and of course, the silver-beaded word necklace that Cody and Carlton had given her.

Alisha, Carlton, and Cody had made the decision that this was the best charity for their family to support. Carlton dropped his daily five dollar donation into the already filling jar thinking, *if only the Amber Alert program had been in place before Lissy.*

Carlton knew his mother kept the jar there so that people would talk about Lissy. Ask about her. Say her name.

Alisha would tell happy stories. Betty added more detail with her memories. It kept Lissy alive for their mother and for Betty, but for Carlton it scraped the wound open, forever gaping and cavernous.

Like Betty, Carlton had lived at home throughout his college years. Unlike Betty, he didn't stay to feel safe. He stayed to keep them safe. To protect his mother and brother. Most people went through life naïve of the threats all around them, not Carlton. He knew predators were in the weeds waiting to attack. Carlton was there to flush them out.

Straight out of college, Carlton started selling drugs. Legal drugs. Carlton was a pharmaceutical representative, or better known as a pharma rep, for Qwonda the global pharmaceutical corporation. Carlton made mountains of money as the pied piper of legal drugs, hawking anti-anxiety, anti-pain, antibiotics, and the zenith of all drugs, erectile dysfunction pills. Qwonda was a multibillion dollar corporation.

Educating doctors on erectile dysfunction and anti-anxiety drugs was Carlton's specialty. He'd travel to hospitals, nursing homes, and doctors' offices, persuading them to prescribe Qwonda's drugs. After three years of pretending to be every doctors' best friend, while manipulating them into prescribing snazzy drugs to unsuspecting patients, Carlton was done.

Yes, the fancy car, six-figure income, and unlimited expense account was hard to break from, but Carlton's ethical side couldn't abide risking other peoples' lives anymore. Each drug's side effects had side effects that required more drugs, and the side effects had side effects.

He'd made enough money to pay off his condo, car, and student loans in three years. With no debt, he decided to focus on what he loved -- the art of the sale. The competitive, face-to-face combat of drawing in your prey, seducing them with words, and sensing the moment to fall silent. That moment when the next person to speak finds themselves ensnared in the trap. The win or lose moment. That joyous instant when a born salesman intuitively knows to close the deal. The gift of selling can't be taught. It's in a person or it's not. Carlton owned it.

He was ready to go to the big show, to go after big ticket items which meant real estate, luxury items, or vehicle sales. Commercial real estate and development sales was where he wanted to go, but then the country took a hard slide down the great recession. The market tanked, and Carlton predicted after that first hard dive it would continue sinking for years to come. Dropping new car sales was the precursor of the crash of real estate sales, which directed Carlton into used car sales.

It was an insane move, leaving Qwonda especially at a time when there was a mega need for anti-anxiety drugs, but the parasitical act of exploiting and profiting from others' pain made Carlton sick to his stomach. Yes, there was a pill for that, but he also knew the cure. Leave. And that's what he did.

After a year at Draeger Autos of Naperville, twenty-six-year-old Carlton was their top salesman with an income back up in the six figures. People needed to get to work if they were lucky enough to still have a job, and he helped them get into reliable and affordable transportation. He liked the auto industry, it was straightforward. They made a product that helped people get from point A to point B. Simple.

Draeger Auto dealerships were a short drive from his luxury condo, and his condo was just a vigorous jog away from Lissy's Bakery and his mother's home. Carlton felt good both physically and mentally, until he saw Lissy's picture every morning. Her picture reminded him that she'd been brutally raped and murdered by Brad Denver ten years past. Denver was thirty-six-years-old and not dead in Collinsville Correction Center. Carlton knew that to be true because he checked Denver's status on the internet each morning before his jog.

Carlton remembered watching Brad Denver at the trial after he was convicted of raping and killing Lissy.

The only remorse Denver felt was for being caught, Carlton thought. *Someday Denver will pay. He'll suffer for what he did.*

Carlton took a sip of coffee and shook Denver from his thoughts.

Carlton stopped to kiss his mother goodbye and dropped a hair net on the counter next to Betty.

"Don't forget your hair net," Carlton said, lightly bumping her shoulder with his. Although he couldn't have his sister, Carlton was thankful Lissy's best friend, Betty, escaped Brad Denver.

Carlton liked teasing her as only an older brother would.

"Asshole," Betty answered with a grin.

He loved how she took his shit and threw it right back at him.

Chapter 21

Back – 2006

The cylinder was full and the taste of metal was in his mouth. He'd gotten the six-shot revolver from his father's night stand. Max probably wouldn't notice it was missing for weeks, or at least until they found Woody's body. Woody planned it so that Max and Opal would find him tonight when they got home from their weekend excursion. They were in Galena, an artsy-fartsy town three-hours northwest.

No, that wasn't true. He hadn't planned this part at all. He planned on getting laid. Woody was sure he was the only male virgin in his high-school graduating class. He'd tried before with an *easy* girl. Got naked and all, and nothing. Only thing that came up was the rancid memory of being raped. It cut right through him and was the perpetual flaccid shadow in the room. The *easy* girl got up, and left.

Woody tried again and again throughout high school, but the shadow always came. He never did. At least not with a real girl.

But this time it was going to work. This time it was a nice girl named Debbie that he'd met in his financial accounting class at community college. They were really into each other.

She spent the night with him last night. Even Sergeant liked her until they put him out of the bedroom. But then it happened again. Every time they got close to fucking his hard-on disappeared.

The moonlight came in with the night breeze and laid on the two naked bodies. "I want to wait," Woody said.

Debbie got up on her elbow and leaned over him. "What? Wait on what?" she asked. "Honey, I'm here now. Nothing to wait on." Her fingers deliberately circled his nipple, slid down his chest, over his firm abs to latch onto a limp dick.

Woody jerked back from her touch. The shadow was in the room, in his head. "I just want to wait. Okay? That's it."

Debbie was up and putting on her panties. "No problem. You can wait all you want. Just don't wait on me."

She was dressed and gone.

Woody held the gun in his mouth. With his finger not yet on the trigger, he stared out the window at the sunrise. That's when he heard the mournful cry of a dog calling from the other side of the door. Its woefulness was deafening.

The barrel of the gun slid out of his mouth. He couldn't leave him. He couldn't.

Laying the gun on top of his dresser, Woody opened the door. Sergeant jumped up with his front legs on Woody's shoulders and kissed him full on the lips with slobbery licks.

Tears rolled down Woody's face. "I won't leave you baby. I'll never do that again."

After putting the gun back, Woody went to his bedroom's sitting room, sat on the couch and turned on his big screen television. Sergeant dropped his chew bone on the couch next to Woody, climbed up, and draped himself over Woody's lap. He chewed contentedly on his bone.

They sat like that watching the morning news.

Woody stroked Sergeant's plush fur. "Sergeant I've got to figure out how to deal with this. You're the only one I can talk to about it with. I can't keep on like this. Doing nothing. Being nothing."

The newscaster reported, "Lance Furner, a Princeton college student was sentenced to six months in jail and three-year's probation after being found guilty of assaulting an unconscious, inebriated sixteen-year-old boy behind a dumpster. The County's Superior Court Judge arrived at the absurdly short sentence and qualified it by adding that 'a prison sentence would have a severe impact on Furner, who is an Ivy League law student with a bright future.'"

"What the fuck?" Woody screamed at the television. "Okay sure, this asshole Furner has to register as a sex offender for the rest of his life, but that poor boy behind the dumpster is going to end up like me, with a gun in his mouth one day. All because that prick is on the street able to do it again?"

Woody got up and paced his room, then stopped to look down at his backyard poison garden.

"No. He won't get away with it. None of them will. Not anymore."

Chapter 22

Forward – 2008

"Okay. What happened again?" Max Futrell asked his twenty-year-old son.

"Woody wait. Wait. Wait." Max hurried to open the used car showroom door and yelled, "Neil. Hugh. Can you come out here?"

Neil, Hugh and Max stood in front of Woody's dealer vehicle, a flashy 2008 Lincoln Navigator with its two huge chrome grilles, complete with a chrome hood mustache and a Lincoln cross logo that was so big it could double for a religious icon. But the three men weren't looking at all that, they were looking at the gaping hole in the windshield. It appeared to have been shattered by a sledge hammer. That's not the story Woody told.

With his ten-year-old Akita, Sergeant Pepper, by his side, Woody relayed the story to the rapidly growing group, as his co-workers, his fellow salesmen and saleswomen spilled out of the showroom.

Max was giggling already. "Okay. Say it again."

With a heavy sigh, Woody began again. "All right, Sergeant

and I were driving here, minding our own business, when out of nowhere came these four turkeys flying straight at us. Now, I understand it's wild-turkey mating season, but this is something I hadn't ever seen before."

While still at the beginning of the tale, Neil and Max were laughing so hard they had to lean against each other to stay standing.

Looking at them Woody stopped, "Can I continue?"

"Oh yeah," Neil said as he tried to control himself.

Max sputtered, "Go. Go. Go."

"Okay. So three turkeys flew to freedom, and I thought the last guy was gonna clear the roof. But he didn't. He went straight through the windshield. His head was bobbing and jerking as he took his last breath."

Woody then pointed to Sergeant by his side. "Now I'm freaking out, but Sergeant here is all business and jumps from the backseat, grabs the damn thing by its neck, and pulls that fricken thirty-pound turkey into the backseat and shakes that bleeding carcass just enough to cover us all in blood. Then he dropped it on the floor."

Woody opened both side doors to reveal blood covering the entire interior. The windows, wood-grain trim, and cream-colored leather seats looked like a slaughterhouse on wheels.

Neil, Max, and Hugh were bent over laughing in tears.

"Okay," Woody continued. "Now Sergeant is sitting there all proud of himself and the fat fuck of a turkey is dead on the floor."

"Whe-where's the turkey?" Max asked pointing to the back seat and wiping his eyes.

"Okay. Well, I got us safely to the side of the road when this passing vehicle stopped."

Neil screamed, "No. No, I can't take anymore."

Woody continued, "Anyway, the guy stops and asked to take the bird home with him. See he had a road-kill permit, which I found out is a real thing when I called the police, because I thought, what are the odds? Right?"

Half of the crowd was bent over laughing.

Woody continued, "Apparently anyone at the scene of a crash like this who has a road-kill permit can take the bird home with him, which he did. But if there was no permit. No bird. And the permit doesn't just apply to birds. No, it applies to deer, squirrels, rabbits, and river otters too."

Max thought he was going to wet himself. "What happens if you don't have a permit and take the bird?"

"That's illegal taking," Woody said flatly. "I learned a lot today."

Woody, with Sergeant by his side, headed toward the showroom to go clean up, then turned back and said, "And before you ask, I couldn't swerve because there was a car coming in the other lane. It was either them or the bird. The bird lost." He added, "By the way, tell mom to skip the turkey this Thanksgiving."

Besides the bloodbath of an interior, two brown feathers with cream-colored chevron markings were lodged deep in the bloodied, cracked glass confirming Woody's story.

Four weeks later, the annual Christmas party had transformed the Honda showroom into a forest of tall oak trees, their branches sloping, and heavy with snow. In actuality, the showroom's steel-support beams were converted into trees with real branches, attached by wire.

Blanketing the branches were bags and bags of the best artificial iridescent white snow fluff money could buy. Twinkle lights looping from 'tree-to-tree' throughout the vast space, and magically lit the twenty-six round tables that were covered in white cloths, accented by pine branches and pine-colored napkins.

Each table seated ten to accommodate Max and Opal's 107 employees, their spouses and their children. At the front of the room stood a fifteen-foot brightly decorated Christmas tree.

On one side of the tree was a throne for Santa Claus to distribute presents to all. The other side of the tree had a large old-school blackboard with chalk, and erasers.

Written at the top of the blackboard were the words *Naughty* and *Nice*, separated by a dividing line down the middle. Under each category were the names of all the employees, their spouses and children. The placement of their names was decided by each employee. Top of the Naughty list was Max, followed by Woody, and on top of the Nice list was Opal, Vette, and Sergeant Pepper.

All of the showroom cars had been moved to the service center to make room for the Futrell Auto Group's annual party.

With the country's recession, the celebration was smaller than prior years, but every bit as festive. The used car sales, Honda's sales, and Toyota's sales were steady. Ford had dipped, but not so low as other dealerships around the country.

Max and Opal were blessed and more than happy to celebrate and share their blessings with their employees. Santa was giving out bonus envelopes to all of the employees, while their spouses received a small wrapped box that held a gift card. Each child was given an age-appropriate wooden or twisted metal puzzle.

Two bars were located in the front corners of the room, and a dance floor with a DJ sat off to the side of the room. A microphone, a grand piano, cello, violin and a drum-set were arranged closer to the dance floor. Dinner had been served. The caterers were clearing plates, and the dancing was well underway.

Vette took the seat next to Hugh's wife, Tammy. "Does Hugh mind being Santa year after year?" she asked.

Tammy affectionately put her hand over Vettes. "Oh Lord no," she said smiling. "It's his favorite thing ever, besides making plastic model cars." They both watched Hugh pick up a little boy and settle him securely on his lap.

"Model cars?" Vette asked. "I vaguely remember him saying something about model cars."

"Yes he has a shelf encircling his craft-room, or toy-room as I call it, that holds all of his model cars. It's pretty impressive. I think he's got forty-two up there now."

"That is impressive," Vette said, looking at Hugh on Santa's throne. "What else is impressive is that Santa suit."

"I gave it to him five years ago."

"That's cool. Mom told me you two have been married since you were nineteen. That's forty-one years? Wow," Vette said.

Tammy leaned back in her chair and took a slow sip of her wine. "Oh no. Hugh and I were married at nineteen and divorced at twenty. We were married again at forty-five and have been married ever since. So in total we've only been married sixteen years."

Vette and Tammy were silent a moment, both watching Opal and Max swirl around the dance floor as if connected ribbons flowing in the wind. Tammy broke the silence, "Hugh and I were never like that."

"What?"

Tammy, having consumed one glass of wine too many, began to overshare. "We divorced because I liked sex too much."

"Oh my," Vette said, apprehensive of the next words to come out of Tammy's mouth. She began to formulate an escape excuse to leave before being too grossed out. She didn't want a lesson in old-people sex. The thought of it made her throat constrict. She gulped down the peppery-hot bile that threatened to come up.

Vette swallowed hard as Tammy continued, "Hugh could go a year without it, no problem. We were the best of friends but I definitely wanted more from a marriage. I wanted a real marriage, course I never got one, and no children either. So I lost out there. Then when Hugh and I connected again, I was going through early menopause and no longer wanted to have sex. Or at least that's what I thought at the time. It's not true. No matter what your age, if you can, you want to have sex."

Vette slid her chair back a bit.

Tammy kept going. "Anyway when we met again, what I really needed in my life was a companion, a best friend, and Hugh is that for sure. He makes me laugh. We love antiquing, going to movies, and just being together. Now with his health issues, we have to be more careful about exercise, walking at fairs and antique shows. His diabetes and heart problems are getting worse. So no, we don't have the passion your parents have, but we have a bond."

Vette watched Tammy's gaze go back to her parents on the dance floor where Max dipped Opal, leaned down, and kissed her.

Vette no longer wanted an escape from Tammy. Now she was intrigued.

Tammy continued, "Times like this, when you see passion actually does exist in other marriages, that it's not a fairy tale, that's when it hits. When I see what I'm missing, what I've missed all along, it makes me angry. Mostly it makes me incredibly sad." She turned to Vette. "Don't settle. Don't ever settle for less. It's too painful."

A curtain lifted the perky façade away from Tammy's face to expose the sorrow that lived there. Vette saw the shine of tears welling in Tammy's eyes and squeezed her hand.

"I won't settle," Vette said. "Thank you."

Neil came up behind Tammy's chair and squeezed her shoulders. "May I steal Mrs. Claus for a dance?" He asked.

Sixty-year-old Tammy sprang from her chair with the zest of a prom queen. "Of course!"

Sergeant rested his steering-wheel-sized head on the table to stare lovingly at Vette. She took his fluffy face in her hands and kissed his fuzzy muzzle. "How's my baby? Did Santa give you a toy?"

"Course he got a toy, a stuffed Santa," Woody said taking the seat next to Vette. "Once we're home he'll put his man-fist of a foot on Santa's legs and rip his head off."

"Even at ten, Sergeant can rip plush toys apart and eat couches?" Vette asked.

"Toys don't last more than twenty minutes, and it was my fault he ate the couch," Woody said.

"How do you figure?" Vette asked. "I was there remember? I went over to your place to let him out and was greeted by a room full of white fluff. All that was left of your couch was a wire-spring skeleton. And sleeping in the middle of it all was this guy," she said, pointing to Sergeant.

Woody rested his hand on Sergeant's back. "I was gone and he was pissed, so he ripped the couch apart. Makes perfect sense to me. I didn't like that couch anyway. Then he graduated to therapy dog and now goes everywhere with me. It was a win-win."

"You're the weirdest person I know."

"If that's true, you need to get out more," Woody said, and took a sip of his Maker's Mark whiskey. "Here come your dates."

Shelley and Cody sat down at the table.

"That dress is wearing you very well tonight Shelley," Woody said, staring at the strapless black sheath hugging Shelley's curves.

"Back off perv," Shelley ordered. "Cody's the one everyone is hitting on tonight." Turning to Cody, she added, "You do clean up good."

"Yes. Yes I do," Cody said, accentuating his point with his signature one-eyebrow lift.

"I'm so glad we have the band back together. At least for tonight," Vette said.

"Yeah," Cody agreed. "Too bad Pete's family moved away, but I'm glad Shelley and Vette found you, Al, to play strings."

Al pulled up a chair.

A musician by trade, Al, the oldest at the table at twenty-eight, gave a nod to Cody. "Too bad you can't come back for the weekend gigs that Shelley and Vette put together. With their school schedules, it's getting harder and harder to get them both in one room. If they let me, I could book every weekend."

"Sorry," Vette said. "I've got five more months to my Master's and CPA. So from now on, my head is buried in books. Tonight is the last time I can come up for air for a while."

"I have eight more years, and towards the end of that, all holidays will be taken too," Shelley said.

"Yeah, but you'll be an orthopaedic surgeon when you're done," Cody said to Shelley.

Shelley looked at Cody, "Well, you're going to be a doctor too."

"Yes, a Ph.D. in Microbiology and Plant Sciences is a doctor, but it's not the same. And I only have four years left."

"You all make me want to puke," Woody said. "Thank God I'm done with school."

"I heard you got your Associates Degree last year," Cody said. "You don't want to go on?"

"Hell no," Woody said. "I started working at the dealership at twelve-years-old, washing cars, sweeping floors, and mowing lawns. Then I graduated to picking up and dropping off customers at sixteen. Started selling cars at eighteen while I went to community college, and now make more money than most people ever will. I'm good."

Woody's eyes lifted to the dark-haired pin-up beauty in red walking toward him. "Well. Hello," he said under his breath.

In the last two years, Woody had found a new means of channeling his rage. As a result, he'd become adept at wearing his mask of normalcy. He'd conquered his shadow by keeping all sexual encounters to one-night stands. He had learned that his fear of intimacy came with the fear of discovery, which made the shadow appear. So quick, meaningless fucks were the answer. The less talk the better. And this pin-up in red coming toward him didn't look like the chatty type. She was just the ticket for the night.

Cody followed his focus and turned his attention back to Woody. "No."

Woody was puzzled, shrugging his shoulders with his palms up. "What? Why? Can you not see what I'm seeing? Look at that."

Cody leaned toward Woody. "I said no. I mean no."

Vette interjected, "Woody." She snapped her fingers in front of his face. "Woody, that's Betty. She's with Cody."

"Ohhhh," Woody acknowledged. "Now I get it. Okay." Then turning to Cody, "Well done, you."

"We're just good friends," Cody said.

"Well then, that changes everything."

"No. It. Does. Not."

Woody shook his head. "Okay. Hands off. You got my word."

"Thanks. Just keep her company while we play and don't let any of these guys near her."

"Can I dance with her?"

"No."

"Can I...,"

"No," Cody shut him down.

Over time Betty had begun feeling safer, especially when she was with Cody. Her oversized, baggy clothing had slowly been pushed to the back of the closet while more form-fitting outfits took their place. Tonight the cherry-red body-hugging dress, with its sweetheart neckline and peplum flounce that embraced her waist, seemed perfect for a Christmas party. The long sleeves and the length, hitting just below her knees, made Betty feel more covered, more secure.

Betty bent down to pet Sergeant. "What a beautiful dog."

Her ample cleavage was in Woody's direct line of sight. "Thanks," Woody said, as he turned to Cody and mouthed the words, *you owe me big.*

Cody returned his comment with a death stare.

Moments later, wearing a jaunty Santa hat and leaning against the grand piano, Vette began to sing. Shelley, Cody, and Al backed her up. The song may not have had anything to do with the holiday season, but it sure warmed up the crowd.

Well, that's all right, mama
That's all right for you
That's all right mama, just anyway you do

Well, that's all right, that's all right.
That's all right now mama, anyway you do

Mama she done told me,
Papa done told me too
'Son, that gal you're foolin' with,
She ain't no good for you'

But, that's all right, that's all right.
That's all right now mama, anyway you do

Vette's slowed-down version of the song channeled Etta James's rich round tones with the soul of Arthur 'Big Boy' Crudup. Together with Shelley, Cody, and Al, the showroom smoldered with the smoke of music drifting low in the room.

Woody couldn't take his eyes off Betty with her long black hair, fair skin, and deep red lips. But Betty's eyes never left Cody, except to smile at Sergeant whose head rested in her lap.

Oh to be a dog, Woody thought. Woody shuddered and brought himself back to reality. Cody would kill him. The least he could do was make her feel comfortable.

"So how long have you and Cody known each other?" Woody asked.

Betty turned to Woody, "Oh, our families have been close for almost thirteen years now." She quickly changed the subject. "The decorations are beautiful and the food was delicious. Thank you for letting me attend with Cody."

"I'm happy to have you," Woody said, thinking *I'd have you any time*. Testing the water he asked, "So you and Cody are a couple?"

Betty's eyes widened, "Uh, well, I love him like…" she felt she should say like a brother, but that wasn't true. It was a realization that shocked her senses. "Like…"

How had she not seen it before? She loved Cody. She was in love with him.

Betty looked Woody straight in the eyes, "I love him."

"Well. That's great. Good for you," Woody said flatly.

The band left the stage for a break and the DJ seamlessly took over.

Betty took Cody's drink, set it on the table, and stood on her tip-toes. She wrapped her arms around his neck. "I'm in love with you," she said before softly touching her lips to his. His moustache tickled her upper lip, then their kiss quickly deepened.

Chapter 23

Forward – 2009

Date of Birth: 10/15/1960 Sex: M Race: W Weight: 130 Height: 509

The Good Samaritan bent his rules and sat in the restaurant down the street from Wendell Jack's apartment. It had been six days since Wendell consumed the muffin.

A waitress stood by the table watching his fork and knife lightly tapping the table like a drum set.

"Afternoon. What can I get for you?"

The tapping stopped. "Your famous cheeseburger, but before I order anything I just overheard your regular cook is out sick. Is the burger going to be as good as all the rave reviews say, or should I get something else?"

"Yeah, Wendell's pretty sick, but he was sent home two days ago. Anyway he's new. Just started this week. And because he was so sick, we all had to stay late the other night sterilizing the place. The owner's cooking again, so you don't need to worry, your cheeseburger will be excellent."

"What's wrong with the new guy," he asked, hoping for details.

"You know, the stomach flu hitting both ends, sore throat, dizzy, and he had terrible bloodshot eyes," The waitress stopped herself. "Oh God, sorry. I shouldn't be talking about this. Like I said, we took bleach to this whole place. I mean top to bottom. And the owner won't let Wendell back in until he's all better. One of the guys is going to check on him later today."

She lifted her pen to her pad and asked, "So would you like fries or onion rings with your cheeseburger?"

The Good Samaritan answered, "Onion rings."

The waitress's description of Wendell's symptoms confirmed that by tonight Wendell would be dead, or near death, from kidney failure, probably right around the time his co-worker arrived. His liver and kidneys had to be shutting down right about now. He needed to be left alone to die in pain.

The Good Samaritan cautioned the waitress, "You know that flu bug is bad. Maybe your co-worker should wait a few days before checking on the cook. He's probably still really contagious and you don't want someone else catching it."

"I hadn't thought of that," she said. "I'll tell him to wait for sure."

The linoleum floor was cold, even with the pillow and blanket Wendell had pulled into the bathroom. Was that yesterday? Two days ago? Today?

It didn't matter. He hadn't moved from this spot except to sit on, or lean over, the toilet. The pretend-brick pattern of the stick-on floor squares waved before his eyes.

Wendell no longer pulled himself up to get on the toilet. That was okay. It was easier to soil himself and watch the baseboards dance.

Then the baseboards stopped moving. So did Wendell's eyes.

Chapter 24

Forward – 2013

It was a small gathering held in Alisha Rayburn's backyard. The yard bloomed with lilacs, and the Mission Arborvitae trees enclosed the backyard for privacy. A robin sang from its nest in the white birch while an early summer breeze lifted a lock of Betty's hair and stroked her exposed skin a moment before she took the first step towards her bike.

The pink Schwinn's baskets were overflowing with bouquets of purple lilacs and pale pink peonies. Next to the bike stood the minister, and to the right of him stood her groom, Doctor Cody Rayburn with his best man, and brother, Carlton.

Betty had never opened herself to another close friendship since her childhood friend, Alice, was killed. For as long as she could remember, her best friend was Cody. Choosing a maid of honor though was tough. Betty had wanted to have Alisha as her matron of honor, but Alisha didn't think it appropriate, and suggested she ask her own mother. In the end, Betty asked a co-worker and teacher from the school where Betty taught first grade.

Betty carried a bridal antique-brooch bouquet of rhinestones and pearls. Betty had fashioned vintage lace into the shape of a bridal bouquet. She then hand sewed all of the rhinestone and pearl brooches, bracelets and earrings onto it to create a stunning sun catcher that sparkled as bright as her smile. At the center of the bouquet was her Great-Great Grandmother's shell cameo, set in 14K yellow gold.

But the two most cherished items on the bouquet were a small wooden heart, and a silver-beaded word necklace that spelled Alice's nickname, Lissy. Both had once belonged to her best friend, Alice. Alisha, Alice's mother, had given them to Betty.

Others may have thought the brooch bouquet gaudy, but Betty felt the sparkle created prisms of magical rainbows that guided her path to Cody.

Betty was escorted down the walkway by her father.

Cody could hardly breathe as he watched Betty walk toward him. She was stunning, and amazingly enough, she loved him. He thought his heart would explode. They both believed this union was forever. They would never abandon one another. Never. God willing, theirs would be a marriage of seventy-plus years. The idea of that long of a marriage might worry most people, but after that first kiss, the most terrifying thing for Betty and Cody was when they were apart.

The first thing Cody did after landing the job as Associate Professor of Biological Sciences at NIU was to go to Johnson's

Jewelers and buy Betty's engagement ring. Now just three months later, the most beautiful woman in the world was about to become his wife.

Betty took Cody's hand under the canopy of the white birch's branches. Cody took her by the waist, bent her back and kissed her full on the lips.

"Ah, excuse me," the minister said. "That part doesn't come until the end."

Cody gently straightened her and steadied himself, "Sorry, I couldn't wait." Looking directly in Betty's eyes he added, "My God, you're stunning."

Betty stood on her tiptoes, wrapped her arms around his neck and tenderly kissed him.

The minister threw up his hands and the small crowd broke into laughter.

Later, after the meal and beautiful cakes, the dancing portion began with Bob Seger's song "Betty Lou's Gettin' Out Tonight." The bass pumped against the trees as Cody slid Betty into his arms and guided her in their now flawless jitterbug routine.

At each place setting was a personalized deck of playing cards that read Betty & Cody's Winning Hand.

They were a beautiful couple, her fifties-inspired, tea-length wedding skirt swirling with each spin, he with his dark hair, thick moustache, and lean build. There was a full foot-and-a-half difference in their height, but they fit perfectly.

A single tear fell from Alisha's eyes, she was so filled with joy that they had finally found each other. Carlton stood next to his mother and gave her a squeeze.

"Tears of joy," Carlton stated.

"Yes," Alisha said. "Now we just need to get you the right girl."

Carlton rolled his eyes and said, "You know I'm never getting married *or* having children."

"Oh you nasty child, you just say that to rile me up," Alisha said. "You watch. Once you meet the right one, you'll be hooked."

"That's a fairy tale. It doesn't happen."

"You'll see," Alisha said, pulled Carlton into her arms and kissed him on his cheek. "You're such a plum, your soulmate is coming. I know it."

"Okay. Sure Ma," Carlton said.

Chapter 25

Still – 2013

There was no celebration at the Futrell house, only sorrow.
Opal did not accept any absences from their Sunday family
dinner and tonight was no exception, but dinner was cut short
when Opal saw fourteen-year-old Sergeant Pepper, Woody's
one-hundred thirty-five pound Akita, whimper and turn in slow,
tight circles in the living room. Opal's throat constricted with
tears as she jumped from her chair and ran to him. From her
reading, she knew. Sergeant was having a stroke.

"It's going to be all right baby," Opal whispered in Sergeant's
ear as she gently held him. He calmed at the sound of her voice
and the feel of her arms, but the moment she let go he began
spinning in circles once more.

Max, Woody, and Vette stood in the arched doorway, stunned
to see Opal weeping with her arms around Sergeant.

"Woody," Opal wept. "Sergeant is leaving us."

Woody pushed passed his father and sister and ran to Sergeant's side. "No, baby," Woody sobbed. "Not yet. Don't go."

Max was on the phone to their friend and Sergeant's Veterinarian, Dr. Heather Turnbauer.

"I'll be right there," Heather said, as she grabbed her bag. Although she lived only ten minutes away, Heather wasn't sure Sergeant Pepper, at his advanced age, would be alive when she arrived. A younger dog could live through a mild stroke and go on to have a good life, but from Max's description of the symptoms and Sergeant's age, Heather knew it was time to let him go.

Sergeant was the sweetest Akita she'd ever treated. Most were aggressive but not Sergeant, he didn't know he was an Akita. He loved everyone. At fourteen, he'd lived a very long life. Normal life span is twelve years, but Woody, Max, and Opal did everything possible to make sure Sergeant had the best of everything. Opal had made Sergeant homemade dogfood since he was a puppy and had taught Woody the recipe specifically created to keep Sergeant healthy. They exercised him exactly as prescribed.

This family loved this dog. Letting him go would be their final, and most painful, act of love.

"He needs his blanket," Woody said as he laid nose-to-nose with Sergeant, keeping one arm under Sergeant's head to elevate it. His other hand softly stroked Sergeant under his front leg. It was Sergeant's spot. The place to comfort, and hypnotize him, and it was working. His breathing was steady. He wasn't scared. Sergeant was calm. Though the slightest movement from Woody would trigger Sergeant to woefully cry out, jerk, and struggle to stand.

Vette asked, "Where is his blanket?"

"Back of my car." A steady stream of tears flowed from all of their eyes. All but Sergeant's. His eyes were unwavering as he lovingly stared at his person, his Woody.

Vette grabbed Woody's keys, ran to the new black Lincoln Navigator, pressed the button, and the back lifted. She quickly pushed aside a trunk organizer for groceries, an organizer for Sergeant's travel toys, and a portable file box, but in doing so, the file box tipped, and a sheet fell out.

Vette lifted the paper and began reading. It was a man's mugshot, and his details.

Wendell Jack
Date of Birth: 10/15/1960
Sex: M
Race: W
Weight: 130
Height: 509
Address: 159 North Jumper Avenue, Fox Lake, Illinois
Victim: Four-year-old boy
Crime: Aggravated child molestation. Sodomized the boy. Threw boy from speeding car going 65 mph. The boy, paralyzed from the waist down, lived.
Time Served: Twenty-five years.
Begin Date: November 6, 2009
End Date: November 13, 2009

When Vette got to the victim line, the crime line, her mind snapped her back to her original task. Sergeant's blanket.

Vette righted the portable file box, slid the sheet back in, and snapped the lid closed. She then reached for Sergeant's favorite blanket. The one with its prominent Akita profile.

The veterinarian, Heather, had arrived, and was inside. She had finished her examination of Sergeant when Vette returned with the blanket to hear her prognosis.

"One of the most wonderful things about animals is how they embrace the moment. When our pets are suffering, they don't reflect on all the great days they have had before, or ponder what the future will bring. All they know is how they feel today. And today all Sergeant knows is pain and confusion. This isn't going to change for him. Woody I want you to hear this. Sergeant is in pain. His pain is only going to get worse. Sergeant will not recover from this. I recommend you allow him to be euthanized tonight so that his suffering can end."

Tears flowed down Woody's cheeks as he held Sergeant close to him with Sergeant's well-worn blanket cradling his massive head. Max and Opal were stock still on the couch, while Vette gulped breaths as if drowning.

Heather had gone outside to give the family time alone with Sergeant.

Woody sat in shock as his mother, father, and sister said their goodbyes to Sergeant. Then it was his turn.

Woody breathed deeply as he looking into Sergeant's eyes. "You are my best and only friend in the world. I couldn't have gotten through it without you. You know. Only you know. I…, I love you. Only you. You're the best…, best dog in this world.

And we'll be together in the next one. Okay? You promise me you'll be there for me in the next. Promise."

Sergeant's breathing was growing more labored. "Okay. Okay. I know baby. It's time."

He looked up at his father, "It's time."

Heather was back in the room. "Do you want to be present while I do this?" she asked.

"Gaa," was Woody's response, accompanied by a nod of his head.

Opal, Max, and Vette circled Sergeant on the floor of their living room, each with their hand stroking his beautiful, thick fur. All was quiet but the sound of sniffling and jagged, open-mouthed breathing.

It was when Heather pulled out the needle that Woody realized he had been holding his breath.

Looking deep into Sergeant's eyes he said, "It's okay baby. It's okay. You go. You can go."

But when life left Sergeant Pepper's eyes, Woody rocked with his beloved friend's body back and forth, wailing with grief. He then lowered his forehead against Sergeants, sobbing uncontrollably.

No one noticed when Heather took the circle of plaster she'd readied ahead of time and pressed it to Sergeant's front paw making a mold. She then wrote Sergeant Pepper Futrell above his paw print. Heather handed it to Opal and began to pack her instruments away.

"Do you want me to take the body and have it cremated?"

"No," Woody said taking a deep breath. "We'll bury him on my friend's farm."

Heather nodded. "I want you to know it takes great strength and love to have helped Sergeant pass with dignity as you did. It was the right decision. He would be proud of you."

For a time Woody continued to rock Sergeant's lifeless body in his arms.

Woody and Max dug a hole in the backyard, across from the poison garden, next to the Juniper bush. The family wrapped Sergeant in his blanket and together they carried him from the house and gently lowered his body into his grave. They each took turns shoveling dirt onto his body, deepening the unimaginable cathartic severing.

They sat silently around the mound. Vette started to softly sing.

> *Amazing grace! How sweet the sound*
> *That saved a wretch like me!*
> *I once was lost, but now am found;*
> *Was blind, but now I see.*

Max and Opal joined in.

> *Through many dangers, toils and snares,*
> *I have already come;*
> *'Tis grace hath brought me safe thus far,*
> *And grace will lead me home.*

Staring at the mound, Woody reached over and held Vette's hand. Sergeant and Vette were the only two Woody allowed in his heart. Yes, he had a fondness for his parents, but his wounded soul wouldn't let them close. He cared deeply for his sister, he trusted her, but sitting there in the darkness of night, Woody realized his one true love was growing cold under that mound.

Vette held Woody's hand, but it was Wendell Jack smirking for the camera that flashed in her head.

Chapter 26

Now – 2018

"It's John Wayne Gacy's fault that I did what I did," Brad Denver told the empty chair in his cell.

Are you referring to Gacy, the serial killer and rapist of thirty-three teenage boys, from Cook County, Illinois? He's to blame for your crimes?

Alice Rayburn's killer, Brad Denver, had been living in a cell for twenty years, and was interviewed daily by the journalist who lived in his imagination.

Wearing his prison blues, Denver continued, "That killer clown picked me up outside a grocery store, drove me out in the country, and forced me to model bikini underwear. Then he made me give him a blow job."

Why would you get in the car with a stranger?

Brad fluffed his pillow on the single bed and tucked his tread bare blanket tightly in place as he spoke, "Hell, it was the summer of 1978. If someone offered you a ride, you took it."

You were a six-year-old boy. Why didn't he kill you and bury you? Wait, 1978? That was four months before Gacy was caught. His crawl space was full. There was no room for any more bodies. Why didn't he throw you in the Des Plaines River with the last of his victims?

Denver sat on the bed facing his tiny desk and the empty chair that was pulled out. "Maybe because I told him my father was a drunk, who beat the shit out of me on a daily basis. Gacy's father did the same to him. Must have felt sorry for me, because he took me back to the grocery store and gave me twenty bucks."

How'd you know it was John Wayne Gacy?

Brad Denver leaned forward and spun the empty chair. Watching it slow to a stop, he answered. "I recognized him from his arrest pictures."

Sorry to interrupt, but you mentioned your father beat you. Was it severe?

"What is severe? A razor strap? Being knocked unconscious by a broomstick? Beaten with a leather belt? Or is it severe to be hammered down by words. Being called a sissy, a queer, or a fat dumbass. He'd belittle me in front of my friends. Laugh as he'd block them from leaving the room. Make them watch as he whipped the hell out of me. I didn't have friends after that."

Your father should have been arrested for child abuse. You must hate him.

"What?" Denver jumped to his feet. "No. That's my father you're talking about. He never abused me. Never!"

Sorry. I misunderstood. So, you believe the rapes and murders you committed are not your fault? That they are a result of these events that happened to you?

Brad sat on the bed again and leaned forward. "Isn't it apparent? They made me like this. I'm the victim here. Everyone is out to get me. Always have been."

An erotic leer came upon Brad Denver's face as remembrance embraced him.

What are you thinking?

Denver sighed. "You know every time I was in the act of killing one of those girls? Holding them under the water. Watching their life drain. I'd have the most mind-numbing orgasm. I miss that part." Goosebumps of anticipation rose on his arms. "Yes. That's the first thing I'm going to do when I get out of here. And the second. And the third."

"HEY ASS-WIPE, SHUT THE FUCK UP!" Came from the next cell.

Chapter 27

Still – 2018

"Why can't I go with you Mommy?" Whenever Luke spoke, his mother smiled, but not today. Vette bent down to help her four-year-old son off with his jacket.

"Oh toodle-bear I wish you could, but you'll have so much fun here with Grandma and Grandpa. I'm going to be cooped up in meetings every day, and that wouldn't be any fun for you, would it?"

"But Mommy when I'm with you, we always have fun."

Vette held Luke's perfectly smooth cheeks in the palms of her hands and kissed him full on the lips.

"Yes I do." Taking a deep breath, Vette tried again. "How about if we think of it this way, today's Wednesday and we'll be together again on Sunday. That leaves only three days we won't see each other, and with all the adventures Grandma and Grandpa have planned for you, you won't even know I'm gone."

Magnified by small, round, wire-rim glasses, Luke's icy-gray eyes filled with tears. "Don't go Mommy."

Vette pressed her son to her, felt his thin arms wrap around her neck with all the strength a four-year-old boy could muster, and let the tears come. One day he'd be strong enough to hold her where he wanted and make her stay. But Vette was no fool. She knew when that day came, when Luke was grown into a man, he'd probably be holding his wife. Not his mother.

Vette tortured herself with the future that lived in her head. Today Vette was Luke's everything, yet before long she'd have to wrestle hugs from him and beg for kisses as he ran out the door. She hoped he'd be gone to university, then graduate school, but then he'd travel thousands and thousands of miles away, meet the woman of his dreams, and stay there. Vette would be left behind. Here. Alone.

Good God, what a depressing thought! Vette shook her head and banished her sad fantasy, at least for now, and quickly thanked the blue sky for the tiny arms that held her.

If it was up to Vette she would never leave Luke's side. It wasn't up to her. Single moms have to work.

Six days after Sergeant Pepper's death, some five years prior, her soon-to-be-husband Frederick Sumner Lieberman III walked into her Chicago office at Armstrong Financial, smoking hot in a black suit, crisp white shirt with one button open at the neck, and eyes that slowly and gently stripped her naked. That was it. They moved in with each other, and after three days of great sex, had tickets booked for Las Vegas to get married two months later.

"What the *fuck* are you doing?" Shelley asked.

Shelley had no filter. She no longer had time for nuances or chit-chat. She said what she meant.

Vette loved her even more because of it.

"Shelley, it's happening. Jump on the train girl," Vette said wearing a semi-permanent after-glow smile.

"Okay. We all know that semen is an antidepressant; that it contains all the happy stuff like endorphins, oxytocin, and serotonin, which is why you're feeling like the world is all butterflies and rainbows. But believe me that's the endorphins talking."

"I didn't know that," Vette said.

"Oh come on," Shelley shook her head in disgust. "Look at yourself, you're like a meth addict, only with teeth."

A dreamy sigh fell from Vette's lips.

"Stop it," Shelly said. "You're going to make me puke. How many times a day do you have sex?"

"Um, three, maybe four times a day."

"Ugh," Shelley said. "Okay. That's good. Less stress for you, but do you really want to make this deep of a commitment this early in the game? Come on. You're logical Barbie, remember? But now your body is being possessed by sex-addict Barbie."

"You bet your ass baby."

"I'm speaking to logical Barbie, if she's still in there. You, yourself, told me Frederick is a horn dog, a player, who has been married three times already," Shelley stated. "Did it ever occur to you that he just likes the ceremony? That he's not into the after party called marriage?"

"Maybe so Shelley, but be happy for me," Vette said. "Be my friend and let me be happy."

Shelley's shoulders drooped in submission. "Okay. I'll do it for you," Shelley hugged Vette. "No matter what, I'm here for you. I promise."

Shelley stood by her friend in Las Vegas at the Little Chapel of the West a week later.

It was a whirlwind romance, marriage, and divorce.

Going, going, and gone in just under four months.

Frederick was an architect turned workaholic Real Estate Broker/Developer who could buy and sell property with great finesse. However, he couldn't turn a phone off, and because of that, Vette had insisted on a divorce. At least that's how Frederick explained it.

After being married for two months, Frederick called around supper time to tell Vette he would be working late. One of his clients had been delayed. Again.

However Frederick wasn't calling from his office; he was calling from another woman's bed. Apparently with all the groping and fondling, the phone's off button was never touched. That minor flaw allowed Vette to overhear her wonderful, workaholic husband in the throes of wild monkey sex with a body-piercing, hairy-armpit, big-busted bitch who—as it turned out—was into psychedelic drugs and orgies. And that was why Vette Futrell-Lieberman insisted on a divorce.

Frederick never could get his facts straight.

When they stood in the Little Chapel of the West, Vette didn't realize it but she was already two weeks pregnant. When the phone mishap occurred she was two-and-a-half months along. Nevertheless she graciously let Frederick go and wished him well. Secretly she hoped he would contract a terminal disease that would make his prick scaly and limp and slowly fall off in pieces. After that, he and the bitch could drop into a gutter filled with bile, and drown.

Was she bitter? Not much.

Shelley was there for Vette, offering to help bury the bodies, but in the end all Vette needed was Shelley's moral support, which Shelley gave readily.

Frederick wanted nothing to do with the baby and signed away all of his parental rights before Luke was even born. He never saw Luke. Never talked to him.

Frederick disappeared from their lives. Vette removed Frederick's name from hers, and never attached it to Luke. As Vette signed the divorce papers, she thought, *Rot in hell, you selfish bastard*, and vowed no man would hurt her like that again.

Vette had always known what she wanted in life. A husband, lots of babies, and if she had the time, to sing in nightclubs on the weekends.

After high school, with no husband on the horizon, she got her master's degree and became a Certified Public Accountant.

While Vette was at university, Shelley was a Purple Line train ride away at Northwestern University. After Shelley graduated from Northwestern, she continued on her path to becoming an orthopaedic surgeon like her father.

Since both Vette and Shelley were living in Chicago, they decided to move in together. They found an upstairs apartment in Pilsen on Halsted and 18th, across from the Express Grill. On weekends, when their schedules allowed, Vette sang, with Shelley on the keyboards, at clubs.

Their apartment was in a safe neighborhood. There were gangs, but the gang's family members lived in Pilsen, so most of the shooting was taken away from the area. That was up until a father of three was shot and killed outside the Express Grill. If they'd been home, Shelley and Vette could have sat at their front window and watched the shots being fired from the silver SUV.

But stuff like that happened all over. Spring time in Chicago was measured by the daily body count from shootings, robberies, and rapes that seemed to escalate with the temperature, and maintain momentum until the first snowfall.

The time came when neither Vette nor Shelley could tell the difference between gun shots and fireworks on the fourth of July. This prompted their decision to move west. After a total of twenty-five years of school and wads of exams, Shelley joined an Orthopaedics Group in the suburbs.

While they lived in the city, Vette had been working in the Chicago office of the choice firm, Armstrong Financial. She worked in their fraud, forensics, and internal auditing department. Once Vette and Shelley decided to move away from Pilsen, Vette transferred to their Naperville office.

Vette was a saver, and with her plentiful salary, she'd built up a huge nest egg. Before her short-lived marriage, Vette used part of her savings to buy a 1934 Colonial Revival home on Benton Avenue, just a few streets from downtown Naperville, where she began nesting; painting, papering, arranging, and gardening. The ten-room house was perfectly suited to her needs. She intended to fill it with children, and would have if Frederick… well as her dad would say, *if wishes were fishes, we'd all have a fry*.

The divorce was amicable, for Frederick. He took everything but the house, the bills, and the baby growing inside her.

After Luke was born, Vette worked two days a week from home, but a year later Armstrong Financial wanted her in the office every day. Vette couldn't do it, and started a financial consulting firm of her own. It didn't work. By Luke's third birthday, Vette had run through most of her savings.

She had to get a real job with real benefits. Max and Opal supplied the answer.

"Come into the family business," her dad said. "Futrell Auto Group needs a Chief Financial Officer and you're the most qualified person for the job."

The upside of nepotism was the swift trust it brought. In a time when dealerships were being robbed from within, Max, Opal, and the company's new CEO, Woody, needed to be able to trust their CFO.

Max said, "The hand that counts our money needs to be a Futrell."

The real question was, would Woody want Vette to be that Futrell?

Chapter 28

Still – 2018

"Happy fifth wedding anniversary, my sweet Betty Lou," Cody whispered into his sleeping wife's ear. Then he dropped a shovel onto the bed.

"If you expect me to dig my own grave so you can bury me in the backyard it's not happening," Betty moaned. She rolled over, and put the pillow over her head.

Cody heard her muffled giggle, straddled her on the bed, and lifted the pillow. "Come on out of there sleepy head, we've got work to do."

"Nooo. We can sleep late. There's no school today. Come on," she whined.

Cody shifted his body to pull the covers off his wife, but then having done so, he was granted with the wonderful sight of her naked body. "Well, maybe we could stay in bed a little while longer."

Betty smiled and pulled her husband to her.

Forty-five minutes later, Cody picked the shovel off of the floor as Betty, now dressed, came out of the bathroom.

"I'm starving," Betty announced.

"Don't touch the plants on the counter," Cody ordered.

"Is it another poison patch for your class?"

"Yep, for my Plants Poisonous to Livestock class."

"Okay. I can't go in the kitchen, so you're taking me out for breakfast. But first, what is the shovel for?"

"Come with me, my love." Cody softly kissed Betty then led her out the back door. There in the middle of their fenced-in backyard was a tree ready for planting.

"For our wooden anniversary I got you a cottonwood tree," Cody said triumphantly.

"Wooden?" Betty asked.

"Yes, the traditional five-year gift is wood," Cody explained and continued. "The Cottonwood is one of the largest North American hardwood trees, although the wood is rather soft. Cottonwoods are deciduous trees that grow up to forty-five feet tall."

Betty smiled and let him describe the plant, first because he loved doing it, and second, because once started, he couldn't stop himself.

Betty got up on her tiptoes, put her arms around Cody's neck at the same moment he lifted her so she could wrap her legs around his waist. "I love you so much Mr. Rayburn."

"I love you so much Mrs. Rayburn," he answered.

"We agreed that the house was our anniversary gift to each other," Betty said.

"It is, but this tree is *our* tree and will grow along with us. It will be the *Cody and Betty* tree. So here we go."

"I love it, and especially you, but could we wait and name it later?"

"Later? How much later?"

"I'm thinking about six-and-a-half months from now when *your* anniversary present arrives," Betty said, with a slight grin. She waited for Cody to catch up to the answer.

"Well, that's a long time to wait for my present," he said, a bit disappointed. Then it hit. "Are you? Are we?"

"Uh huh," she said nodding.

"Oh my God!" Cody held her tight then twirled her around. Gently he put her feet on the ground and held her shoulders until he was sure she was steady. "We have to get you food. But you can't go near the kitchen until I get all of that stuff out of there."

They ate that morning at the Dearborn Café, best breakfast around. Back home after cleaning up the kitchen and bleaching the counters, Cody deemed the area inhabitable for her. Later he sat Betty under the shade in the backyard with an iced tea.

"Tea is very good for you and the baby. Hot tea is warming, and helps with relaxation and settles the stomach. Teas are rich in antioxidants," Cody said. He filled in the final shovelfuls of dirt around the cottonwood tree and trained the hose on it. He wiped his brow with the back of his hand and sat next to Betty. "But you shouldn't drink more than one cup of coffee a day. I'm not going to be crazy about this. I won't tell you what to do. I promise."

Betty laughed and shook her head. "Oh. Sure. You won't get crazy about this. Want to know what I'm worried about? I'm freaked out about how much larger my breasts are going to get. They're already a triple D."

Cody looked to the sky with his palms up, "My prayers just keep getting answered!"

Betty leaned over and smacked him on the back of his head.

Sitting back in her chair the smile left Betty's lips, "Weirdo. No." She sighed. "Did you see today's mail? That monster sent me another letter."

Cody took Betty's hand. "I saw."

Betty took a sip of her tea. "What if this is a girl? How? How do we keep her safe from predators? The government could decide it's too expensive to keep pedophiles in prison. They could allow pedophiles to live anywhere. They could live here in our neighborhood. Brad Denver could get out. He could move here."

Betty pointed to the house. "You saw the mail. If they let predators mail letters to their victims, what's to stop them from letting them out. He could come here."

Cody knew Betty was working her way into a full-blown panic attack and gently pulled her chair to him. He touched her cheeks with the palms of his hands until she was looking into his eyes. He kissed the tears forming in her eyes and then her lips.

"That won't ever happen. I will always keep you and this baby safe. There are no pedophiles anywhere near here. That's why we bought this house close to the grade school. They can't come here. I won't let them. And as to Brad Denver, someday he will get what's coming to him. Someday he will pay. I promise you that." Cody laid his hand on her belly. "I promise you both that."

Chapter 29

Still-2018

Date of Birth: 10/15/1963 Sex: M Race: W Weight: 198 Height: 600

The Good Samaritan carried the muffin in a paper sack as he turned the corner to Kent Soto's decaying home on Willow Street. What was left of the exterior-white paint had peeled to the ground years ago leaving gray rotting wood exposed to the elements. He turned to go up the walkway and jolted to a stop. Walking toward the porch was a woman and her small son.

"Excuse me," he said just loud enough for them to turn back toward him. "Are you here to see Kent Soto?" The Good Samaritan worked to hide the terror in his chest.

"Mr. Soto is my piano teacher," The little boy offered.

Staring directly at the mother, he said, "Could I speak to you for just a moment?"

"Uh, sure," she said coming out to the village's sidewalk.

Speaking in hushed tones so that the little boy didn't hear, he said, "I'm Jason Hall and I learned that Kent Soto is a pedophile who has committed aggravated criminal sexual abuse, meaning rape, molestation, and statutory rape against a six-year-old boy, an eleven-year-old boy, and a nine-year-old boy. He lured them in with piano lessons. How many times has your son been here?"

"Oh my God. Oh my God. Only, only once. We've been here once. I got his name from the post office community wall for piano lessons. I didn't leave Teddy alone with Mr. Soto, I sat in the outer room. I never left. Oh my God."

The mother got down on her knees in front of her seven-year-old son. "Teddy sweetheart, did Mr. Soto touch you in any way the last time we were here."

"No mommy. I just sat on Mr. Soto's lap at the piano and he showed me where to put my fingers. He was nice. He rubbed my legs and my back while I played. You're not staying this time are you? Mr. Soto said you didn't have to stay anymore."

"Wha…, What? No. No honey. We're never coming back here. You're never to come near this house or that man ever? Do you hear me? You have to promise."

"I promise mommy. But can I still play the piano?"

"Of course, we're getting a new teacher right away."

Gripping her son's hand, she stood up next to the Good Samaritan and said, "Thank you. Oh my God you're an angel. Thank you."

She hurried away with her son as the Good Samaritan walked up to the door and rang the bell.

The door opened four inches. "What," Kent said. He seemed annoyed that his plans for the day had been disrupted.

"Mr. Soto, I'm Jason Hall and I saw your ad for piano lessons at the post office. I met up with Teddy and his mother just now and she wanted me to tell you she had an emergency. They had to leave in a rush but she asked that I tell you. She will contact you to set up Teddy's next lesson."

The door opened, fully exposing the fifty-five-year-old man with an exceedingly long, horse-shaped head propped up by a sloppy neck. Eyes too close to his nose were accentuated by wire rimmed glasses. He looked like nobody and everybody.

"Well that's a shame," Kent said. "Thanks for letting me know." He began to push the door closed.

"Oh that's not why I'm here," The Good Samaritan said. "I was hoping to take piano lessons and now that you have a free slot, could I take Teddy's time?"

"Ah, sure. Come on in."

Kent was eating the poisonous muffin. "This is really good. Where did you say you got it?"

"A bakery in Marengo called Fred & Meg's."

Kent swallowed the last bite. "I've heard of that place. I'll have to go there. Okay, our time is up. Just keep practicing those exercises. Do you want to set up a time for next week or sooner?"

"My schedule is crazy lately, which is why I just showed up today. As soon as I'm free, I'll give you a call okay?"

"Sounds good, and if you bring another muffin, I may just give you a discount."

The Good Samaritan smiled. "Oh, that can be arranged."

Chapter 30

Still- 2018

Sixty-five-year-old Max had been retired for a year. Opal pushed him into it so they could travel, and most importantly, so he could know his grandson. It was the best decision Max ever made. Luke was his best buddy.

It had been a smooth transition handing over the reins of Futrell Automotive Group from Max to Woody. Woody had twenty years of experience under his belt. Having learned the business from the ground up, nobody was more qualified than Woody to run the dealerships. Max had to admit, Woody ran the dealerships as well as Max ever could.

Woody wasn't alone, he had Vette, and both Neil and Hugh were there to help him. Neil was a healthy young man of fifty-two and wasn't going anywhere. He and his partner, Kent, married the moment it became legal and were blessed with a daughter named Lola via a surrogate three years back. No one knew if Neil was the biological father or if Kent was, and it wasn't anyone's business but their own. What mattered was Lola was a most wanted and loved little girl, and she had both of her daddies wrapped around her tiny fingers.

Hugh on the other hand was not so good. He was the GM of all the dealerships, but having just turned seventy, his health was declining. Hugh was a Vietnam Veteran who'd been, like thousands of others, covered in Agent Orange and a bunch of other herbicides during his tour. Those herbicides gave Hugh a Molotov cocktail of ailments starting with type 2 diabetes that led him to high blood pressure, chronic obstructive pulmonary disease, ischemic heart disease, peripheral neuropathy, and an aorta packed like a summer sausage with cholesterol plaque. Every so often a glob of plaque would break free and travel to his brain for the added bonus of a transient ischemic attack. He'd survived a multitude of those mini strokes.

"Better a mini stroke than a maxie," Hugh said. "They're just hit and run episodes. Don't last more than an hour if that and then I'm fine. Anyway, I think Tammy's making it up. I feel fine."

"Making it up, my ass!" Tammy said at the dealership in front of Max, Neil, and Woody. "You've all seen him when he's having a TIA. His left side goes slack, he leans over and back like he's going to fall backwards and he has to grab hold of something or sit down before he falls over. On top of that his mouth droops and he's totally out of it. Sometimes it shows up as double vision and then he does a contortionist's back bend. God knows how it will present itself next. It's a crap shoot!" Looking at Hugh with anger built out of terror, she added, "You know I'm right. After fifteen TIA's we stopped counting."

"Oh, but I haven't had one in a year," Hugh countered.

Max wished he hadn't popped in for a visit that day. He, along with Woody and Neil, felt they were watching a train wreck and couldn't turn away.

Tammy threw her hands up in the air and slapped them down to her sides, "You had one last week. And another two weeks before that. But. But, whatever," she turned to Max. "I can't get him to go to the hospital anymore and if I do, he signs a medical waiver saying he's leaving against medical advice. He packs up and we go home as if nothing has happened."

"Why do they want to keep him for twenty-four hours?" Max asked knowing he should have keep his mouth shut.

"Because after a TIA your risk of having a massive stroke is outrageous."

Hugh shrugged his shoulders, "Which is why I might as well be at home. I'd much rather die there than in a hospital."

"It's all because of his diabetes being so out of control," Tammy said.

"I take insulin every morning and at night, and, if I remember, before every meal, *and* I take all the pills Tammy lays out for me." Hugh put his arm around Tammy and gave her a squeeze. "You could be poisoning me for all I know."

Tammy scoffed, "If I wanted you dead, you would have been dead years ago. I like you now and am working hard to keep you alive. Which is why I'm so upset. Here I brought you a salad for lunch today and find you eating fried onion rings and a triple-fat cheeseburger."

"Ah, but you love me," Hugh smiled at his wife.

"Yes. Yes I do." Tammy gave Hugh a quick kiss and went to her car.

Woody turned to Hugh, "Man you better start listening to her. She may be little but she's scary."

Chapter 31

Back- 2014

Cody and Betty Rayburn met Brian Phants and his wife, Chanya, at the Ellwood House Museum's, 'Wine on the Terrace' event, where they learned they all shared a common interest in wine. A pretty easy assumption given the nature of the event. Even so the two couples became friends fast.

Brian and Cody were the same age. Betty and Chanya were just a few years apart. It was definitely the wine talking, but by the end of that first evening they had made plans to go on a long weekend together for a wine tasting themed vacation.

Of course the next morning both couples questioned the sanity of going on a vacation with strangers, to share a cabin no less with another couple they barely knew. But neither couple backed out and the trip was happening and happening soon.

Cody and Betty talked about how it could go so many ways of wrong but then again if it worked they could be hitting the jackpot in the couple's friend category.

Back home in southern Illinois, Brian and Chanya had the same conversation.

Still, three weeks later over the long Columbus Day weekend, the two couples took that first vacation together exploring the northern Illinois wine trail. They rented a two bedroom, two bath cabin, at Starved Rock Park in Utica that had a porch overlooking the Illinois River. It was the perfect spot to bring a bottle, or better yet a case, of wine back from the vineyards and relax by the fire pit in the evening. October in northern Illinois is prime time for watching trees morph from green to vibrant yellow, red and orange.

Brian and Chanya's home was three hours south of Cody and Betty, close to Bloomington. At that initial planning session, the couples decided to trade off vacation locations every year. The first year they would travel the northern Illinois wine trail and the next year they'd go to the Shawnee Hills wine trail in southern Illinois.

They agreed that if the first year went well they'd keep going back and forth, north then south, until they'd hit all of the wineries in Illinois. Once completed, they'd move on to another state. Their vacations together could go on for as long as their bodies and the friendship allowed. It all depended on that original trip.

The first year Cody and Betty learned something important. Brian and Chanya were avid card players and equal opponents when dealt a hand of euchre. Brian and Chanya discovered their new friends loved to dance as much as they did. The four had deep philosophical discussions about politics, world peace, and how to grill a steak. Brian and Chanya introduced Cody and Betty to the board game The Settlers of Catan, and Cody and

Betty taught them to jitterbug.

They'd gone on their fourth adventure in as many years and had extended their trips from long weekends to a full week together.

Forward- 2018

This year's vacation was over spring break. At the end of March, warm weather and wild flowers were much more prevalent in the Shawnee National Forest rather than in northern Illinois where snow was still melting into the ground. The beauty of the Shawnee hills was always a joy to come back to. The wine was good too.

Chanya never left home without her paints and canvases.

"I love your work," Betty said looking up from her book. As Chanya was with her paints, Betty was with her books. She had brought a bagful of hardcovers and was currently re-reading *Rebecca*.

"You're so sweet. Thank you," Chanya smiled.

They'd shared much about their backgrounds over the years, although Betty hadn't spoken about the nightmare. One day she would. Possibly.

Chanya described her childhood so vividly that Betty could smell the roses in the air near the shores of Lake Naivasha. Chanya was born in the United States to Kenyan parents who had then moved back to Kenya for the first twelve years of Chanya's life. Chanya's memories brought to life the Great Rift Valley, home to the Maasai people, the nomadic group of her family. She walked Betty closer to the shores of the lake where the scent of chemicals and pesticides replaced the roses to sting her nostrils and burn into her throat. The profuse use of pesticides created the thriving flower industry while killing the fish and wildlife. When the Maasai people saw their animals getting sick from drinking the lake's water they stopped bringing their cattle there. When the people became sick, most had nowhere to go.

Along with her artwork Betty loved Chanya's accent, how she never pronounced the letter R and how vowels slid from her mouth in warm tones. It had taken Betty a bit to glide with the cadence and pronunciations of Chanya's version of the English language but now understood her perfectly. And Betty loved how the minute any music sang through the air, Chanya's body moved. Shyness lifted from Betty's shoulders when her friend bid her to dance with her. Chanya's intuitive sway of her hips flowed fast and yet fluidly as she taught Betty how to do traditional tribal dances. Betty's movements were initially stilted, but with time she relaxed into it. Cody was ever so thankful. Thinking of that made Betty smile to herself.

In a few months they would learn how fruitful this vacation truly was, with news of their baby, but for now Betty sipped her wine as Chanya continued to answer Betty's question about her art. "I'm influenced by many artists but I lean mostly toward Loïs Mailou Jones's work. I love the fact that she wanted to be remembered as an artist and not specifically for her race or gender."

Chanya was working on an acrylic painting that combined a Midwestern landscape with three Kenyan women. She planned to layer this one with oil.

Her work was recognized in art galleries and museums around

the world. "I will paint one for you and Cody," Chanya said.

"We can't afford one of your paintings," Betty laughed.

"Don't be rude. I would never charge you for a gift." Chanya smiled.

Betty stood, stretched and walked barefoot through the grass next to the creek-bed toward her friend and outstretched her arms in a full air hug. Chanya turned, smiled and mimicked Betty's actions as the two friends enveloped each other in a loving embrace.

Chanya's parents were lucky. They came back to the states, to Illinois, where friends helped them resettle. Chanya was thirteen when her father succumbed to cancer of the kidneys. And just after Chanya graduated from high school, her mother was diagnosed with leukemia and was gone within weeks. Chanya had no one left except her high school sweetheart, Brian.

Brian was a few years older than Chanya. He'd signed up for the military right after he had graduated. Although they were apart, they were a couple.

Brian was home on leave from his deployment in Iraq when Chanya found a lump in her breast. They married three days later. Chanya learned she had the BRCA1 gene and immediately chose to have both breasts, her uterus, and her ovaries removed. She was nineteen-years-old. Twelve years later she remained cancer free.

That evening when canvases and books were put inside the cabin, Brian asked, "What's this?"

He was staring at the heavy wooden crate Cody set on the floor.

"It's a combination graduation, welcome to your new job, and housewarming gift for your new home," Cody answered. "It's a case of Alto Vineyards wines, which includes your favorite award-winning dry Chambourcin. Seeing as how Alto was one of the first vineyards in Illinois, Betty and I thought it would be a fitting gift for all of your upcoming firsts."

Brian stood and wrapped his friend in a firm man hug, then held Betty in a sisterly embrace. "Wow. What a great gift! Thank you." Cocking his head toward Chanya he asked, "Did you know about this?"

"Of course, my love," she answered with a gleaming smile. Her white teeth contrasting with her jet skin was stunning. Brian never saw a more beautiful woman in the world. He'd loved her from the moment she walked into his high school sixteen years ago and over time loved her more than he ever knew was possible.

"Oh, and then there's this," Cody added as he quickly ducked out through the kitchen door to return carrying a five-and-a-half foot tall Epicureanist sixty-bottle wine cabinet. It was more like an impressive wine jail, made of wrought-iron grapevines climbing and intertwining.

"Holy shit man. That is amazing!" Brian said.

"Chanya helped me pick it out," Betty said. "We wanted to make sure you would actually use it in the house and not relegate it to the garage."

Jokingly Cody asked, "Now that you've earned your Master of Science in Business Intelligence and Analytics do you feel superior to us all?"

"When it comes to euchre, you bet your ass."

"Will it be hard to leave police work to become the city of

Carbondale's Chief Information Officer? Or do we call you CIO? Which is it?" Betty asked.

"Either one, but chief geek will do for you guys," Brian smiled. "And to be clear, yes I work in law enforcement, but I'm not a police officer."

Cody looked puzzled, "Really? All this time I thought you were a cop or detective. How crazy is that? It's cool. Don't tell us everything at once. It's cool. Here we are four years later and I'm learning something new about you."

Cody dealt their hand of euchre as they sat around the table. "So we know you had a few tours in Iraq. We know you're going to be CIO for the city of Carbondale. So what is it you've been doing in that in-between time?"

"Hey, I thought you knew. But then I don't know what courses you teach at university and it makes no difference to me."

"Don't get me wrong," Cody said, holding his hand up as if a stop sign. "I really don't care what you do as long as you two go on these vacations with us once a year."

"Pass." Chanya said looking at her cards.

"Pick it up," Betty said to Cody. He quickly scooped up the jack of spades and discarded the only heart in his hand.

"Me too," Brian said going back to their conversation of occupations. "Makes no difference to me either. No, I've worked at Collinsville Correction Center for twelve years now on death row. Although there is no death row anymore, we still call it that. Yeah, I'll be happy to leave that job. I drive forty-eight miles to work and forty-eight miles back every day because I couldn't bear to live anywhere near those terrors."

Brian hesitated for a moment, and said, "Really a lot of them aren't so bad. Those are the ones that just need to go home. But then there's the heinous ones, like this forty-six-year-old serial pedophile, rapist, and killer, Brad Denver. Every day that I have to deal with him, I just want to...," Brian's hand quivered into a fist. "Anyway, that's one of the reasons it's way past time for me to get out of there."

Betty's cards fell to the floor. Brian quickly leaned down to pick them up for her.

"That's too bad. You had the left bower *and* the ace, king and queen of spades. All the better for us honey," Brian looked up at Chanya, who directed him to turn to Betty in time to see a ghastly whiteness spread over her face.

Chapter 32

Still- 2018

A year had passed since Woody convinced Vette to come to work at the dealerships. Sitting in her office with her suitcase near the door, Vette remembered the conversation that brought her to this wonderful job.

Last year Woody came to her house.

"You've got to do it," Woody had said, which prompted Vette to reach in her pocket, pull out her two-inch pocket knife and set it directly in front of Woody.

Without hesitation Woody placed his pocket knife next to hers. Since that day in the trailer, the throw-down of the junk-drawer knives was an unbreakable promise, their signal for absolute truth.

Vette asked, "Is this charity? You know if it is, I can't do it. Yes, you're the CEO, but I'm worried mom and dad are making you hire me, and I don't want to step on your toes."

"No Vette. This was my idea. Sometimes. You know. Sometimes it feels like I have no one I can trust." Woody pointed to his furry friend, whose head was resting on the table next to Woody's elbow. "Except for my big boy here." Woody leaned over and kissed his Akita, his new love named Jag, on his head. "I have no one but Jag to help me now that dad has retired. Sure dad drops in to the office whenever he needs a break from whatever it is that he and mom do, but mostly I'm on my own." Woody felt something tug at his sleeve.

Vette and Woody both scooped up their pocket knives and put them away.

"Uncle Woody, can I take Micker Bag outside to play?" Luke asked as he wrapped his little arms around Woody's two-year-old Akita's massive neck. Luke's face, half the size of the dog's head, was pressed tightly against Jag's face. Jag looked as if he was smiling.

"Course you can Luke," Woody smiled. "And his name is Mick Jaggar. Remember to call him Jag."

Luke jumped with delight. "Come on Micker Bag. Let's go." Jag looked at Woody for confirmation.

Woody nodded to Jag, "Go. Watch." His assignment confirmed, Jag hopped twice like a bunny on his front legs then raced after Luke.

Jag wouldn't let anyone within ten feet of Luke. Luke could wrestle with Jag, use him as a pillow, play ball with him, and race around the yard. Whatever Luke wanted, that's what Jag allowed. Except when Luke tried to go outside the yard. Jag put an end to that instantly by blocking Luke's passage and barking to alert Woody and Vette every time. Jag was gentle as a lullaby with

Luke and kept him safe. They'd been best friends since Luke was one-year-old and Jag was eight weeks.

While Luke was out with Jag, Woody reinforced Vette's decision to take the job by offering a financial package that made her last job at Armstrong Financial pale in comparison.

The slam-dunk decision came when Woody said, "If you want to, you can work remotely from home the majority of the week."

As a celebration gift for taking the job, Max and Opal gave Vette a present. The week before she began work, they gave her and Luke a trip to Disney World. With Max at the controls, her parents flew Vette and Luke to Orlando in the Cessna 421. After refueling and many hugs and kisses, Max and Opal left them to go on to the Florida Keys.

The second Vette and Luke walked into the Magic Kingdom, Luke's delight was infectious. Her parent's gift to Vette was to view the kingdom through Luke's eyes. Max and Opal knew as parents that joy doesn't come from making their own dreams come true. It came from seeing their children's dreams come true.

Luke rode every ride, skipped all his naps, and never stopped smiling. While standing in line for Mickey Mouse's autograph, Luke lost his first baby tooth. On their last day, Luke proclaimed their vacation was the biggest fun he'd ever had. It was the biggest fun Vette had ever had too.

Vette curled her life around Luke.

Since starting the job at the dealerships a year ago, wrapping her life around Luke was so much easier, until now. Now they were making her go on this dealer trip alone. Without Luke.

Vette sat in her office waiting for the limo to pick her up and take her to the airport. She could have had them pick her up at her parent's house but she knew she would have never gotten into the damn limo with Luke crying for her to stay.

Hell, remembering their actual goodbye from this morning was like being throat punched.

"Don't go Mommy," Luke cried.

Yes, she was in the best of all situations. Her parents were Luke's babysitters and loved him as much as she did. Luke had stayed overnight at Max and Opal's many times before but only for one night at a time.

Vette was scheduled to be away from Luke four nights. Four full nights.

Vette looked towards Woody's office thinking, *this is all their fault.*

Woody, Opal, and Max ganged up on her and ordered her to go. The Toyota dealership won a trip from the manufacturer. They were always winning trips to Las Vegas, or on an African safari, or to Palm Springs, or to LA. The more cars they sold, the more trips they'd win that sent them all over the world. Hugh and Tammy went on some of the trips. Neil and Kent took some of them. Woody went to Vegas once in a while, but on the whole, Max and Opal gave the trips to managers. Once Max retired, Woody kept up the tradition.

Woody, Max, and Opal could pay for their own vacations. Giving the contest trips as job perks to their employees was a great incentive for keeping them loyal and happy.

However when this trip to Bermuda came their way, everyone insisted Vette had to go. She pleaded with them to give it to someone else, that she would take the next Walt Disney World trip they won. That way she could take Luke with her, but no. No one agreed.

Right after the word came about this trip, Woody sent Vette to their parent's house to have the conversation.

"You have to get out on your own," Max had said.

"You're too young to be sitting at home every night. You should be dating or at least taking time to cultivate your own interests," Opal chimed in. "Did you know…"

Max and Vette were sitting at the kitchen table, knowing a history lesson was coming.

Opal didn't bat an eye as she continued, "around 1790, the transportation revolution had roads extended and railroads built to allow more people to travel. You mustn't squander your chances to see the world. We only get so many chances and then they're gone. So you see, you must go on this trip."

It was an all-expense paid, first-class trip to Castle Harbour Resort on Bermuda's largest private beach. Vette was booked in a waterfront villa with a balcony overlooking Castle Harbours' pink beaches. It was decided. She was going.

Poor. Poor. Pitiful her. She was leaving for paradise today, Wednesday, and not getting home until Sunday.

The pain of missing Luke all of those five days and four nights was going to be her undoing. After Frederick and the divorce, Vette made a vow she would date. And she'd start the day Luke left for college.

Vette had explained how she felt to Shelley. Shelley totally understood and then told her to pack her fucking bags or she would come and drag her by the hair to the plane.

"Don't go Mommy," kept repeating in Vette's head. Her memory was on a continuous loop repeating the morning goodbyes.

"I love you more than the whole wide world and I'll miss you more than the rising sun, but I won't be gone long. And I'll think of you every minute of every day. The hotel's phone number is on the refrigerator where I showed you and so is my cell-phone number. You can call me anytime you want."

Luke's tears slithered into her veins and sucked her heart dry. Vette lifted Luke's glasses, dried his tears with a lace handkerchief, and kissed his eyes.

"Okay?"

"Anytime?" Luke whimpered.

"Any ole time you want."

Replacing Luke's glasses Vette whispered, "Want to know a secret?"

Preceded by an arduous sniff, Luke answered, "Uh-huh."

"I happen to know Grandpa bought a shovel and a whole bunch of gardening tools just your size. And Uncle Woody promised that Jag would come by and play with you every single day."

Luke's glistening eyes grew wide with excitement. "Really?"

"That's what I heard, and Grandpa is out back right now waiting for someone to help him dig a new garden and plant seeds. Do you think you could be his helper?"

"Okay!" Luke was itching to bolt out the back, but Vette held him a moment longer as she watched Opal open the front door to take her to the dealership where the limo would be picking her up. The time had come for goodbyes.

Vette hugged Luke one last time. "Oh Toodle-bear, I love you so."

"I love you, Mommy." Luke couldn't wait one second longer. The lure of tools and dirt sent him darting from his mother's arms and scrambling for the back door. "Bye Mom."

A tear ran down Vette's check, "Goodbye Toodle-bear."

Vette suddenly realized she'd been staring at her suitcase sitting by her office's door for the last fifteen minutes.

Sure she could have stayed another few hours with Luke, but this in-between time at the dealership was supposed to be like decompression surgery; it was supposed to relieve some of the excessive pressure. Three more hours of decompressing and Vette would explode.

She left her office in a rush to find Woody. That was the best thing about being in the office. There was always someone to keep you company.

Thank goodness for her co-workers. One of her most favorite people, besides Woody, was sixty-year-old Roberta Gerard. She was a direct person, not one for chit-chat, and militantly opposed to any form of sexual misconduct anywhere, whether at work or on the street.

A wholesaler made the mistake of calling her Bobbi-My-Baby once.

You contemptible, narcissistic, misogynist. My name is Roberta. Not Bobbi-My-Baby. If you're asking to be sued for sexual harassment, say it again.

He never made that mistake.

Vette was certain if the situation arose, Roberta could verbally take down a terrorist. No one screwed with her. Not Max, Hugh, Neil, or Woody, and Vette would never try.

Roberta had been Futrell Auto Group's Office Manager for over twenty years. She was a living databank of vital information. If you needed anything, anyone, or instructions, you asked Roberta.

"What do you need honey?" Roberta's loud nasal tone could be heard across the room.

Vette stood next to Woody and both took a brief moment to absorb Roberta's costume of the day. She was the most colorful woman either of them had ever known. The more salt that came in to her peppered hair, the more bohemian her clothing became.

Today above her teal reading glasses was a skull cap of red, blue, green, and yellow embroidery that matched an equally colorful knee length vest. It was trimmed in black faux fur circling her armpits and ran up one side of her front zipper around her neck and down the zipper's other side. Her high-heeled boots were embroidered in another pattern of purples, brown, and pink. Bangles covered both forearms and poking out of her modest bob haircut were huge silver chandelier earrings of the moon and stars. She wore a conservative black long-sleeved tank top and leggings under it all to make it office friendly.

"You look absolutely lovely today, Roberta," Woody said.

"Why, thank you dear. Now what do you want?"

"I have a fleet buyer coming in twenty minutes and just realized I left my backpack at my house. Could you go get it for me? I don't want to miss this meeting but there are some vital documents I need for the deal in my backpack."

Roberta tilted her head and scoffed as if to say 'are you insane?' "Woody, you know I don't make unprotected left turns and the fastest route to your house has three. So in order for me to get there and back in the time frame you require is impossible. I would need at least one hour to make the round trip."

"Come on Roberta," Woody pleaded. "You don't need a stop light to turn left. You can cowgirl up and jump into traffic. I know you can."

"Why on earth would I do such a thing at this late date in my driving career?"

"I can go get it for you," Vette suggested.

Roberta quickly lifted her palms up in a what-the-hell pose that slapped her bracelets together, clanking like a cacophony of tin cans. "Don't you have a plane to catch? Literally. A plane to catch?"

"The airport limo isn't picking me up for another three hours and Luke's already settled at Max and Opal's house so I have nothing but free time."

Woody said, "Great! Thanks."

"I'm going to need to take your car, mine is at home," Vette said.

"Here you go," Woody said handing her the keys to his house and the Lincoln. "My backpack is right next to the front door." Woody gave her a perfunctory hug. "Thanks. I really appreciate it."

Vette turned to leave, and almost ran smack into Hugh.

"Have a great trip Vette," Hugh said. "I know Max and Opal are thrilled to have Luke for the next few days. Which made me think. You know, I teach a course on building plastic toy model cars."

"Yes, I remember hearing that," Vette said.

"Well, while you're away, maybe I can have Luke come to my house where I have a toy room, perfect for teaching him how to make a model car or plane," Hugh said. "As a matter of fact, I just got a Star Wars authentic Luke Skywalker X-Wing Fighter model that would be perfect for him and me to build together."

Even though Hugh was kind to offer and seemed eager to teach Luke how to make a toy fighter plane, Vette knew Opal and Max were not about to give up a moment of their precious Luke time. They had a fun-packed schedule.

"That's good of you to offer, Hugh, but Mom and Dad have Luke's time all booked while I'm away. Right now, I think Luke may be a bit young for that kind of intricate work. Maybe in a few years, I'll take you up on your offer, okay?"

"Sounds good to me. Well, have a safe trip." Hugh turned and walked to his office. At seventy, Hugh was moving a little slower.

Vette turned to Woody. "Have you ever seen his toy room?"

"Yeah," Woody said. "It's damn impressive."

"Yes, it is that," Vette agreed. "Tammy says he labors over each one of those models like a work of art. I guess they are. She told me it takes him months and months to finish one."

"Hey, are you going to go to my house?" Woody asked.

"Going now. Going now," Vette shook his keys in the air.

"Don't eat any of the stuff on the counter. I baked some No-Fail Fudge early this morning and it turned out to be an epic fail. Milk had gone bad and I didn't realize it until after I cooked them. Took one bite and almost lost it. I didn't have time this morning to clean up and pitch them yet."

"I can do that for you when I'm there."

"No. Don't bother. I'll take care of it. Just don't touch them."

"Okay, you whack-job," Vette said wiggling her fingers in front his face as if casting a spell. "I won't touch them."

"I mean it."

"Okay. Okay. I promise I'll just grab the backpack and be right back."

Roberta called to Vette as she headed toward the door. "Mind those unprotected left turns!"

Chapter 33

Still- 2018

*F*antasy Fudge, the No Fail Fudge recipe card sat on Woody's breakfast counter along with a mountain of brown squares piled high. The chocolate mountain resembled something Jag would leave behind a bush in the backyard. In the sink was a gallon milk jug, turned upside down in the drain, next to an empty jar of marshmallow cream. Before Vette saw the mottled yellowish-pink hues of bacteria clinging to the inside of the upside-down plastic container, the powerful funk of sour, lumpy milk assaulted her nostrils.

"Good God," Vette said to the empty room as she turned from the smell. "That's a definite fail."

As she walked around the counter, a well-used recipe card peeked out from beneath the fudge instructions and caught Vette's eye. The ingredients and footnotes kept her attention. Reading it twice, she pulled out her phone to capture the recipe in a photo. She checked the readability of her picture and put everything back as it was.

Woody bought this 1980's house, not for the wood kitchen cabinets, the beige backsplash, the russet-colored granite counters, or for the living room's wood-burning stove. He bought it for the land. Woody had over three acres of beautifully mature landscaping. The house and front yard filled up one full acre, while the backyard took up the remaining two acres. All of it was breathtaking and meticulously cared for by Woody. He had even transplanted his poison garden from his parent's backyard to his new home.

Opening the specially made wrought-iron gate with the skull and crossbones at the peak and the words, '*These Plants can Kill*,' written just below, Vette went inside her brother's poison garden. Compared to the fenced two-plus-acre backyard, the garden didn't take up that much room. If it had been found off a countryside road, it could be comparable to the size of a generational family plot. Vette moved to the fifteen-foot-tall plants with the large leaves in section number four, and pointed her phone's camera to the base name plaque. Next was a photo at section six of the beautiful purple flowers, then over to section twelve for the low-growing ground cover.

Vette grabbed the backpack and locked Woody's house. With the touch of her finger, she opened the tailgate of his Lincoln. She tossed the backpack in, but in doing so she knocked over Jag's travel-toy organizer prompting a stuffed Woody Woodpecker to laugh maniacally. The other toys rolled randomly across the spotless carpet.

Vette climbed awkwardly into the back, pushed aside the trunk grocery organizer and a box of files. She stuffed all of Jag's toys back in his travel organizer, then leaned against the back of the back seat with her legs stretched to the tailgate opening. She pulled her phone out and found the picture of the recipe card, and focused on the bottom section.

> *Use mortar and pestle to grind seeds to fine consistency.*
> **Puree roots and berries. Mix all together.*
> *See research file number one, section four.*
> **See research file number two, section six and twelve.*

Vette enhanced the photo looking beyond the recipe card to see a small grey ceramic mortar bowl sitting on the counter and inside the bowl was its pestle wand with a perfectly shaped curve for smooth grinding against the mortar. She put her phone back in her pocket, and leisurely scooted her way out.

"Ha." Vette said to the open air. "Finally got it."

Turning to the left she noticed the padlocked file container once again. Lifting Woody's key ring she found the matching key for the lock and scooted back against the back seat again. She began pulling out files from the Dog List section, the In-Progress section, and the Completed section.

Words jumped from the page. *Search Type: Registered Sex Offender. Victim age. Victim gender.* The offender's *date of birth, sex, race, weight and height.* Names. *Janice Stanley Knight, Amy Miller, Kent Soto* and it went on and on and on. There were court records. Victim stories. And finally sex offender's obituaries. There had to be twenty-five or more in the Completed section. Only two in the In-Progress file. And the Dog List section was an inch thick with Troy Coomes' file at the front.

Vette found she was holding Wendell Jacks sheet. The one she'd held before. Vette knew. She'd known since Woody's dog, Sergeant's death.

Vette did the math. Woody started killing sex offenders when he was seventeen. When he was lost and she was at university.

Vette was horrified. But she read it again. And again.

> *Victim: Four-year-old boy*
> *Crime: Aggravated child molestation. Sodomized the boy.*
> *Threw boy from speeding car going sixty-five mph. The boy, paralyzed from the waist down, lived.*
> *Time Served: Twenty-five years.*
> *Begin Date: November 6, 2009*
> *End Date: November 13, 2009*

Vette's son was four years old. *This could have been Luke,* she thought. The horror dissipated and was replaced with an ease of contentment. Woody's manner of dealing with these people was deplorable. Yet now, Vette could see. It was oddly justifiable. Almost poetic.

She knew she had to get back. There was no time to search the files to find out how he was killing them. But she was sure in the last eleven years her baby brother had killed at least twenty-five convicted sex offenders, with that number rising by two according the in-progress file. And he was getting away with it. There was nothing to stop him, except maybe her. But why would she do that? How could she do that?

This was her fault. They should have talked about his rape, their attack. They should talk about it with each other, with doctors. She had to get him help. She had to.

Chapter 34

Still - 2018

After Betty's cards fell to the floor, Brian, Chanya, and Cody gathered Betty, some wine and glasses, and went to the fire pit. This was the night for real horror stories told by the fire.

Brian leaned forward and stared into the flames. "Jesus," he said, shaking his head in disgust. "Brad Denver abducted you and Cody's sister when you were eight years old. You got away and he…" Brian turned to Cody. "That asshole did that to your sister? God, I'm so sorry."

"No need to say you're sorry," Cody took a sip of wine. "You had nothing to do with it."

"No," Brian agreed. "But I brought it forward by being here, by working there. And for any renewed pain I have caused you two, for that I'm sorry."

Betty said, "It's been twenty years now. And lots of therapy to help put it away, but it's like locking your crazy uncle in the attic. Every so often he tromps around above your head just to let you know he's still there. That it happened. We accept that Alice will never come back. That this thing, this horrific thing, it will never go away. But I do wish… I wish Brad Denver would. Maybe then that crazy uncle in the attic would finally be gone." Betty looked at Chanya. "You know, he sends me letters from prison. He always writes the same thing."

A memory jerked Brian forward in his chair. In the memory he was walking past Brad Denver's cell. That dumb fuck always talked to himself. Brian remembered hearing him say something.

"Yeah," Denver had said. "That dark-haired one that got away. I'd like a chance at her. Maybe I'll write her another letter."

Simultaneously Brian and Betty said, "Dear Betty… come back. "

Betty slowly turned toward Brian, "How do you know that?"

"Brad talks to himself," Brian said. "He won't be quiet. I heard Brad, just before his next-door cell mate screamed at him to shut up."

Brian could hear Jack Osteen scream at Brad Denver in his head, *"HEY ASS-WIPE, SHUT THE FUCK UP!"*

Brian continued, "Anyway, just before that, I heard Brad say those exact words. *Dear Betty… come back.* God. I'm sorry."

Cody put another log on the fire while Chanya refilled everyone's glass.

"There had been multiple attempts on his life before I started working there," Brian said. "Guys jumped him in the shower and in the hall. Inmates have a pecking order and pedophiles rank at the bottom. The general population has a way of eliminating pedophiles rather quickly, but that only happens if an inmate is stupid enough to tell what he's done to be put there, otherwise the other inmates have no way of finding out."

"So you think the inmate population has no idea what Brad Denver is in there for?" Cody asked.

"I'd bet my house on it," Brian said. "He spends most of his time alone. With overcrowding in the prison system the turnover of inmates is high. The new guys in there don't know what he's in for. It has to be how he's stayed alive all these years, and it's how he will continue to stay alive."

"That can't happen," Cody said looking Brian in the eyes.

"No." Brian stared back through the flames at Cody. "It can't."

Within days word began to circulate at Collinsville Correction Center. Brad Denver was a pedophile. He preyed on little girls. Little girls.

Chapter 35

Still- 2018

Dating wasn't something Vette had to give up. She chose to give it up.

Shelley, Vette's closest friend, wasn't dating either. As an orthopaedic surgeon, Shelley was the only other woman Vette knew who was living a celibate life. The only logical explanation why Vette and Shelley were single, was they were too stunning and too powerful. They were intimidating without realizing it. And Shelley was dateless due to her schedule, although it didn't stop her from badgering Vette to get started.

"Come on," she said. "Let me fix you up with my next door neighbor, Wendall."

Although a really nice guy, Wendall was a combination of Quasimodo and Howdy-Doody. On a good day Wendall could button his shirt and make it came out even.

"I don't think so," Vette answered.

"Okay. Then we'll go to a club and you can pick out one of your own."

"I'd rather be tied to a bumper and dragged around town. Anyway, when do you have the time, or the energy to go to a club?"

"Yeah, we're screwed." Shelley scoffed, "No. To be literal we're not, and therein lies the problem."

It had been almost six years since Vette's last date and that was with Frederick. It would take another six years to build the courage to try it again. It wasn't that Vette had no propositions. She was asked out many times, but each offer was met with a polite refusal.

Going on this trip without Luke was flinging her way over her comfort border. Vette's fingers slid into her pocket to skim the small knife. Holding her pocket knife gave her a sense of security. She knew Woody felt the same about his.

I have to put this in my suitcase before I check in, she thought.

As the limousine came to a stop before the American Airlines terminal, tears welled in her eyes to underscore that point. All was good, but now here she was at O'Hare Airport actually doing the leaving. Leaving her Toodle-bear. But she was also leaving her baby brother who needed her even more than she knew. She knew Woody was silently hoping for her to help him. And she would as soon as she got back.

She wanted to scream at the limo driver to turn the car around and take her home. Instead she blinked back her tears, tucked her knife inside her suitcase, and headed for the ticket counter to check her bag and confirm her seat assignment.

O'Hare airport was packed. She'd allotted two hours to check in, the amount of time recommended by the powers that be. Apparently the early arrival time was in case the bomb-squad felt you warranted a strip search. Vette carried a lighter in her purse, but could that really be considered an explosive device? She wasn't sure.

After getting her boarding pass, Vette carried a large coffee along with her backpack slung over her right shoulder, and her purse, and stepped outside O'Hare departures just far enough away from the door to be legal. Wedging her backpack between her legs so that no one could grab and dash with it, Vette pulled out a Silver Pack of Virginia Slims, ripped off the cellophane, popped out a cigarette, and lit up. She didn't really smoke. At least that's what she told herself.

She wasn't a thief, axe-murderer, or vamp. She was a smoker. Vette had started smoking when she was twelve and quit before she became pregnant. She hadn't gone near a cigarette in four years, but last year one of the guys at work offered her one, and one couldn't hurt. Right? Wrong. She'd been smoking ever since.

Smoking cigarettes used to be glamorous. All the best people did it, but oh how times change. Now cigarettes are vulgar and cigars are macho. Cigar smokers get a mahogany-lined bar and a movie deal. Cigarette smokers get a rat-infested alley and as much respect as a package of body odor. Though in the end all smokers are created equal. They all die writhing in pain. With that in mind, Vette seriously considered getting the patch as she leaned against a post, inhaled deeply, and filled her lungs with luscious smoke. Okay, maybe next week she'd quit.

Anyway, no one knew she smoked and she'd deny the habit until her dying day. But oh man, that first drag filled her lungs and gave her the sweetest hint of a buzz. She hadn't had a cigarette in, well about an hour ago. Maybe she was a smoker but she only smoked in certain places, like outside or in the garage, anywhere away from her family, and never around Luke. And yeah, sometimes hanging out her bedroom window.

Whatever, she thought. *Fuck it. I'm a grown-ass woman and if I want to smoke I will.*

A gray-haired woman walked by giving Vette the stink eye. Vette smiled while mentally giving the old bitch the finger, then snuffed out the last of the butt, took a final pull on her coffee, and threw out the cup before heading for security with an Altoid dissolving on her tongue.

She sat at gate F27 in Terminal 3 and opened the latest *US* magazine. Reading a celebrity gossip magazine was her guilty pleasure. Every so often she'd blink back a tear over Woody and his files, which for some odd reason made her miss Luke even more, but at that very instant she remembered what Roberta said.

"Get the hell over it." Roberta ordered. "That boy is going to grow up and leave you sitting in your living room to watch your plants die. So get the hell on with it. Enjoy your life and stop waiting. I don't want to hear one more belly-aching word about missing Luke, because it's going to get a hell of a lot worse. Kids are put on this earth to break their mother's hearts and you're no exception to that rule. He will never think about you as much as you think and hope and worry and pray for him. Eventually he'll figure it out, but you'll be dead when he finally gets it. Long dead."

"Roberta," Vette said. "I hate to point this out, but you're tad cynical."

"Honey I'm a realist. And you have a ticket to Bermuda so get the fuck out of here. Drink too much. Find a man. Have sex on the beach. Go to parties. Have sex on a balcony. Dance all night. But above all, have sex. When you get home, you'll be relaxed. Luke will be happy and life will go on."

Vette smiled thinking of the conversation that took place just a few hours ago. Roberta was right, she was going to make herself have fun.

Vette laid her backpack flat on the chair beside her, slid her iPad out of the front pocket where she'd put it for easy accessibility, then created a makeshift coffee table of her backpack, where she laid her ticket, and set her bottled water.

Before coming on this trip she downloaded some movies and a bunch of books including two her mom recommended by an author named Sidney Sheldon. He'd been long dead but his novels promised a perfect storm of romance, suspense, and mystery that apparently stood the test of time. If she couldn't be with Luke, at least she could be with a good book. It was always fun to find a new author, even if he was dead and gone. For now though she was happy with her celebrity gossip magazine.

Her first class ticket showing her seat 2B was exposed for all to see, including him.

It was an aisle seat. He had one too, but he'd move to the window this time. Coming back from the gate desk with a new boarding pass in hand, he sat across from Vette and watched.

"Our flight time today will be three hours and twenty-two minutes," the pilot said over the loudspeaker, but Vette wasn't listening. Hollywood's Hottest Hunks held her full attention. The guy sitting next to her was no slouch either, but she couldn't talk to him yet. Rule is to wait until five minutes before landing to strike up a conversation. That way if the guy snorts when he speaks or is a religious zealot or a conspiracy theorist, Vette would only have to deal with him for a few minutes rather than hour after hour after hour.

Vette connected her noise cancelling headphones to her iPad and was about to slip them over her ears.

"I normally don't sit next to smokers but I couldn't take my eyes off of you. So I changed my seat to be next to you."

Chapter 36

Still- 2018

Okay, this is stalker bad, Vette thought. Looking into his dark raw-honey eyes, Vette stammered, "Uh, I don't smoke." It was all she could think to say to this sex-on-a-muscle man.

"Oh yeah you do," he said.

"Well. Okay. But no one knows."

"Trust me," he smiled showing his Hollywood white teeth. "Everyone knows."

Vette sat straighter in her chair. "No they don't."

"If they come within four feet of you, they do. You reek of it."

"Well then, why in the hell would you want to sit next to me," Vette said, instantly loathing the five-o'clock shadow he sported.

"Because I haven't talked to you in like twenty years and thought we could keep each other company. That was a mistake," he said turning to look out the window at the passing clouds then back at Vette. "You know, I had an aisle seat."

"Yeah. So?" Vette challenged.

"So, I hate window seats."

"Who doesn't?" Vette said. "When you have to go to the bathroom…"

He cut her off. "You have to climb over the sleeping blob next to you."

"Yeah." Vette stared at the man. "Carlton? Carlton Rayburn? You're, you're Cody's brother."

"Yes," Carlton said. "Yes I am."

"Wha? How? What are the odds? You going to Bermuda. Sitting next to me. Either you're a fricken stalker or this is the biggest coincidence ever," Vette said.

"I'm going for door number two because I'm not a *fricken* stalker," Carlton said, stating the obvious. "Could it be that we are going on the same Toyota trip?"

"But you're a drug seller, drug dealer," Vette said a bit too loudly.

All heads in first class turned to Carlton.

"What the hell?" Carlton said so all could hear. "No, I'm not a pharmaceutical salesman anymore." Lowering his tone he added, "Vette, you are making this so much more difficult than is necessary. I can see you're going to have to switch seats with someone here."

"I'm not switching seats," Vette announced.

"Well neither am I," Carlton countered.

"Fine."

"Fine."

Both faced forward. Not a word was spoken for all of ten seconds.

"What do you do now?" Vette asked.

"GM at Draeger."

"No kidding," Vette angled her shoulder toward Carlton. "How long you have been there?"

"Not long," Carlton said. "Twelve years."

"That's a lot longer than not long, you know."

"And you're the CFO at Futrell," Carlton stated.

"How do you know that?" Vette asked. "You are a stalker."

"Okay. I'm that, or could it be that I listen to what's happening in my own industry, in my own town?" Carlton pointed to the plane's ceiling as if having an epiphany and said, "That's it."

"You're making fun of me."

"It's so easy," Carlton chuckled. "I'm sorry. Let me buy you a drink. I hear you get the best service up here."

After the lunch was served and removed, Vette asked, "Why are you here alone? Bermuda is supposed to be one of the most romantic places to go."

"I'm not seeing anyone right now and wasn't about to take the chance of being in Bermuda with someone that isn't…, well that isn't."

"I know what you mean. I haven't dated in so long, I wouldn't know where to begin," Vette said.

"I date. I date a lot. Just haven't found someone I feel compelled to carry on a long-term conversation with." Carlton looked a bit startled at his own comment. "Don't get me wrong, I'm not an intellectual snob. I just want someone that has more depth than I've met yet. Does that make sense?"

"Actually it does," Vette smiled. "My most interesting conversations are with my four-year-old son, Luke. He's fascinating."

"Kids usually are. They're very insightful," Carlton said. "Did you know Cody and his wife Betty are going to have a baby around the first of the year?"

"No I didn't. That's wonderful. Good for them."

Vette stared at Carlton a bit too long.

"What?" he asked.

"You're like a Chippendale dancer with brains."

"I believe I should take offense to that statement on behalf of all Chippendale dancers. But instead I'll reciprocate by saying, you're a stunning piece of art yourself."

"Piece of what?" Vette said.

Carlton shook his head and chuckled, "You are so easy. I said, piece of art."

"Oh. Uh. Thank you?"

As the plane touched down Carlton said, "Seeing as how you and I are both here stag, do you want to hang out some? When we get in we're supposed to sign up for activities and dine-around restaurants. I really don't want to sit next to some twenty-one-year-old fourth wife of a balding beer-belly executive, and pretend to give a rat's ass about the latest episode of *Keeping up with the Kardashians* and their preposterous scandals. So would you like to? Join me, I mean? No obligation, just company if you want it. I think we could have fun, and if not we can go our separate ways."

"I'd like that." Vette smiled and said, "I'd like that very much."

Chapter 37

Still

With both arms full of groceries, Tammy slammed the kitchen door with her foot.

"Hugh?" she called.

"Hey you're back early," Hugh said coming in the room. "Have you got more in the car?"

"Yes," Tammy said, laying her first load on the table. "Was that little Hudson I saw leaving just now?"

Hugh stopped at the opened door. "Yes, we were finishing up the 1951 Hudson Hornet model, but for some reason he didn't want to stay. So he called his mom to come and get him. I'll finish it up tonight."

"That's too bad that he couldn't finish it with you," she said as she unpacked the first bag and began to put things away. Refrigerator and cabinet doors opened and closed. "Will you take it to him tomorrow then?"

"Nah, Hudson said he didn't want it anymore," Hugh answered, as the door closed behind him. Carrying in another load of groceries, he added, "I'll keep it with the others."

"You need to go sit down," Tammy said looking at Hugh's sweaty brow and red face. "Have you tested your blood sugar lately?"

"Yep. It's high."

Tammy left the groceries and went to the corner of the counter and opened the white-marble bread box where Hugh kept his test kit, needles, syringes, insulin and his emphysema inhalers. She kept his pills in a plastic bin in the cabinet below. He took twenty-three pills in the morning and fifteen at night. His eye drops for glaucoma and dry eyes were in the refrigerator, in addition to his Lantus insulin glargine that he shot into his stomach every morning and every night.

Tammy took out Hugh's test meter to check his latest numbers. She clicked the button to see 361, then clicked again, 297, and again 385, 316, 313, 310, when she reached 392 she stopped pressing the back button. Normal levels were 72 to 108. She knew all too well the long lasting effects Hugh's sustained high blood sugar levels had already taken on his body. He had severe heart disease and had experienced so many TIA strokes they stopped counting. He had eye problems, nerve problems, and was dropping protein in his urine, so yeah he had kidney damage along with a shitload of other health issues.

The other side of high blood sugar was the inevitable drops. Hugh's sugar would spike high, he'd then shoot himself up with too much fast-acting insulin then his blood sugar would plummet. Every time his blood sugar dropped, Hugh lost more brain cells. He had more and more drops lately with some going as low as 40, a figure that usually put people into a diabetic coma to die.

Luckily every time a drop happened, Tammy had been there with the glucagon emergency kit. Hugh would be disoriented, and the next instant unconscious. Tammy immediately gave him the injection and turned him onto his side because she knew what was coming. He would vomit. He always did. But the injection worked to raise his blood sugar to 70 mg/dl and above. Hugh would then wake up fifteen minutes later and all was fine again. Until the next cycle.

The first time this happened, Tammy had called 911, but only the first time. Hugh was furious. She never called again.

On their last visit to the VA, Hugh's doctor announced, "You've tested positive for Hepatitis C."

Tammy exhaled sharply when the doctor said it so matter-of-fact. "Isn't that fatal? What do we do to stop the liver damage?"

"Oh, you don't need to worry about it. He'll die long before the Hep C kicks in."

"Wha?" Tammy couldn't believe her ears. That's when she realized the Veteran's Association just wanted their Vietnam Veterans to die. These men and women were costing the government too much money and their inevitable deaths would save the government a ton of money in medical and compensation costs.

Hugh was a ticking time bomb. But a time bomb that Tammy worked to keep alive by fixing him healthy meals, accompanying him on nightly walks, and monitoring his health as best she could.

"Did you give yourself a correction shot of insulin?" she asked.

"Yes, but it doesn't matter anymore," Hugh said sitting at the kitchen table. "Nothing changes. No matter what I do, my blood sugar is high. So I'm going to eat and do whatever I want. Makes no difference anyway. And I might as well have fun." He added, "Hell I'm seventy. If I make it another year that's a bonus."

"Stop talking like that," Tammy said. "We just had our twenty-fifth wedding anniversary and I plan to celebrate our fiftieth anniversary with you."

"Well you'll have to bring the cake to the cemetery and eat it sitting on my grave because there is no way in hell I'll make it to ninety. You heard the doctor this week."

"Screw that doctor," Tammy said. "We need to go back to Mayo Clinic to have you checked over."

"There's nothing they can do," Hugh said. "My body's just caving in on itself. Got two more grocery bags to get." Hugh went back out to the garage.

Tammy picked up the package that came in the mail for Hugh and walked it into his toy room. It contained model car chrome tires and a new precision knife. There, on the work table, was the 1951 Hudson Hornet model with the top part completed. It was just waiting for the rolling chassis, or bottom part with the wheels as Tammy called it, to be glued together.

She looked up at the shelf that stretched clear around the room, now filled with fifty-one model cars. There was one space open for the Hudson, the fifty-second. Tammy laid the package next to Hugh's partially opened briefcase. Looking back at the briefcase, she noticed a plastic baggy that appeared to have hair inside. There were letters written in black marker on the bag. Hu…

"What are you doing?" Hugh said, slamming his briefcase shut.

"I was just looking. Why'd you do that?" Tammy asked.

"What?"

"Slam your briefcase like that. You scared me."

"Sorry," Hugh shrugged. "I just closed it, didn't mean to do it so hard. Guess I don't know my own strength. What do you think of the model so far?"

Tammy knew she was never to touch a model on the table because it could easily fall apart if the glue wasn't completely dry. She never touched Hugh's models, and refused to clean in here for fear of breaking one. She leaned closer to the emerald green 1951 Hudson Hornet with its bloated body and unibrow visor above the windshield. It had red tear-drop back lights and on the trunk was a chrome emblem shaped like an eagle's wing span. The word "Hudson" was carved ever so elegantly in the center. Next to the top part of the model sat the chassis with white wall tires.

"Oh Hugh," she said putting her arm around his waist. "I think this is one of your best models yet. So much intricate work. It's beautiful."

"Thank you," he said giving her a squeeze.

"Now I have to go put the rest of those groceries away and start lunch," Tammy said leaving the room, closing the door after her.

Hugh opened his briefcase and looked at the blonde tuft of hair in the baggy marked "Hudson," next to the Polaroid of the eight-year-old naked body facing the wall. The white face mask was inside the case and hidden from sight in the false top compartment.

Over the last few years, it had become easier. Not easier in that he had more victims annually. Increasing the number would be reckless. Hugh was exceptionally cautious. He only allowed himself to choose one boy a year, but the manner in which he got them was easier. Hugh found a way to draw the boys to him rather than hunting them down. He was getting too tired and old for an aggressive hunt.

He devised a more efficient method. He had gone to the park district and proposed teaching a course. The district jumped on it. Hugh taught a four-week summer course on scale model building for eight-to-ten-year-olds. Most mothers liked the strong grandfatherly figure he offered their sons.

Hugh liked having a group to choose from. Making his choice was easy. Look for the most vulnerable. The shy one. From a single-parent household. The runt of the litter was always good, too, meaning small of stature for their age. And, of course, a boy.

The cost of the course was not cheap as many materials were necessary to build a model car to scale correctly. At each work station, Hugh meticulously laid out all of the tools on an individual gray-blue measurement mat that each student would need. There was a knife, tweezers, paper towels, sprue cutter, tape, clothes pins, toothpicks, glue, emery board, paint brushes, paint, putty, and cotton swabs. And, of course, the model. This year it was a Jaguar E Type Car Starter Set 1/32.

At the end of each class the students took all of their tools home with them to bring back and set up their own work station for the next class. That way they would know the proper way to maintain their tools for years to come.

Hudson Terry sat in the last row of work stations. He didn't initiate conversations and he didn't ask questions. Hugh recognized the lost look in his eyes. He could smell the fear of firsts on him. Hugh made a point to draw him out. To help him.

When Hugh spoke with Hudson, he put in a special effort to always be smiling, keeping eye contact, and nodding to show that he was truly focusing on what Hudson was saying. In those four weeks, Hugh confided in Hudson's mother that he felt Hudson was quite gifted and a kind boy. Hudson became more animated around Hugh, speaking faster, gesturing and nodding, and sitting up straighter whenever Hugh approached.

It was Hudson's mother who did the asking. "Mr. Johnson, would it be possible for you to help Hudson with another model now that the class is over? He has loved this class so much and I hate to see him have to give it up."

Hugh smiled, "Help him in what way?"

"I know you only teach this course once a year, but could you make time to work with Hudson a bit more until he feels confident to build them on his own?"

Hudson stood next to his mother looking hopeful. Hugh bent down and looked him straight in the eye, "Of course I would love to work with you on another model. I have one I picked up the other day that would be perfect. It's a 1951 Hudson Hornet."

"Hudson? Like my name?" Hudson asked.

"Yes, exactly like your name." Hugh smiled.

Hugh looked at Hudson's mother. "Thursday mornings are good for me, I'm off work that day. My wife volunteers at our church's food pantry distribution from 9:00 to 11:00 a.m., then does our grocery shopping, so we wouldn't be disturbing her either. Would that work with your schedule?"

And so the first Thursday of July they began. Hugh grew closer to Hudson, and Hudson was grateful for his attention. But the last Thursday of July at 9:30 a.m. it all changed.

Chapter 38

Still

"Well, crud," Hugh said to Hudson, as they sat side-by-side on tall comfortable stools at the work station.

"What's the matter, Mr. Johnson?" Hudson asked.

"We're out of plastic cement," Hugh said, going to the supply closet to double check. "Yep, we're out." Hugh turned back to Hudson, "Will you be all right here for about fifteen minutes while I run to the store and grab some? You can watch TV and have anything you want to eat from the kitchen."

"Sure, I'll be good," Hudson said.

Hugh picked up his keys and said, "I'll be right back."

He drove to the back alley and parked his car out of sight. He opened the gate to the six-foot privacy fence and walked into the back yard. Inside the work shed, he changed into black slacks and a black long-sleeved t-shirt. From the cover of the high bush cranberry, he watched.

He saw Hudson sitting on the leather couch with his hand in a bag of chips. The huge TV above the fireplace was turned to *Ghostbusters*, the real version with Dan Aykroyd and Bill Murray not some flimsy remake.

The white face mask slid like butter onto his face. Hugh was ready. A soft breeze followed him through the back door as the Ghostbusters on TV stood on top of Spook Central, the super-conductive antenna created to bring forth Gozer in its Destructor Form. Hudson's eyes grew wide at the sight of the red-eyed, spiked-hair creature.

Behind him stood the man in the white mask.

The man watched Hudson reach into the bag of chips. Gozer's arms electrified, purple veins of lightning spewed toward Hudson from the TV.

Hudson's nightmare began.

Hudson's legs kicked wildly at the air as he was carried into the bedroom. His naked body shook as he faced the wall. He felt the smooth, cold metal of scissors touch the back of his neck. The crunch of the blades sliced together, cutting his hair. Pulled to the bed, the lid of the petroleum jelly fell inches from his check.

After.

"I'll slice your mother from her crotch to her mouth in front of you. She'll bleed to death and just as she is about to die, she'll watch me do the same to you. Tell anyone this and I'll do that. You live at 1365 W LaSalle Street. Do you understand? I know where you live. I know where your mother lives."

With his back to the man, Hudson nodded vigorously. He did as he was told. Clean up. Wipe off. Don't look at the man. Get dressed. Sit on the couch. Don't move. Don't look. Don't tell. Don't ever tell.

"Hudson, I'm back," Hugh called from the front door. It had been twenty minutes. He was getting slow in his old age. Changing back into his khaki slacks and white collared Polo shirt took longer than usual. His knees were giving him trouble again.

"Hudson?" Hugh walked around the corner and saw the boy sitting on the couch facing the television's black screen.

He was smaller now. Less interesting. Less.

"I've got the cement. Ready to finish this model?" Hugh feigned enthusiasm. Hudson didn't move. "Hudson? You all right?"

Hudson bolted from the couch. "I'm fine. I want to go home." The man told him he had to wait until the old man returned before calling his mother. Wait. Wait.

Hudson gripped his cell phone, punching the numbers.

"Hi mom. We're done. Come now. Please come now. It's fine. I'm all right. Just tired. Can you come now? Okay. I'll be outside waiting. Me too."

Hugh went to Hudson. "Is everything all right Hudson? Did something happen while I was at the store?"

"I'm fine. Nothing happened, I'm just tired."

"Are you sure nothing happened?" Hugh pressed. He got down on his knees, which hurt like hell to do, and looked Hudson in the eyes. "You can tell me anything you know. Anything and I'll never tell."

"No. Nothing happened. I just watched Ghostbusters, and I don't feel so good."

"Do you want to come by tomorrow to finish the model? I can make time so you can get it done and take it home."

"No. I don't want it. I'm not coming back here. I'm bored with making models. I don't want to do it anymore." Hudson grabbed his backpack and went to the front door. "Thanks, Mr. Johnson. Bye."

"Bye Hudson." As the door closed Hugh smiled, walked into the laundry room and threw in a load of dark towels along with his black slacks, black shirt, and his underwear.

Chapter 39

Still

Carlton and Vette were inseparable. Carlton's dry sense of humor kept Vette entranced. The man could make her laugh at the most inappropriate times, and she loved that.

By their second dinner together Vette found herself spilling her story of Frederick. "So yeah, we got married after knowing each other for two months and divorced a month-and-a-half later."

Carlton nodded, "Well at least you worked hard at it. I'm sorry, did you say your names were Nicolas Cage and Lisa Marie Presley? Nope. Wait. Wait. That's not right. They were married for three months. You two are more in league with Kim Kardashian and that NBA player she blinked at. What was his name? Oh yeah, Kris Humphries. They lasted, I think, about a month longer than your marriage."

"Hey!" Vette protested. "I had to divorce him. He was having wild monkey sex with a body piercing, hairy armpit, big-busted bitch who was into psychedelic drugs and orgies. "

"Oh. Well," Carlton shrugged his shoulders. "Who could blame the guy? Choosing between you…" His gaze went slowly up and back down her body-hugging cream cocktail dress, her piercing blue eyes, and flawless skin. He quickly shook his head as if to clear away his awestruck mind. "Or choosing hairy armpits and body piercings." Carlton pondered a moment. "No contest. I'd go with the pits."

Vette was hooked. He didn't coddle her. He shot straight from the hip and told her exactly what he thought. Vette gave it right back to him. They were a match.

Friday Vette climbed on the back of their rented scooter and held on to Carlton as he drove to Gibb's Hill lighthouse for what the brochure read was the best view in Bermuda. They walked the shops on Front Street, then snorkeled at Horseshoe Bay's pink beach in Southampton, where Vette almost drowned in two feet of water.

"Why the hell do people do this shit?" Vette said. She sputtered and coughed as she stood up, then immediately fell full face in the water again. She struggled to her feet revealing her white Brazilian scrunch bikini with the bottom outlining her muscular butt that was now brown from days in the sun.

Carlton was trying unsuccessfully not to laugh while aroused at the same time. "When your tube is under water, you don't breathe in."

"Fuck-wad. Remind me to never do this again." Vette wiped the snot from her nose.

"Come on, you've got to try it one more time. They say there are sea turtles over there."

"I'll do it. But only because you took me shopping."

Carlton nodded. "Yeah you owe me big for that."

That evening she paid in full. Carlton came to her room to escort her to the formal dinner. When the door opened, all he could do was take a step back and gasp.

"Damn. You have to warn a man if you're going to look like that. That dress is a loaded gun."

Vette smiled. She wore an elegant, body-skimming gown by Hervé Léger. The strappy navy knit with its sweetheart neckline exposed her long neck and highlighted her cleavage. She wore no necklace, no bra and no earrings. Nothing to take away from her curves and smooth muscles.

"That dress is worth every penny you paid for it."

"It's a rental," Vette said, matter-of-factly grabbing her clutch bag.

"What? A what?" Carlton looked startled. "Rented like a high school prom tux?"

"This would cost one thousand, six hundred and ninety dollars retail. Who in their right mind would spent that kind of money on one fricken dress?"

"How much was it to rent?"

"Two-hundred twenty-five bucks for the dress and thirty for the clutch. So don't spill anything on me."

"You rented a purse? Now that's just weird," Carlton said.

Vette held up her sparkly clutch. "I'll have you know this a Diane von Fursternberg sequined envelope clutch that would have cost me about two hundred bucks. So this total outfit would have taken me for around two grand. That's a trip to Disney World."

Carlton slowly waved his hands in front of her body as if to outline her. "I'd much rather go on this world trip."

"Good, then it was worth the rental fee," Vette smiled and sauntered in front of him, down the hall.

Carlton was admiring the outline of her hips swaying to and fro before him, and sighed heavily.

Vette looked over her shoulder, "Did you say something?"

"Can't talk just yet," Carlton said. "I'm contemplating a trip to Happy World."

Carlton held her hand as they rode the elevator.

After cocktail hour, the six-hundred and forty Toyota guests filed into the main ballroom with its massive stage. In front of the stage was a dance floor and fanning out from there were table rounds for the evening dinner. They were covered in Toyota-branded colors of silver with red accents.

Like magic, Carlton secured two seats for them next to the dance floor center stage.

After the filet mignon, wine, and dessert, the room went dark. Lights shown through the stage curtain revealed a circle of fig leaves around a crown, and at the base of the crown was the name MARS. The drum beats punched and colors flashed against the curtain turning it red, green, and white.

The very familiar artist sang, "Tonight, I just want to take you higher..."

The room erupted.

The stage curtain lifted to an exclusive, Toyota-attendee's-only concert of the twenty-four karat magic world tour. Everyone including Carlton and Vette were on their feet as Bruno Mars and his group of eight men, a drummer, two on keys, a bass player, a guitarist and three singer-dancers jacked up the room.

The screams and cheers couldn't drown out the percussion that beat against their chest. The announcer shouted, "Toyota! Welcome to the twenty-four karat magic world tour. Let's go! If you came to party tonight get up! Get up! Get up!"

The men jumped on stage wearing baseball shirts and black sweats with a white stripe on the outside seams. Bruno Mars shirt was white the others were in pastels.

Halfway through the set, Carlton's hand slid low on Vette's back. Vette turned to Carlton as he leaned down lightly touching his lips to hers. Vette was ready for Carlton.

Bruno shouted to the crowd. "Come on ladies, dance with me." Carlton couldn't take his eyes off of Vette's hips dipping and swaying.

Too soon it was done. Bruno Mars and his eight friends left the stage. The crowd screamed and screamed and screamed for more.

Carlton said, "He'll be back. Don't believe me just watch."

"Uh!" The sexy sound coming from the back of Vette's throat nearly made Carlton sit down and cover himself.

Just as Carlton predicted the band was back, singing "Uptown Funk."

Carlton and Vette danced down the hallway toward Vette's room.

Carlton sang, "Uptown funk you up. Uptown funk you up."

Vette answered, "Say what?"

Inside her room, Vette put the *24K Magic* CD in the player. All of Toyota's guests got a CD in their gift bag along with a t-shirt when they left the event. As if they needed any more than they had been given already, the trip, the place, the food, and then there was the exclusive concert.

Vette thought, *Could life get any better?*

It was about to as Vette turned to Carlton inside her room. Her hands went to her dress straps. She flicked the right strap off her shoulder and took a step toward Carlton. She stopped, turned to look at her left strap, then looked back at Carlton as she flicked that one down her arm too.

"Oh honey, you are waking up the rocket." Carlton said.

"That's the idea." Vette reached behind herself.

Carlton heard the zipper go down.

As the Hervé Léger gown slipped to the floor, Carlton learned Vette had nothing on under that rented gown. No. She had on everything he needed.

By "Chunky," the second song on the CD, Carlton had taken her on the floor. "That's What I Like" was playing while Vette savored the taste of him as he leaned against the wall of balcony curtains. When "Straight up & Down" burst from the speakers, Vette was coming on the couch.

"Finesse" filtered through the shower curtain while Vette soaped up her breasts, abs, and her fine full woman bush. She held Carlton's shoulders as she slid her body against his in a slow dance.

"Too Good To Say Goodbye" brought them to the CD's close with Vette snuggling into Carlton, his muscular arm gently wrapped around her with his hand resting on her breast.

Vette looked down at his hand. "Is that going to be a thing? Or is that something you always do?"

"What?"

"Sleeping with your hand on a woman's breast?"

"Actually I've never lain like this with anyone, and yes, I believe I would like it to become a thing. But only with you," Carlton said as he kissed her forehead. Carlton started to move. "I need to go now."

"What the hell?" Vette blurt. "Where are you going?"

"Over to the desk," he said matter-of-factly. "I have to write Bruno Mars a thank you note."

Vette grabbed his arm and pulled him back to bed. "Get back here and shut up."

But they didn't shut up. Conversation was not a problem.

With her head on Carlton's shoulder Vette said, "I haven't done that in almost five years."

"I could tell around the sixth time."

Vette slid her body on top of his.

"Oh no, not just yet," Carlton eased her back on her side. "Give me a few more minutes. You don't want to kill me on the first night."

"No," Vette kissed his shoulder. "I want to keep you around. Okay, we can talk for a bit. Then it's back to business, big guy."

"You're going to be the death of me."

"Not for a long, long time if I have a say so."

Changing the subject, Vette snuggled into her pillow and faced him. "It's nice that you still help your mom at the bakery."

"Not all the time," Carlton said, stroking her hair away from her eyes. "Just now and then. Mostly I help by finding new recipes, like that deconstructed cheesecake recipe from Tempest Bistro we had last night. Mom will love that one."

"I just found a new recipe, or rather, I stole a new recipe for jelly glazed oatmeal muffins from my brother," Vette said. Not wanting to think about the files she found there too, Vette kept her mind on the recipe. "I've been wanting that recipe forever. Woody kept telling me he would give it to me but then he always forgot. Well I was at his house picking something up for him, just before coming on this trip, and there it was. The recipe card on the counter. So of course I took a picture of it. I'm going to make a batch when we get home." Vette looked in Carlton's eyes. "You can come over and try them if you still want to hang out with me after we get back."

Carlton got up on his elbow and stared down at her. "Okay. We need to clear something up right now. As I told you on the plane,

I'm not seeing anyone because I hadn't found anyone, ever, and I mean ever, that compelled me to carry on a long term conversation, let alone spend my life with. It sounded crazy to me that one person like that even existed. My mom always said there's someone for everyone and I'd know it when I find them. But who believes their mother anyway. Now here I am with you, and it feels like home." Carlton thought he saw panic in Vette's eyes. "I know I'm setting off every psycho alarm in your head, but I'm going to say this anyway. I'm falling in love with you."

"Ahh," Vette stammered.

"Don't freak out and don't you go running for the hills," Carlton said. "Just don't say anything. I want you to know my intentions toward you are honorable. So much so that when we get home, I want you to meet my mother. Of course prior to your meeting, I will have to tell her to put all of her recipes under lock and key, seeing as how you're a known recipe thief."

Vette pulled Carlton to her and gently kissed his eyes, neck and lingered on his lips. She then whispered in his ear, "I'm falling for you too."

Her fingers circled Carlton's nipple and slowly moved down his body. "Oh good," Vette kissed his neck. "Look who is ready for more."

Carlton masterfully flipped her on her back. "I'm here to please."

"Oh yes. Yes you do."

Chapter 40

Still

Woody was a high functioning alcoholic, at least that's what his self-diagnosis revealed once he looked up his symptoms on the Internet. And the Internet never lies.

So what if he came home from work and had four whiskeys, neat, sometimes five. It wasn't like he was drinking a case of beer a day. He didn't like beer, it tasted like warm piss even when it was cold. His normal go-to drink was whiskey, Maker's Mark, Jack Daniel's, or if he could find it, Four Roses. Sitting out back in his perfectly landscaped private yard sipping a drink while staring at the stars with a fire in the fire pit made for a perfect date, especially if he was alone.

He didn't drink and drive. He just liked a nice buzz at night by himself.

Everyone was after him to find a woman, a wife, or even a string of dates. It was never meant to be for him. He was a one-night stand kind of guy. Most of the time he could get it up, but sometimes not. The rancid memory of being raped lived forever in the corner of his mind. It was the perpetual flaccid shadow in the room. When the dark shadow crept into his mind, he became impotent. If she, whoever she was, expected share time before the fuck, that was a deal breaker. Share time invited the shadow into the room. Woody was not a share kind of guy. He was the hot sex and out the door guy.

He didn't trust anyone enough to tell his secrets. Any secrets. He didn't even talk to Vette about it, but then she already knew. She'd been there and had insisted they never talk about it. So no one else would ever know. No one. He'd issued a self-induced restraining order on everyone else, to keep them away from his thoughts. He wished he could keep his thoughts away from himself.

Woody had been practicing liquid therapy for the last twenty years. He learned early on that the only way to keep his own thoughts at bay was by floating them in whiskey. He'd tried other methods along the way, but nothing numbed the memory like whiskey.

It was their first Sunday family dinner since Vette got home from Bermuda looking rested and tanned, when their mother, Opal, cornered Woody in the kitchen.

"Vette just told me Shelley isn't dating anyone, Woody," Opal said. "Why don't you ask her out? Just for company, nothing more."

"Mom," Woody shook his head. "She's Vette's best friend. It would never work. Anyway, I think I'm one of those people who is meant to be alone. I'm a confirmed bachelor."

"You're gay?" Opal asked. "Not that there is anything wrong with that. Not at all. Dad and I are supportive of you no matter what. We will march in the pride parades and do whatever else you need. Did you know the first gay pride parade was on June 28, 1970 when people marched into New York's Central Park?"

Woody's mouth fell open. "How do you know this stuff mom? That's just weird that you know all these random facts."

"Well, it's true."

"No mom," Woody chuckled. "I'm not gay. You'd be the first person I would have told if I was. No, I'm a heterosexual man who doesn't want to have children and is not willing to put up with the mess most relationships bring. Marriage gives a lot of advantages to women and men who want that lifestyle, but from my vantage point, there is nothing I can get from marriage that I can't get as a bachelor."

"Oh Woody," Opal looked close to tears. "That is so not true. A good marriage is magical. Sure it takes work and fights, but the outcome is more than words can describe. And that's what I want for you. I want you to have someone to watch over you, and for you to watch over. Someone who is your best friend, who loves and adores you."

"Why mom? Why do you want that so much for me?"

"So I can stop worrying about you."

That will never happen, woman or no woman, Woody thought.

Woody believed his mother was born worrying about her own birth, and she would continue worrying, not so much about herself, but about her family until the day she died. She carried the worry gene. Thank goodness it wasn't passed on to him, although it was pressed on him. Like now.

"Mom, I had Sergeant, and now I have Jag, who is my best friend, and who loves me and adores me." Woody leaned down and rubbed the sides of Jag's fluffy head and kissed his massive forehead. "Don't cha' buddy."

Jag looked indulgently into Woody's eyes, stood up, and left the room.

Opal rolled her eyes. "Okay. What about Roberta's niece, Joan?"

"Mother!" Woody looked appalled. "I went out with her once. Hell, she turned over faster than a prom date with a wine cooler."

"Oh my god," Opal gasped. "Why do you tell me these things?"

"You asked. That's why."

Woody noticed the familiar fragrance of warm muffins cooking in the oven fill the kitchen. "What smells so good? Is that dessert?"

"Yes. I'm so excited to taste it," Opal agreed. "It's *your* secret recipe for jelly glazed oatmeal muffins that Vette came across in your kitchen. She texted me the photo of your recipe card. Vette hasn't even tried it yet."

"What?" His eyes locked on the new granite mortar and pestle on his mother's kitchen counter. Remnants of bean grounds were in the bowl. Jelly glaze covered with plastic wrap waited on the kitchen island to be drizzled over the warm muffins. An image of his recipe sat next to it.

"Did you taste any of it?"

"No, you know you can't taste raw batter ingredients," Opal said turning to the sink. "It could make you sick."

Woody lifted Vette's phone that had been left on the counter, found the recipe photo and deleted it. He then did the same with his mother's phone, erasing the text. Woody walked to the oven to check on the muffin tin and immediately screamed as it burned his fingers, "Damn!"

The half-baked muffins splattered on the floor. Woody's foot slipped in the sludge. He grabbed for the island and instead sent the bowl of jelly crashing to the floor. For a second, his hand steadied on the paper recipe, then took a fast slide off the counter sending the paper and Woody to the floor. The recipe and Woody were covered in jelly and batter. It was ruined. All of it.

Vette came into the kitchen to see what the fuss was all about, with Luke following close behind.

Lifting the tattered recipe for Vette to see, Woody said, "This is the recipe for poison muffins I make to kill the rats in my backyard shed." Woody struggled to his feet. "Not only would it have tasted like crap, it would have killed us all."

Luke dipped his finger in the batter on the floor and opened his mouth.

Vette, Woody, and Opal screamed in unison, "NO!"

Vette scooped Luke up, holding his hand far from his mouth, and took him straight to the sink for a vigorous scrubbing.

Chapter 41

Still

Date of Birth: 09/20/1953 Sex: M Race: W Weight: 208 Height: 5'11

The Good Samaritan was outside Troy Coomes' house at 1534 Kornom Drive. Troy was convicted of aggravated child molestation of his twelve-year-old stepson, Randall. He'd made the boy perform fellatio, and followed it up by systematically burning a line of circular cigarette burns from Randall's wrist to his forearm. Once done, Troy happily passed out in his recliner aided by his nightly case of beers.

After working the graveyard shift, Randall's mother got home, passed by Troy out cold in his chair, to find Randall cowering in the corner of his bedroom closet. She divorced Troy while he served a fifteen-year prison sentence.

It started the same as the others. He laid Troy's sheet on the passenger seat, took out a toxic muffin and closed the plastic container. Parked in front of the home where Troy rented the downstairs apartment, he put the muffin in a paper bag and went to the door.

The Good Samaritan saw Troy push the curtain back from the front door window and smile. The door swung open wide. "Hi there," Troy said enthusiastically, almost as if he was expecting him. "What can I do for you, son?"

The Good Samaritan blinked once as he stared at the old man. Troy was a sixty-five-year-old father figure with fluffy half-circle bags under his eyes. He had a little gray hair on his sunburned scalp, and the hair he did have was shaved neatly and close. His wide, toothless grin made his large ears wave a comical greeting.

"Hi. I'm Robert Sewell, but you can call me Bob." As always the Good Samaritan used another pedophile's name. "I live down the street in the upstairs apartment of that house," the Samaritan pointed quickly down the street, not allowing Troy to pinpoint a location. "and I wanted to welcome you to the neighborhood."

"Well hell boy, come on in here and have a seat. Let me go find my teeth." Troy left the front door wide open as he turned and went deeper into his home.

Troy's voice echoed from another room, "I'm always losing these damn teeth," he said coming back to the front door. "These teeth and reading glasses. Guess that's what happens when you get old." Troy chuckled at himself and waved the Good Samaritan into his home, but the younger man at the front door hadn't moved.

"I'm sorry, I can't come in right now. I have to get to work at the grease plant."

"I hear that's a good company to work for. I work at the food packaging plant on Forest Drive, but I work the third shift. I like it, it's quieter," Troy said. "Come on in. I don't get many visitors, Bob, and it'll be heartening to have someone to talk to. I'll get you some coffee. You got time for a cup of coffee, don't 'cha?"

"Well, if you already have it made, sure." The Good Samaritan couldn't believe the words that just popped out of his mouth. Couldn't believe he allowed himself to be drawn into Troy's home.

He felt comfortable sitting on Troy's brown plaid couch with the dip in the middle cushion. No hairs were going up on the back of his neck. No chest tightening.

A few picture frames held photos of a farm. A stack of old newspapers waiting to be scooped up and taken to the trash cluttered the floor between Troy's stained recliner and the metal TV tray masquerading as an end table. There was no other furniture in the room.

Troy watched the young man look around. "Yeah, I have to get some furniture but that will have to wait for next month's check."

"You can go on Craig's list and look for free furniture. Most times all you have to do is go pick it up and it's yours. I've gotten some pretty amazing things that way." The Samaritan sipped his coffee. Why was he in here? What was he doing?

"Don't know anything about this Craig person, you'll have to tell me more about him. What you got there, son?" Troy asked pointing to the paper bag sitting next to him on the couch. Troy groaned slightly as he leaned forward in his recliner. "Sorry, I got a bad back. What'd you say you got there?"

He didn't want to do it. The Good Samaritan didn't want to give the muffin to Troy. Something was wrong.

"It's ah. It's a welcome muffin I made for you, but um, it may not be good," He started to get up to go. "I'll make a fresh batch and bring you one."

"No. Don't be silly. Hand that over here, son." Troy took the bag as the Samaritan stood. "Sit back down while I eat this Bob."

He sat and watched as Troy took the muffin out of the bag and began to eat it. With each bite Troy took, the Good Samaritan felt bile rise in his throat.

"This is really good," Troy said swallowing the last bite. "I'll have to repay your kindness and have you over to dinner. Are you free Saturday night?" Troy shook his head and laughed. "What am I thinking? Of course a good-looking young man like yourself wouldn't be free Saturday night. How about we make it Sunday night?"

The Good Samaritan swallowed hard. "I'd like that very much, but this Sunday I'm booked. How about next Sunday? Give me your phone number and I'll call to confirm next week. I'm getting a new phone number this week so I'll call you with that."

Troy wrote down his number and handed it to the Good Samaritan. When they reached the front door, Troy took his right hand in both of his blue-veined, brown-spotted hands. "You've made an old fellow very happy, Bob. You're a good man."

"Uh, thank you." The Good Samaritan cleared his throat, "I'll see you soon."

Troy waved.

The Good Samaritan waved back at Troy, drove past Route 20 with the windows down, and fresh air blowing on his face. He stopped on the side of the road, quickly walked into the ditch, leaned forward and vomited.

Something wasn't right. He knew he had to find the truth. He wiped his mouth with the back of his hand.

"I have to find the ex-stepson, Randall," he said out loud.

Chapter 42

Still

The room held darkness within, while outside the sun polished bright. The bar, more like a long murky hallway, was papered with dollar bills tacked to the walls and ceiling, all marked in black sharpie with a patron's name.

He sat at the bar's counter that ran the length of the right side of the room. He assumed a kitchen was to the left where the smell of grease spilled out. At the far end of the room, next to the back exit, a hook and eye lock held the one-person bathroom door slightly closed. One could look through the gap to see if the room was in use.

He watched as the bartender emerged from the bathroom after not washing his hands. The bathroom was now vacant. The bartender was dressed in jeans with a grease-smeared t-shirt. The outline of a pack of Marlboros jutted out of the breast pocket. The bartender walked around the front of the bar, removed a handful of signed dollar bills, stuck the tacks back into the wall, and shoved the bills deep into his pocket.

The deep rumble of the Screamin' Eagle mufflers announced Randall's approach even before the Harley turned the corner. Elburn used to be a spit-of-a-town and Fat Boy's was the place hardcore bikers met, but when the town got a Chicago Metra train stop, everything went to hell.

It pissed Randall off so bad. He'd just driven past a fucking Starbucks, for Christ's sake, and across the street was a yuppie bicycle shop. When he pulled up, Randall parked next to a lone Softail thinking, *it's early*, and threw his half-smoked Camel to the curb. As he made his way to his favorite bar stool, Randall thought again about moving south or west or anywhere, provided that it was far from a city.

The Good Samaritan had watched the olive-gold-and-black Road King pull up. He sat back at the bar, opened the day's newspaper, and ignored Troy's ex-stepson, Randall Vahl, as he walked into Fat Boy's.

The patch on the upper left of Randall's black-leather vest-cut read, "Screech," his road name. Above it was a small circle patch of a flaming skull that matched the extra-large center-patch on the back of his cut. Above the small front circle patch was an American flag. On the back of his cut was a top rocker just above the huge center-flaming skull that read "Gypsy Bandits." The bottom rocker read "Illinois" and on one side of the skull were the letters "LE" with "MC" on the other side.

With the back center enlarged, one could see the skull was on fire and had cross bones slicing through the eyes to the jaw on both sides. It took up Randall's massive back. Looking closer, the Good Samaritan saw that the skull was centered over a tire's hubcap that was also on fire. Other smaller patches peppered Randall's cut including a U.S. Army Operation Enduring Freedom veteran patch.

Through his research, the Good Samaritan knew Randall had done a number of tours in Afghanistan and was biding his time until retirement as a recruiter. Randall, only seven years to go.

"Man, I like your bike. Those sliders in gloss black are slick. It's a 2018 Road King, right? Or is it a '17?"

Randall turned to see the mustached, buttoned-down urban professional sitting two stools down. Randall wanted to ignore him but what the hell, there was nobody else to talk to until the regulars rode in after work.

"It's an '18. Yeah, I like the gloss black. You ride?" He highly doubted it but you never knew.

"Yeah, just sold my '06 Heritage Softail. It was pearl white with enough chrome to burn holes through your eyes on a sunny day. But I got an offer I couldn't pass up and now I'm looking to move on to my next ride."

Another Gypsy Bandit filled the door before moving toward Randall. The Good Samaritan saw his road name was Oak, which wasn't very original because he was quite tall. "Hey Screech, sorry to hear about your stepfather. The flu is a rough way to go for Troy or anyone." Screech rolled his eyes. Oak added, "Or not."

"Thanks brother, but there is no love lost."

"I get it," Oak said. "Meet you at the back table, gotta go to the head first." Oak walked to the one-room toilet.

The Samaritan looked from his newspaper, open to Troy Coomes' obituary, and back to Randall. "You're Randall Vahl. I remember hearing your story. I'm sorry man, I went through that same kind of…"

"Okay, it's been good talking to you about bikes, but I have to stop you right there," Randall said abruptly. "I'm sick of bleeding hearts. Hey, I'm sorry you were... that someone fucked with you, but my mother's been dead awhile and now that asshole, Troy, is dead too, so I don't have to pretend anymore.

I was never abused, touched, looked at sideways or anything like that from anybody, especially my ex-stepfather. Humph," Randall stopped for a second. "That's the first time I've said it out loud. Go figure. But it doesn't change the fact that I don't want to hear anyone else's sick, sad story, okay? I don't mean to be callous man, but I'm really done with it."

The Good Samaritan was genuinely surprised at Randall's frank response. "What?"

Randall continued. "The guy was a deadbeat alcoholic who convinced my mom to marry him and I didn't like it. So I set him up. Yeah giving myself the cigarette burns up and down my arm wasn't fun. As a matter of fact it hurt like hell. But doing that made my story real. It made it easier for me to tell the story about what he did, when in fact, he didn't really do it. It got him out of our lives for good, and look at the bright side, he quit drinking in prison. My mom went on to meet a nice old guy when I was away on my first tour in Afghanistan. They got married. He bought her a nice house and after they both passed away, I inherited the house free and clear. So all's well that ends well."

The Samaritan nodded, "Huh. Well I'm glad to hear that. No one should ever have to go through that shit. So back to your club. Do you guys go for weekend rides or just day rides?"

"We do both," Randall said, relaxing into his stool now that they were discussing the club. "The Gypsy Bandits' National meeting is this weekend in Madison, Indiana. All the northern Illinois chapters are taking the run tomorrow. Kickstands up at the crack of dawn. It's a good time, and a nice ride." Randall looked at the guy and asked, "Are you a cop or veteran of a foreign war?"

"No. Is that the criteria for your club?"

Randall watched four more Gypsy Bandits come through the door, each giving him a man hug and a 'hi brother' before heading to the long banquet table in the back. Randall turned back to the hipster and said, "Yeah it is. Good talk."

The Good Samaritan had been dismissed. Randall got up from the stool and moved to the back table with his brothers.

The Samaritan looked from Randall back to Troy's obituary and said, "Look what you made me do."

Having heard him, the bartender peered at the hipster from the corner of his eye.

Chapter 43

Still

Lush five-foot tall, five-foot wide bean shrubs, with leaves the size of bear paws, were planted in Randall's backyard along with the special ground cover, along with the black-berried bushes that are often confused with blueberries in mountain forests. Worn out aged mulch littered the ground around the full bushes in the back corner making the plants look at home. As if they'd been living there for years.

In the back of Randall's kitchen freezer, behind a stack of french bread pizzas and a quart of neapolitan ice cream, was a reclosable zip bag holding a dozen toxic jelly-glazed oatmeal muffins. A label issued from Randall's home printer was stuck to the muffin bag that read: *Science Project.*

A folder on Randall's desktop computer was also named *Science Project.* In that folder were files with all of the pedophile names, addresses, and dates of progress and completion for every pedophile the Good Samaritan had ever targeted and killed in the past twelve years. He'd been very prolific, killing on average three a year since he turned seventeen. Although the last five years, he'd deliberately been slowing down, being more careful. Killing only one a year.

Troy Coomes would be his last, bringing the grand kill total to twenty-eight. He made sure that the *Science Project* folder also contained his precious recipe for the toxic jelly-glazed oatmeal muffins.

The Samaritan had made a batch of muffins in Randall's kitchen using Randall's muffin tin, mixer, spoons, and the pestle and mortar that now resided on Randall's counter. He'd made the muffins with the berries and beans from the plants in Randall's backyard. Those muffins, which were now frozen through in Randall's freezer, were ready. It was time.

The Good Samaritan stood on the street, next to the storm drain, in front of Randall's free-and-clear inheritance house, when he made the call.

"Yeah, well I don't know if I should do be doing this but I was at Randall Vahl's house in Elburn the other night and like, yeah, uh, we were drinking and stuff? And Screech, well that's what I call Randall you know, Screech is his road name. Anyway, Screech had a bunch of beers and stuff and started talkin' all this crazy shit about killin' baby-rapers you know? And I'm freakin'. Then he showed me these big muffins he made that are in his freezer and told me how they were poisonous and shit, and the bag they were in was marked *Science Project*. Then he told me how he'd been killin' baby-rapers for like twelve years and he was like braggin' that he'd finished off twenty-eight of 'em including his ex-step-dad, Troy Coomes."

He paused for effect then went on, "Well, yeah so then he shows me a folder on his computer called *Science Project* with all the names and pictures of these guys and the recipe for those kill muffins and then he takes me outside to show me the poisonous plants he uses for ingredients. Now I'm totally freakin' out, cause I don't know if he's gonna kill me once he remembers he's told me all this shit. So I decides I better call you. My name? Hells to the no man. I'm not steppin' in that shit. His big-ass biker buddies will kill me dead if they find out it's me who called. I've said what I've said. You're on your own."

The line went dead.

The Samaritan, wearing latex disposable gloves, pulled the battery out of the burner phone, opened the zippered plastic bag full of bleach, and dumped both the phone and battery inside. He sealed it up and tossed them like chicken legs in a sack full of flour. Once thoroughly cleaned, he pulled the battery out and threw it down the storm drain. Carrying the bleach baggy containing the remainder of the phone, he walked to the 7-Eleven kitty-corner from the house, and dumped the phone in the dumpster. He poured the rest of the bleach onto the ground and shoved the gloves inside the zipped baggy. He walked down a side street toward his car, slowed near a storm drain, and precisely dropped the baggy through the grates. He didn't stop.

Driving away, the sound of sirens bounced against buildings in the distance, ping ponging ever closer.

Chapter 44

Still

The missions, the unit, and the brotherhood was what got him through. When dwell time finished, it seemed only minutes before the Army's muscular tentacles were suctioning him back, drawing him in for another tour.

The distinctive throbbing of air slapping his chest and cheeks that he felt now hit him like the *chuff-chuff-chuff* of helicopter rotor blades, but the buffeting he felt wasn't from being airborne. It was from lane splitting two semis going ninety-miles-per-hour on his bike as he thread the needle.

Randall Vahl was howling through traffic, waving around cars, lane splitting between semis. He'd been through five tours in Afghanistan and yet nothing was as terrifying as this. Not the ride. The ride pumped adrenaline through his veins. The ride was propelling him from the horror that was directly behind him. Stalking him. The ride was the only thing keeping him from reaching into his leather cut, drawing out his old-school revolver, putting the barrel to his chin and pulling the trigger.

Randall had been four beers in and bellying up for another when the BOLO was issued. Be on the lookout for Randall Vahl. Within the hour, the authorities knew where to find him. They knew Randall was at the Ferguson Lodge, attending the Gypsy Bandits' Annual Meeting. The meeting that had members from all over the world converge in Madison, Indiana on the Ohio River. Randall's specific location shot the BOLO up to an all-out manhunt.

His very own Gypsy Bandits brothers were hunting him. The Gypsy Bandits only accepted members who were police or veterans of foreign wars, no exceptions. It was an elite law enforcement motorcycle club and growing larger every year.

They called each other brothers, all club members no matter where they were from, they were his brothers. So when his brother Hammer, a Cook County cop who got his road name from the brutal way he handled suspects, told Randall to get the fuck out of there, it seemed ironic. Like a joke. It had to be a joke. But it wasn't.

"The poisonous plants are growing in your backyard. Forensics has the killer muffins matching up to the victims. The muffins are in your freezer. All the victim's files are in your computer along with the recipe. It's all there man. In your house. Your kitchen is dripping evidence from the pans in your sink. A tip came from an anonymous call that got the warrant. Forensics finished twenty minutes ago and they're coming. Coming for you man, guns-a-blazing."

"What the fuck!" Randall said. He was freaked. Hammer had taken him from the bar to stand outside in the gravel parking lot next to his bike. "This is crazy. I didn't do it. I don't know anything about any of this. You know I didn't do it!" Randall guzzled the beer in his hand, then crunched the empty can against his thigh. "I'll tell them. They got no real proof."

"Screech, I don't give a good goddamn if you did it or not. Hell, you're doing us all a favor by putting down baby-rapers. The world's a better place without 'em, but you can't tell that to those bleeding-heart tree-huggin' liberals that are coming for you with burning torches." Hammer hesitated. "There's more."

"Fuck me! More?" Randall threw the crushed beer can away from the hundreds of parked bikes.

"They hadn't gotten around to burying Troy's body yet and forensics was able to test him for the poison-platter muffin mix. It's done. They got 'cha. They got you hard man. And now they're about to exhume the other twenty-seven on your list."

"My list. WHAT LIST?" Randall screamed. "I don't have a list. I didn't do it."

Hammer grabbed Randall's massive arms and snapped him to attention. "I don't give a shit. You hear me. I don't give a shit. They got you either way. You're going down for it. You're an inch away from staring out the ass-side of a prison cell for the rest of your life unless you get on that bike and ride like a mother fucker through hell's back door."

"Where? Where can I go that they won't find me? There's no place to hide. Nowhere." Despair smeared Randall's features like an old-man stroke and compressed his short thickset frame. "Thanks for being my friend Hammer. For telling me."

"We're not friends, we're family."

The moment he heard the word family, Randall knew where to go. His grandparents on his mom's side, Gurtis and Verneda Gadson, were born and raised in Evarts, Kentucky.

Randall had visited his mamaw and papaw during summer vacations. Gurtis took him a few miles east to Black Mountain, the highest mountain peak in Kentucky. After a day of hunting, Randall would follow Gurtis through the front door of their shack in the holler where Verneda would have soup beans and cornbread ready on the cook stove for supper.

Those summers gave him his favorite childhood memories. He knew it was the place to go. It didn't matter to him that ten years had passed since the roof collapsed on that shack. Or that a sucker-tree grew next to the rusted-out cook-stove, and a family of weasels nestled happily inside Verneda's pantry. Gurtis and Verneda were long dead but that didn't stop Randall from going.

Over the Ohio River, off of the Mountain Parkway onto Kentucky 15, Randall fled until he locked down the stand on his bike in front of a dilapidated house. There were two gas pumps out front with a rusted pole between them that dangled one long, florescent-yard light high above. Large, pealing white-painted words were tacked on the front of the house. They read "*Gas 'n Food*," and below that, "*Pay Inside*."

Following orders, Randall went in. The screen door creaked open and a millisecond before it slammed shut, Randall minded his manners and eased the door closed. The floor boards could be heard groaning under his boots.

Flea market shelves of dust-laden windshield-washer fluid, motor oil, and expired snack food littered one side of the room; the other side held three long shelves full of liquor. No dust there.

Randall went to the card table that doubled as a checkout counter. Behind it sat an old man with an inch of white beard on his chin. The man's globular nose, broken fifty or more years before, sat flat against his pock-marked face. His eyes were in a permanent squint from brows bowed low, like an old woman's breasts. Tacked to a wooden beam above the man were black-and-white and sepia photos of a younger life, and hanging below the pictures were long curly strips of fly paper peppered black, with tiny-winged corpses.

Chemically manufactured pine car fresheners hung about the room. They only served to sting Randall's nostrils and churn the contents of his stomach. Fortunately, a few steps in, the smell of fried fish wafted from a back room and folded the scents together nicely to sooth his belly.

Upon Randall's entry, the old man's beefy hands whacked the card table to kill a fly. He cleared his throat in a long, syrupy three-pack-a-day gurgle that sent what had been stuck down there spewing from his lips into a nearby tar-slimed pot.

"Looky what we got chere. What can I do you for son?"

"I'm in need of gas, sir." Randall's eyes followed the old man's gaze to a television screen set on a nearby shelf. The newscaster said Randall's name and his photo blazed across the screen.

"Randall Vahl is wanted for questioning in the alleged murders of twenty-eight convicted pedophiles. Vahl is armed and dangerous. If you see this man, do not approach. Call the number listed on the screen below."

Randall slowly pushed a fifty-dollar bill across the card table toward the old man. His grandparent's southern tongue came back in a rush. "Sir, if it obliges you, could I pump that gas now?"

"You can fill 'er up son, but first you need to sit and eat." The man pushed Randall's money back toward Randall then lumbered into the next room. He came back with two plates overflowing with fried food.

Randall was riveted to the floor. No clue why, except he was sure it would be rude to move.

The old man set the plates down, utensils clattering. He turned and went back for another trip, picking up two empty jelly jars. Back in his chair, he filled the jars to the lip with clear liquid.

"My Missus made catfish and hush puppies. Best you'll ever have in this life. They go together like corn pone and pot liquor. Name's Bascome Click, and Nell in there is my bride of fifty-four years."

Bascome's legs spread wide in the folding chair. "Sit down son and eat." He pointed to the clear liquid in the glass. "That there is my own white lightnin'."

Bascome tapped his jelly glass against Randall's creating a dull thud rather than a clink. "Here's to a safe journey."

Randall took a long soothing pull, set the jar down and started talking. "My mama's folks were Gurtis and Verneda Gadson from…" Randall started.

"I know'd Gurtis and Verneda. They were good people." Bascome tilted his head toward the TV. "No matter what those citified news people say, you're good people too. Everyone in these hills knows that so you got nothin' to worry about son. We take care of our own."

"I appreciate that Mr. Click, but I won't put you or any of your folks in harm's way." Randall and Bascome finished their meal and drank two more jelly jars of moonshine.

Bascome handed Randall a thirty-two-ounce mason jar full of moonshine for the road, and said, "I'll be seeing you then, good Lord willing and the creek don't rise."

Back inside, Nell shuffled toward the card table in her house shoes to clear the plates. She was surprised to see a thick wad of money. Before leaving, Randall had emptied his wallet thinking, *don't need this anymore.*

Twenty minutes later, Randall turned off Black Mountain Ridge Road onto the one-lane gravel drive, past multiple radio towers, to the large rock summit. Trees on both sides of the towers had been chopped down so that on a clear day the Great Smoky Mountains on the Tennessee and North Carolina borders were visible.

Randall parked on the summit to clean out his saddle bags. He'd given all his cash to Bascome Click and his wife. On the rocky clearing, he carefully laid out his leather coat, helmet, full-fingered gloves, three stocking caps, a skull-face mask, his good day-and-night protective glasses and goggles, and a practically new rain suit in its pouch. It was his death-cleaning. He kept his beloved Gypsy Bandits full-patched leather cut on. That item was never to touch the ground.

Although today it would touch the ground. With him in it.

Randall wrote a quick note and tucked it in full view for someone to find.

> *To whoever finds this.*
> *All this is yours for the taking. I'm leaving this world and have no more use of it.*
> *Forgive me, my brothers.*
> *Signed,*
> *Randall Vahl*

Randall sat on a rock at the edge of the summit, and looked down at the tops of pine trees some two-thousand feet below. They filled the valley with a sculptured 1970's shag carpet look. Directly across the valley was a rock formation, a summit much like the one he was sitting on, but from his perspective the mountain's bones and layers were exposed showing balding rock formations that sprouted tufts of pine trees on top. Randall smoked the last of his Camels, one after another, while finishing off Bascome's lightinin'. He was thankful for it. Thankful for a stranger's kindness.

What he couldn't figure out was why anyone would accuse him of killing all those people. Killing Troy. No one knew he lied about the attack. No one… but the hipster. He had told that hipster in Fat Boy's Bar. So no. Nobody knew. And yet, all that evidence was planted on him. Whoever the killer was, he knew about Troy. Knew where Randall lived. That hipster knew. His thick black mustache, the professor square glasses. He wore an easy smile, and asked the right questions.

He asked just the right…

A light from above flicked in front of Randall causing him to look up and to the left, where the fire tower stood. Inside the fire tower, the sun reflected off a man's binoculars.

Faster than a knife fight in a phone booth, Randall chugged the moonshine and sat astride his bike. Soon he was punching sixth gear at eighty-miles-per-hour, headed straight for the deep valley's shag carpet.

It was time to go. Time to die. His biggest regret was taking down his pristine Road King, but he was thankful for the last ride.

The bike flew four-hundred feet away from the precipice before his thighs released it into the abyss below.

Leaning forward he thought, *I'm fixin' to go down the road a piece.*

Time gentled, and rolled Randall's body into a summersault, easing him down to the tree tops below. His arms were opened and legs wide, floating on the air, staring up at the clouds, when the abruptness of a dead white trunk of a pine tree impaled him through the back center patch of his cut. His body, lubricated by blood and propelled by his weight, slid down the dead trunk. Spears of branches reached inside his gut and disemboweled him, slithering thick snakes of intestines, pieces of liver, and ruptured organs, decorating the pine's trunk like a Christmas tree.

Driven by Randall's hefty weight, the hollow tree waved subtly to the man in the fire tower. It swung back and forth, back and forth, creaking further downward until an earsplitting crack echoed through the valley. It threw the wooden dagger 500-feet below, to stab deep into the ground by a gully at Dry Bottom Road trail. It would be two weeks before hikers found the entrails of intestines hanging over the path, and looked up in horror to see Randall's body displayed like a fat bug gored by a pin. His arms and legs dangled, pointing to the ground. Feasting maggots kept his eyes, nose, and mouth alive with movement.

Chapter 45

Still

The Good Samaritan realized his focus had wavered over the years. His code was true but had rippled too wide. And now he'd killed an innocent. Not Randall, but Troy, the step-father. Just because it was on paper. Just because they were convicted, he realized not all were guilty. He'd never make that mistake again. He couldn't live with it. He would find his true target.

The Good Samaritan craved one more kill. Only one. The shadow maker with the white mask.

Chapter 46

Still

DATE OF BIRTH: 09/23/1956 SEX: M RACE: W WEIGHT: 176 HEIGHT: 511

"Brian you cannot do this," Chanya said. "You will put us, and all that we've worked for, in jeopardy. You only have two days left at Collinsville and you will be done. Please my love, just walk away."

Brian Phants's wife was pleading with him. "If not for yourself, think of me, of Cody, Betty and the babe she carries. The babe that will be here in just five months. Brad Denver is not worth risking your life, risking us."

Brian finished buttoning his uniform and rubbed the ache in his shoulder. It had been over nine years since he'd had total shoulder replacement surgery, but it was still bothersome, mostly when he set the metal detectors off. There were a cacophony of alarms each time he walked into work, but after all these years everyone was used to it. In any case, he only had two shifts left and then he'd be out of that storage cesspool of humans.

Chanya was right. It was a risk, but some things are worth the risk.

Brian was sickened by the stacks of letters Cody showed him that came from Brad Denver, his sister Alice's rapist and killer, and the man from whom Betty had escaped. Brad Denver had been sending vile letters to Betty for the last twenty years. Brian saw the photos Cody had kept hidden from his wife Betty, pictures of his sister Alice's ravaged naked little body found lying face down, under water in a drainage ditch, just two days after Alice's eighth birthday.

Alice had only been seven-years-old when Denver took her. Seven-years-old when he raped her and raped her and raped her again. She was alive when he ripped his ten trophies from her fingers, her tiny pale fingernails. She was alive when he held her head under the muddy water.

How long did it take before she surrendered to the darkness of death? How long before Alice drowned? Brian knew from his correctional training a person has three minutes before losing consciousness. Denver would have had to hold her under water for another five to ten minutes before she died. But Denver didn't hold her. He piled rocks on top of Alice, wedging her in place and strolled away.

Do the dead remember? Brian wondered. He hoped not. No one, especially a child, should have to keep those memories throughout eternity.

Being caught didn't frighten Brian as much as the thought of Brad Denver getting out to torture another child. And Brad Denver would.

Cody had come south to Brian and Chanya's home the weekend before, alone. He insisted Betty stay home and rest. She was in her second trimester and stress wasn't good for her or their baby.

"Brian you don't have to do this," Cody said and meant it. "Denver can rot in that prison for the rest of his life and we will go on with our lives. Betty and I will have our baby. We'll grow old. You and Chanya will grow old. We'll be happy. It will be good."

"I'm doing it Cody." Brian said.

Chapter 47

Still

Last week, Jack Osteen saw Officer Brian Phants pause in front of Brad Denver's cell for a moment, before he stopped to talk to him.

Jack thought Officer Phants wasn't so bad, as guards went. Phants would talk to Jack like a person not a thing. The other guards weren't like that. Phants sometimes brought him a book, then they'd talk about it afterwards. Phants had a way of nudging the madness an arms-length away when he walked onto the block, and for Jack, it was a miracle.

Having spent his teen years and all of his adulthood in a cage, Jack learned to encapsulate and embrace the madness. Sanity was the alien that Officer Phants brought to the block just by describing the world outside.

Jack had been inside since the age of thirteen, back when OJ Simpson was found innocent and Jack wasn't. Jack was tried and convicted as an adult, maybe because he looked like one, when all he wanted at the time was a PlayStation, a Stretch Armstrong, and to escape with Martha.

Instead Jack got twenty-three years of long-term solitary confinement with a side order of hallucinations, agitation, aimless violence, and delusions. The SHU was a dehumanizing, high-tech torture chamber that drove men to madness, and Jack was no exception.

When Officer Phants discussed the latest book he'd given Jack to read, or described the season as fresh-cut grass blown on the road, it was jarring. Like an old-fashioned camera's flash bulb popping before his eyes, it shocked Jack awake.

So when Phants asked last week, Jack said yes. That, and because Phants was going to search for Martha.

Five days ago, Officer Phants brought him the bible. They'd talked about this particular exchange. Phants asked Jack to look over the special contents and to decide if they could work a deal.

Once Jack saw the extra pages tucked inside, he knew he would do it even if he got nothing in return. *But what the hell*, he thought, *why not get what I really want*. And what he wanted was to search for Martha. Jack couldn't do that from inside a cell but Officer Phants could from out there.

"HEY ASS-WIPE. SHUT THE FUCK UP!" Jack screamed, as he shot up from his slab of a bed.

Jack Osteen lived in the cell next to Brad Denver and for the fourth time today, he had to yell at the son of a bitch. Brad's horrifying crimes, his constant ramblings, and the putrid smells of his diarrhea and vomit drifting from Brad's cell into Jacks, to push Jack over the edge.

Sure Brad had been sick for the last five days, apparently with the flu. The guards brought the in flu. The prisoners caught it, and generously passed it around. Jack was fine. He never caught anything. All the same, he didn't want to breathe in Brad Denver's rancid flu by-products, all day and all night.

Jack sat down on his bed with his back to the bars and slid Phants' bible off the shelf. It automatically opened to Matthew 18:6 where the verse was highlighted in yellow marker.

"it were better for him that a millstone were hanged about his neck, and that he were drowned in the depth of the sea."

The newspaper clippings and photos that had been hidden inside were given back to Officer Phants two days before, but Jack sifted through his mind's eye and could still see Alice Rayburn, seven-years-old, abducted, raped and killed. Connie White, twenty-seven-years old, abducted, raped and killed. Stacy Swenson, ten-years-old, abducted, raped and killed. Five more raped, and who knew how many more he'd raped and killed that were never to be found?

The photos of the three girls pre-rape, pre-kill, were all pretty school pictures with dimples and ruffled dresses, except the oldest, Connie. Her photo was like a blonde Farrah Fawcett with a flip-back hairstyle, sitting in front of a community-college graduation cake. Tucked under those photos came the post-rape, post-kill pictures. Naked bruised bodies, stark white leathery skin, fingernail beds without nails. Little legs, little legs, long legs all spread-eagle, genitals exposed, bloated faces down, hair waving in water. All waving in water.

This is what Brad Denver did. Raped and killed little girls, while adding in a rape and murder of a young woman.

Jack thought, *Monsters don't live under the bed, they live in the car parked outside your house. Once caught they move into the cell next to me.*

It'd be over soon. Officer Phants said it would be today. They'd do it today. When it was done, Phants would fulfill his promise. He'd find Martha for Jack. Phants promised.

Sure Jack was no saint. He was on death row too, but he wasn't a monster like Brad. Jack was a savior. Denver's deeds re-opened a chamber Jack had locked inside of himself for the rage. That rage took him to the bars closest to Denver's cell.

The heaving and gagging had stopped. The antibiotics had kicked in. Denver was over the flu and on the mend but the putrid smells still hung in the air to slither through the bars.

Jack whispered at the bars to Brad Denver. "*Alice, Connie, Stacy. Alice, Connie, Stacy. Alice, Connie, Stacy.*" Over and over he said their names until he got his reply.

"Betty," Brad said as a prayer.

"She got away," Jack poked the bear. "She doesn't count. That all you killed? That was it? Three? You're pathetic." Jack scoffed. "I killed that many in my own living room one night."

Jack hadn't really. Only one in the living room, one in the kitchen and the other in the bedroom but Brad Denver didn't know the difference.

"Oh, there were more. Eight more," Brad whispered. "Nine if I'd gotten to Betty, but the cops got me seconds before I could reach her. She was going to be mine for the second and last time. Just a front yard away. I was so close. So close. I don't think she knows how close I was to having her, again. I should write her and tell her. She'd like that."

"Women or little girls?"

"What?"

"What did you want? Women or little girls?

Brad liked this conversation. He answered, "Little girls are my calling. Older ones take too much effort. The little ones, I perfected that. I'd watch and watch and wait. The hunt was my favorite part. The doing was pleasing, but not as satiating as the hunt." Brad inhaled deeply. "How about you? What part did you like?"

Jack had gone on his own killing spree but for a righteous purpose.

"The saving," Jack said.

"Oh I saved things too," Brad said.

Jack didn't mean saving trophies like Brad. He meant it in its real sense. To save Martha. He'd saved himself too, but Jack had envisioned their death long before he pulled the knife. At least the death of the two. The third one was a bonus kill.

Brad Denver preyed on little girls like his Martha. Jack hungered to kill Brad Denver, his fourth and final kill.

Once done, he'd have Martha again. Officer Phants promised.

Jack was big for thirteen at five-foot ten-inches and 140 pounds. Kids at school called him Barkley, like Charles Barkley, the basketball player. Jack was more tall than big, but compared to the other guys he stood out. He didn't want to stand out. Being the new kid was bad enough. Being the big new kid sucked.

His mom moved him and his sister, Martha, away from their dad in Indiana to one of the top ten drunkest cities in Illinois. At least that's what Jack thought. It had more bars and liquor stores than any town he'd seen. His mom didn't want to take either of the kids, but she took them just the same. All she wanted was asshole Todd, the guy she was screwing.

Todd moved them into his white-trash neighborhood with his white-trash neighbors and hooked Jack's mom up with dope. Used syringes were re-used and left on the stained coffee table, on the kitchen counter, or hanging from their drug-filled arms.

Jack did his and Martha's laundry. He got Martha's breakfast, made her sack lunches, and fixed her dinner. Martha had just turned nine and didn't understand why Todd and their mom were always passed out on the bed. Why, when they weren't passed out, neither one made any sense. Their mom was gone even though her body was there.

It got worse when the money and their mom's looks ran out, which didn't take long at all.

Jack came out of his bedroom in his pajama pants and followed the muffled screams to Martha's bedroom door. The door was opened a hand's width. Jack's eyes darted from his mother at the head of the bed with one hand holding Martha's arms high and the other holding a cloth over Martha's mouth, to Todd's naked body rocking on top of Martha.

Jack burst through the door and knocked Todd against the wall. It was good to get in the first blow before Todd was up and on Jack. There was nothing to be remembered after that.

Jack woke on his bedroom floor to find the door locked from the outside and his window boarded and nailed shut. Jack was missing four teeth, his left eye was swollen shut, he was wobbly, his thoughts were dippy, and he had no idea what day it was.

He found the bucket his dear mother left for him to puke, crap and piss in, sitting next to a pitcher of drinking water. After three days living with the smell of his own shit and hearing the screams coming from Martha's room, Jack had had enough. After five days when the screams became mere whimpers, Jack knew rage.

Other men were visiting Martha. Jack listened to the many voices coming from the hallway. Apparently Todd's job was to break in Martha like a wild mustang so they could sell her to the many men beating a path to their door.

Peddling emergent human flesh was a lucrative business. Between visitors, the house was quiet while Todd and their mom partook in the best smack money could buy. It was during the quiet that Jack pried the last of the wooden planks from his window and escaped his prison. He didn't go far.

After putting the wood back up on the window, Jack doubled back through the unlocked front door and went straight to Martha's room.

Quickly covering her naked little body with a blanket, he whispered, "I'm getting you out of here." He untied the thick rope that stretched from her right wrist to the headboard.

"No one will hurt you again." He worked on the rope from the footboard to her right ankle. "But right now you have to be quiet, because mom and Todd are working off their high."

Jack needn't have worried. Martha hadn't made a sound, not even when he entered the room. No gasp of deliverance. No fearful outburst at seeing a person, any person. By the time he'd released her left leg and left arm, he recognized the silence, the purple tracks in her arm, the constricted pinprick pupils. Her arms and legs had fallen limp but remained in position; open, ready for the next customer even though she was free. But she wasn't.

A nine year-old heroin addict is so much easier to sell. No thrashing. No screaming. Compliancy made easy.

Jack heard Todd and his mom stir in their bedroom.

Jack bundled Martha in the blanket and stealthily carried her outside to the makeshift shed that doubled as a garage, and tucked her between a broken mower and the mound of black garbage bags full of trash.

"Martha? Martha?" Jack gently shook her when a tiny hum escaped her lips.

She saw Jack. Silent tears began streaming from her eyes.

"You're safe now. Stay here and don't make a sound." Jack's thumb softly rubbed away a tear. "I'm going to go get you some clothes and stuff, so I'll be a little while, but don't worry. I promise to come back and we'll get out of here together. Okay?"

Nothing.

"Okay? Martha?"

Fear has a sound and that sound wormed its way up Martha's throat.

Jack held her in a quick hug. "It's okay. I'll be right back. Promise you won't move?"

Two soft grunts echoed in her throat. Jack took it as a yes.

Back in the house, he pulled the dime store four-and-a-half inch serrated utility knife from the kitchen drawer and waited behind the open pantry door. Through the crack Jack saw an overweight, white, fiftyish-year-old man slip in the house just as his mother came in the room.

"Wish one are you here for?" She slurred.

"The boy."

"Oh yeah. You're here all the way from Chicago," she said. "It's a thousand bucks. Cash."

The man pulled out a stack of bills. "I've driven much farther for a boy. This is closer than most, so I'll be back real soon."

"Good." She counted and said, "Like I said on the phone, he's a cherry so we're going to give him something to loosen him up for you. Go in the living room over there," she pointed off to the right. "I'll come and get you when he's ready."

His mother called down the hallway to Todd. "Get him ready."

She went to the fridge for a beer when a dry cloth was shoved down her throat.

Jack could hear Todd walking toward the back of the house to Jack's bedroom, presumably with a syringe full of smack to plunge into Jack's veins before the fat fuck in the living room was escorted down the hall to rape him.

Jack held his loving mother's head firmly against his chest as he plunged the knife deep in her left jugular, sliced through her windpipe and around to her right jugular in one swift movement. Ear-to-ear.

As she bled out, Jack put his weight to the pantry door smashing her spindly rag of a body inside until he heard the door latch. He switched out the dime-store serrated knife for a sturdy six-inch chef's knife. Todd required more heft.

Todd turned the key in the padlock on Jack's bedroom door, unhooked it and flipped the steel arm back. Just in case the kid was hiding behind the door, he held the syringe above his head ready to plunge. The smell of fresh shit hit him but nothing else. Taking a step in, Todd stopped. His head turned right, left.

Soaking in his mother's blood, Jack stood directly behind Todd in the doorway. A pregnant bubble of blood fell from his belt to kerplop on his knock-off Nikes. Todd flipped around.

Todd didn't realize he was dead. The knife drove in, tip to heel, just below Todd's left breast. With both hands on the handle, Jack angled the blade upward to Todd's left shoulder blade, slicing his heart in two. Jack released the handle with a little push forward and watched Todd slump to the floor. Jack emptied Todd's pockets, taking money and keys, then lifted the shit bucket the two had so lovingly provided him. Jack dumped the contents onto Todd's face.

Jack went through the kitchen to retrieve the serrated knife and a kitchen towel before walking in on the fat man whacking off.

Fat-man's eyes were closed tight anticipating his own finale. Jack stepped behind the recliner before the crescendo, and in one easy movement, cut Fat-man ear-to-ear. He cleaned out a huge wad of cash from Fat-man's pockets, leaving his identification and credit cards. Draping the kitchen towel over Fat-man's shrinking dick, Jack gripped the thing with the towel and began to saw back and forth with the short knife. It came off much easier than he thought, in one full package that included the two sacks. First, in Fat-man's mouth went his balls, prompting the now limp dick to slither from his bottom lip like a dead snake.

With Todd's, Fat-man's, and his mother's cash, Jack and Martha drove away from the white-trash torture chamber. They had 3,452 dollars and 68 cents. Two trash bags in the back seat held their clothes and their chest of drawers treasures: Martha's music box, two knock-off Barbie dolls with wonky painted eyes, and stuffed in Jack's back pocket was a stub from the only Indiana

Pacer game he'd attended with his father. Nothing else in that place needed to come with him and Martha.

They were asleep in a mom and pop motel when the police rammed through the door. Martha cowered in the corner with her forehead pressed against the wall as the police handcuffed Jack and dragged him away. Jack hadn't seen or heard from Martha since.

But Officer Phants promised. Once Jack killed Brad Denver, he'd know where Martha was. He'd see her again.

Chapter 48

Still

Brian and Chanya Phants researched both Jack and Martha Osteen's story. What they found turned their stomachs.

When it happened, Jack and Martha's father back in Indiana wanted nothing to do with his killer son or junkie daughter. Didn't matter that they were just thirteen and nine.

Jack went to jail, and after an evening in the ER, Martha was shipped off to a children's psychiatric hospital. Back then there were no bright colors or fun toys for the kids in the insane asylum. Instead they were treated to peeling lead paint and feces-covered walls.

Their heads were shaved for lice, both boys and girls, and all were given hospital gowns. Most chose to go without. It was a hog confinement packed tight with no play therapy, art therapy, or survival manuals. Just one large room filled with cots, steel-barred doors, and a waiting game to see who could outlast hell.

Martha lost.

Brian Phants walked through the prison's metal detector and as usual set off all the bells and whistles. A new guard walked up to Brian with his hand-held detector to wave over Brian's shoulder area when he was stopped by another guard. "That's Brian Phants, no worries there. Just a bionic man with a shoulder replacement," he said. "Only one more day, Brian, and you're out of here."

Brian answered, "Yep. Our things are moving into the new house as we speak." Brian started to walk away.

"Oh, almost forgot to remind you," the guard said. "The new camera system will be installed in your area from noon to 12:30. So no cameras will be working then. You'll see the red light come back on once they're up again."

"Good to know." He'd known this was happening and had planned for it.

Brian went about his morning ritual, waiting until noon to give Jack the four-inch serrated knife that Brian had taped to his bicep, all the while thinking about how in the hell he was going to tell Jack about Martha. Deal was, he'd tell Jack once the job was done.

Brad Denver was right on schedule for his noon shower. Another guard on the block had that lucky duty. Brian passed Brad Denver and the other guard on their way to the shower room. Denver looked healthier than he had over the last week but the stench of being sick needed to be washed off.

Earlier, Brian had taken the knife from his arm and taped it to the inside of his pocket. Before cuffing Jack, Brian slipped him the knife. Jack taped it to his stomach and walked with Brian to the west entrance of the showers.

"Hey," the guard manning the east entrance to the showers yelled at Brian. "Denver's in there now."

"Can't help it," Brian said. "Osteen must have caught Denver's flu. He puked all over himself."

Most showers are open so the guards can see in but not on their block in Collinsville. Theirs had old-school single stalls with curtains, and were not visible from the two doorways.

Jack took off his clothes, stuck the tape to the inside of a dry stall, and held the knife. He watched through the gap of the curtain as Brad Denver lifted his forty-six-year-old flabby stomach apron to scrub his balls. Water swirled yellow piss down the drain. Jack waited until the water was clear again before pulling back the curtain. He knew Denver couldn't fight off a younger man or stop him from shoving the threadbare towel down his throat.

In one easy movement Jack cut Brad Denver from ear-to-ear, while whispering: "Here's a message from Betty, Alice, Connie, Stacy and those five other girls."

He pulled the threadbare towel out of Brad's mouth and watched Denver's body slide to the concrete floor. As he had done years before to Fat-man, Jack draped the towel over Brad's shrunken appendage, got a good grip, and began to saw back and forth. It came off in one full package, dick and both balls, just as it had with Fat-man. And just like Fat-man, Jack shoved his balls into Denver's mouth leaving the tiny dick sticking out like a little girl's tongue.

Jack stood over Denver's lifeless body, letting the shower wash away the evidence.

Dry and dressed, with the knife again neatly taped to his stomach, Jack was escorted back to his cell.

"Did you throw the knife down the drain like we agreed?" Brian whispered.

"Yep."

Jack was back in his locked cell with his hands free of cuffs.

"Thank you Jack."

Jack nodded.

"I'm sorry, but what I found out about Martha is bad. It's really bad. She's dead."

"Wha-What?" Jack came close to the bars.

Brian felt his heart break through the bars. "God knows I wish I didn't have to tell you this."

"When? How?"

"Right after you two were found in that motel they took Martha to the ER to assess her. There was nothing they could do with a nine-year-old child severely addicted to heroin. They let her detox on her own in a children's psych ward. Withdrawal is an awful, awful thing for the body to endure, but it's not life-threatening. Martha had a hard time. It took her twenty days."

Jack gripped the bars. "How did she die? When?"

Brian sighed deeply. "Boys and girls lived together in that same ward. The autopsy showed she had been raped... repeatedly, in the psych ward. Toxicology confirmed there were numerous attackers. She was beaten and died of strangulation."

"When?" Tears were spilling down Jack's cheeks.

"Just a week after she was clean, so about a month after you last saw her."

Jack took a step back from the bars. "She's been dead all this time. I didn't save her. I saved nobody."

Brian looked up to see the camera's red light come to life. The blare of an alarm screamed down the block. Denver's body had been discovered.

Brian turned back just in time to see Jack lift his shirt and grip the knife. Brian heard Jack say, "Ear to ear."

The shock of Martha's news and the adrenaline from his recent kill dulled the pain, and fortified him to raise the knife. In one swift movement, Jack sliced open both of his carotid arteries and throat.

Brian screamed over the alarm. "Open this cell!"

Before the bars jerked open, Jack convulsed backward and died.

"After I gave Jack Osteen the Bible with the documents Cody had put inside," Brian said., "Jack seemed to come alive with purpose. Like he'd been waiting for the chance to release someone's pain." He turned to Betty and Cody, adding, "It was your anguish, but somehow by killing Brad Denver, Jack felt he liberated himself and his sister, too."

Betty and Cody were sitting in Chanya and Brian's new home in a rural subdivision of Carbondale with its spacious lot and incredible views of the rolling hills of Southern Illinois. A deck of cards sat untouched in the center of the table.

Cody said, "I'm sorry about Jack Osteen. I'm really sorry."

"Maybe it was for the best. Jack was holding on to the thread of hope that he'd see his sister Martha again. When that thread broke, it was too much. I tell myself, he would have found out eventually. Still, it doesn't lift the culpability I feel for his death. I pray heaven exists, because then at least, they're together again," Brian said.

Just then Betty remembered her reoccurring dream with Alice and the man, their rescuer in the front seat of the car, who was waving at a little girl running toward the car.

"Who is that?" Betty asked in her dream as she pointed to the man who was out of the car hugging the little girl.

"Oh that's Jack. He saved us," Alice said.

"But, Alice. You weren't saved. We weren't saved," Betty said.

"Oh yes we are. You'll see," Alice said.

Betty realized her dream was a premonition, a delicious dream come true.

"Don't you dare blame yourself for his death," Betty said to Brian. "Jack Osteen was a hero. It's heartbreaking that he and his sister had such sorrowful lives. I believe they're together, maybe they're in heaven, maybe not, but consider this; if there is no heaven, then there is no hell, so either way their torment is over," Betty said. "I thank God for Jack Osteen and the peace he has given me. He saved me, and Alice. I will keep him in my thoughts forever."

Chanya put her hand over Betty's hand. "I will too. Mr. Osteen deserves peace and so do you. You and Cody and Alice."

Cody nodded, "And Alice."

Cody stood.

"I promise you both," he said looking from Chanya to Brian. "Betty and I will take this to our graves. No one. No one will ever know the details of this."

Cody slowly paced and spoke as if giving himself instructions. "Betty and I will leave tonight and in the morning, I'll call my brother Carlton. I'll tell him the details of how Brad was found but no more. Then Carlton, Betty and I will go to my mother."

Chapter 49

Still

Date of Birth: 05/04/1948 Sex: M Race: W Weight: 223 Height: 600

Mornings began with a warm hand covering Vette's left breast. Carlton Rayburn and Vette Futrell were… what? It? An item? Vette couldn't think of the word as she stared at his hand. In love wasn't enough. It was more like they'd been fully assembled for each other. He made her feel safe, and she hadn't felt that in twenty years. He was her confidant and lover.

Vette was safe with him, which allowed her to release the memory. When Carlton shared his sister's story, Vette unlocked the door to the trailer. Now Carlton knew. He knew more than Shelley, more than her parents, more than anyone.

Shelley would forever be Vette's best girlfriend, but Vette had never told her. She wasn't sure if her silence was to protect

Woody, or to protect the way she was seen by Shelley. Vette needed the constancy of their friendship, not pity. Someday she might tell her, but not just yet. One thing was certain: Shelley approved of Carlton.

They were having lunch overlooking the Fox River when Shelley blessed Vette and Carlton's union by saying, "I call dibs if you ever dump him."

"What the hell. Back off babe," Vette said. "Go find your own."

Shelley shrugged, "Just saying. If he ever needs a knee replacement, I wouldn't mind looking up that hospital gown."

"So you approve of him?" Vette asked with a chuckle.

"For you? Definitely. He's perfect for you and Luke. I'm really, really happy for you." Shelley said. "Now it's my turn."

"Finally!" Vette opened her arms to the heavens, but actually it was just to the ceiling of the restaurant.

"Don't get so excited. And don't expect me to go on FindMeAHusbandNOW.com. That's never going to happen."

Now looking down at his hand covering her breast, Vette thought about how she loved Carlton, especially how he cared for Luke. Carlton genuinely pondered Luke's thoughts and responded with respect. It tickled her how many of their conversations were actually battles of trivia.

"The Average American opens a refrigerator twenty-two times a day," Luke started.

"That sounds excessive, but okay." Carlton said. "Did you know that in California you can't legally buy a mousetrap without having a hunting license?"

Luke giggled. "It's illegal in Georgia to eat fried chicken with a fork."

Vette's heart melted listening to their conversations. Nothing was as sexy as this man who loved her Luke.

What combined Vette and Carlton into a couple wasn't one thing, it was the deluxe-combo-platter of it all.

Vette didn't like to be away from Luke at night, and Carlton didn't like to be away from Vette, or Luke. Days after returning from Bermuda, Carlton began sleeping over at Vette's house. Luke was surprisingly okay with it and their combined lives became the norm.

Luke climbed in between Carlton and Vette, who were luckily wearing pajamas this morning.

"In Kansas it's illegal to eat cherry pie with ice cream," Luke said.

Vette wrapped her arms around Luke. "You, little man, with your bizarre trivia knowledge, are becoming more and more like your Grandma Opal every day."

Carlton sat up straight addressing Vette, "Hey, I happen to love Grandma Opal's trivia."

Luke lightly bumped Carlton's shoulder with his, in a high five of approval. Carlton feigned he'd been shoved hard and theatrically fell off the bed.

"Vette leaned across the bed, making sure to protect Luke as she went, "Are you all right?"

"That guy up there is stronger than he looks," Carlton said, as he climbed back up. "Scoot over Hoss, give me some room."

Luke giggled and leaned into Carlton. "Did you know the odds of dying from falling out of bed or over furniture is one in 4,238?"

Vette's mom, Opal, had said *when your true love comes along you'll know it.* Opal was right. When Vette first met Carlton, she felt as if the heel of a hand thumped her on the forehead and she'd heard an inner voice shouting in her ear, *you're going to marry this man.*

Carlton felt the same. Alisha Rayburn, his mother, was psychic. At least that's what Carlton believed, as he remembered their conversation at Cody and Betty's wedding some five years past.

"I'm never getting married or having children," Carlton had told his mother.

"You watch. Once you meet the right one, you will be hooked," Alisha predicted.

Did she foresee Vette coming to him five years ago? Carlton stretched his arms around both Vette and Luke. It didn't matter if his mother saw them coming or not, he was grateful they were here.

Then his phone rang.

"Hey Cody, what are you up to?" Carlton asked, as he put his feet over the side of the bed.

"What?" Carlton stood and walked out of the bedroom.

Chapter 50

Still

Vette would be home alone tonight. She'd lived in the Colonial Revival for over five years with only a few tainted months occupied by that philanderer, Frederick. Once all remnants of him were removed from the house, it became a loving home filled with laughter. But no laughter tonight.

Tonight Grandpa Max and Grandma Opal were taking Luke into the city to see his first play, Charlotte's Web, at the Broadway Playhouse, then on to dinner. The night would end with a sleepover at their house.

Carlton was meeting his brother, Cody, and Cody's wife, Betty, after he got off work. The three of them were going to their mother's to process Brad Denver's murder, but mostly to remember Lissy.

"I thought I'd feel…, I'd feel different," Carlton said to Vette that morning after Cody's phone call. "I thought when Alice's killer died, there'd be this great weight lifted off my chest. Instead, it's like one brick falling off a high rise. It's nothing. Nothing changes. His death, even as stunningly gruesome as it was, can't undo it. It can't make me un-see pictures of her brutalized body. Un-know what he did to my baby sister. His death doesn't un-lose Lissy. She's gone."

Sitting next to Carlton, Vette lifted his hand to her lips. "I'm so sorry."

Their bond became stronger by baring their darkness. Vette and Carlton spoke with no restraints, no judgement.

"I'm glad Brad Denver's dead," Carlton said. "I'm glad he can't hurt anyone else. I only wish he'd been killed the day before he saw Lissy."

"I wish so too," Vette said. "I would have loved to have known her."

Luke would be with Tammy, Hugh's wife, for part of the day before Vette's parents picked him up for their big night. With Luke at her parent's house for the night, and Carlton with his family, Vette would go from work at the dealership to a quiet evening of wine, a bubble bath, and a good book. She hadn't had a spa night in a long time and was secretly looking forward to it.

Vette slid the morning paper into her leather backpack when the headline froze her.

Serial Pedophile Killer Impaled!
Authorities confirm the Muffin-Man Killer, Randall Vahl, has murdered over twenty-eight pedophiles since 2006...

"Did you read about Randall Vahl, the pedophile killer?" Vette asked Woody. "He killed twenty-six convicted pedophiles."

"Twenty-eight," Woody said, his gaze not leaving the inventory sheets on his desk.

From across the dealership, Vette watched Hugh Johnson, their dealership's general manager, hurry out the front door, albeit a bit wobblingly. Discounting his unsteadiness to old age, Vette turned back to Woody, lifted her chin, and stared at her baby brother. "Yes, twenty-eight. He fed them a jelly-glazed oatmeal muffin, then a week later they'd be dead. Apparently their deaths were originally ruled natural causes due to influenza, but now they know it was the muffins. Poisonous muffins, like your rat recipe."

"Is that so," Woody lifted his gaze to hers.

"The article hinted at a bean and a berry plant, like the plants in your poison garden, the ones used in your rat-poison muffins."

"I dug that garden up. Too dangerous to have it that close to Jag."

Hearing his name, Jag lifted his head from a deep sleep, saw Vette and moved to her side. Vette put her hand on Jag's humongous head and began rubbing his lush fur.

"The killer kept files on his victims, like the file box you keep in the back of your car."

"Those files are gone. Shredded."

Vette reached in her pocket, pulled out her two-inch pocket knife and set it directly in front of Woody.

Without hesitation Woody placed his pocket knife next to hers. Their throw down of the junk-drawer knives. Their signal for absolute truth.

"Ask," Woody said looking straight in her eyes.

Tears welled in Vette's eyes. "I don't have to."

"Ask." Woody leaned forward.

"Woody, I hate to interrupt you," Roberta's nasal voice pierced the room before her costume of the day made its entrance. "Oh, hi Vette, I was actually looking for you."

Both put away their knives. Vette quickly wiped her tears to focus on Roberta's pale-blue peasant dress casually flung over a long-sleeve silver tank top and silver ruffled bloomers. Bloomers that touched the tops of her silver open-toed sandals. Bangles filled up both forearms, as usual, and five beaded necklaces hung from her neck to her waist. Today, sprouting from sixty-year-old Roberta's salt and pepper head, was a five-inch mauve-colored flower. Not a silk flower. A real flower.

"Hugh's wife, Tammy, just called to let you know she has to run to their church for about an hour or so. She'll be back before your parents come to pick up Luke. She wanted me to tell you that Hugh is there now with Luke and will watch him until she gets back." Roberta fluffed the flower in her hair as she spoke. "No emergency, she just wanted you to know. I'm sure Luke will have fun with Hugh."

Chapter 51

Still

Hugh was laying out the bath sheet on their king-sized bed. The petroleum jelly jar was open on the nightstand, and the Polaroid camera was across the room on the dresser next to the scissors.

When Tammy called and asked him to come home and watch Luke for an hour or two, he'd rushed out of the dealership fast to get home. This was an unexpected and exciting opportunity. The anticipation was so intense that Hugh forgot his briefcase at work that held his white mask. *No problem*, he thought, as he pulled out his extra mask from the back of the closet and laid it on the dresser.

Luke watched silently from the doorway. "Mr. Johnson?"

Hugh jumped, knocking the jelly jar to the floor and watched in horror as it rolled toward Luke.

"Did you know elephants are the only land mammals that can't jump?" Luke asked. Luke picked up the jar, walked further into the bedroom and handed it to Hugh.

"Thank you, Luke," Hugh said, as he set the jar back in place. "No I didn't know that." Hugh lifted a lock of Luke's hair. "Your hair is so soft. So pretty."

Taking his hand away, his tone changed. "Didn't I ask you to stay in the living room and not come in here?"

"Yeah, but," Luke said.

"No 'yeah buts.' When I tell you to do something, you need to do it, no questions. Do you understand?"

Luke shrunk back toward the door. "Yes sir. Can I go in your toy room?"

"I told you no already. You're not allowed in there." Hugh was irritated. Luke was wasting their precious time. Hugh only had a short window before Tammy would be back.

"I saw a Star Wars fighter plane model on your work table in there with my name on it. It says Luke Skywalker. I can read good. Can we open the box and look at it?"

"No."

"What are you doing? Can I play with your camera? Are we going to play dress up? Can I try on your mask?"

Hugh had enough. He grabbed Luke by his arm, dragged him to the living room couch and pushed him onto it.

"Ow," Luke said rubbing his arm. "That hurt."

"Now sit here and don't move until I tell you."

"Why are you being so mean? Your face is white. Are you sick?" Luke asked looking at the gray pallor of Hugh's face. "You don't sound good. Is that why you put a towel on the bed? Are you getting sick?"

"No," Hugh said, panting. Sweat covered his brow as he leaned against the couch. He didn't care anymore. Time was up.

"Woody, I need you to help me to the bedroom now."

"I'm Luke. Woody's my uncle."

"Yes Luke. Come on," Hugh didn't care if Luke saw him, or that he could tell the world. Hugh was tired of the charade. When Hugh was done, Luke would stay silent forever. He knew how he'd kill him and where he'd dump the small body. No one would ever know. No one would ever find him. It was perfect.

His heart was racing faster than his first time. Hugh was trembling with anticipation.

Luke's glasses fell from his face as Hugh's clammy hands lifted him off the couch.

"We're going into the bedroom now."

It was time.

Tammy came in through the mudroom to find Luke sitting on the couch facing the blank television screen.

"What are you doing Luke?"

"Nothing. Just practice reading and waiting on you." Luke said reaching into a bag of chips. He set down his *Toad on the Road* book.

Tammy scanned the room for Hugh. "Where's Mr. Johnson?"

"He's laying down. He was tired."

The doorbell took their attention. Luke ran to the door and flung it open. "Grandma!" He exclaimed and jumped in her arms.

"Have you been having fun?" Opal asked.

"Yes, Mrs. Johnson and I made cookies before and then Mr. Johnson came home. Is it time to go?" Luke asked.

Opal nodded and turned to Tammy, "Thank you so much for watching our little man, Tammy. I really appreciate it."

"Oh, anytime. We loved having him."

Tammy walked into the bedroom to find Hugh lying on top of the covers on the bed. A bath sheet was on the floor.

"Hugh? Hugh?" She shook him. Hugh was unconscious, not moving.

Chapter 52

Still

"I know you killed those pedophiles and I don't blame you. I blame me." Vette said to Woody in his office.

"Why on earth would you blame yourself?" Woody asked shaking his head.

"Because I should have told what happened. I should have made mom and dad send us to therapy. We needed help. We needed to talk but I put a gag on us both, especially you." Tears welled in Vette's eyes. "We need help now. You need help and I'll make sure you get it."

"You don't need to worry about me," Woody said. "I'm not doing that anymore. I made a mistake. I killed an innocent man. I'll never make that mistake again."

Woody took a deep breath. "There's only one more I want. The one that did it to me. I have to find him, but that may never happen."

Roberta ran into the room. "Tammy just called in a panic."

Vette jumped to her feet. "Is Luke okay?"

Roberta put her hand on Vette's arm to calm her, "Oh yes, he's fine. He's off with your parents having a great time. Opal called a minute before Tammy. I was just coming in to tell you when I got Tammy's call."

Roberta went on, "Tammy's the one that needs your help. When she got back from the church and after Luke left, Tammy found Hugh passed out in the bedroom with a massive blood sugar drop. His diabetes you know. Anyway, Hugh left his briefcase here with the glucagon emergency kit.

Tammy said she was able to rouse Hugh enough to get some orange juice with added sugar down him before he passed out again in the bed. She's searching the house for another kit, but no luck so far. She thinks he might have one in the briefcase. She's going to pieces, says he's falling into a diabetic coma, so one of you must to get that briefcase, make sure it has the kit in it, and get it over there right away."

Woody, with Jag following, jumped to his feet.

Hugh's old-school briefcase, the size of carry-on luggage, was open on his desk. Thankfully the dual three-digit locks hadn't been bolted. Woody and Vette riffled through the bottom section but neither saw the emergency kit amongst his calculator, business cards, iPhone, iPad, or under the plethora of papers, pens and files.

"I understand Hugh was excited to get home to watch Luke but don't you think it's odd that he left his phone and iPad, and all here?" Vette asked. "Not many people get that excited to babysit a four-year-old boy?"

"Well I do," Woody said, "but Luke's my nephew."

Vette puzzled at the depth at the top of the 1980's pilot-lawyer attaché. It seemed disproportionately wide. She unsnapped the four interior buttons making the fan-files flop forward.

Woody saw it first, reached in, and grabbed the orange plastic emergency kit that held the vial and syringe.

"Here. Found it."

On the way out of the bag the container bumped a metal tab on the underside of the handle which dropped the fan-files further into the bottom of the case, the false top sprung open exposing a five-inch wide compartment.

Vette jerked just as she had in the single-wide trailer's bedroom when the petroleum jar hit her foot, when she expected to be pulled to the bed. Looking in the false compartment of Hugh's briefcase, her mind's eye saw the man open the bedroom door to leave. He was taller than their dad, and wore a mask that wiped his face away exposing only small sections of a balding scalp. The man wore this mask, this white, full-face mask with the eyes and nasal holes cut out. The mask was inside Hugh's briefcase. Hugh had the mask. Hugh. It was Hugh.

"Vette. Vette!" Woody held his sister's body close as she started to crumble to the floor.

Vette whispered in Woody's ear, "It was Hugh. All this time. Hugh, is the man. The man, the bad man in the trailer."

Vette leaned against the desk and pulled the mask out of the bag and with it came a closer memory. Hugh's offer just before she'd gone to Bermuda.

"While you're away, maybe I can have Luke come to my house where I have a toy room, perfect for teaching him how to make a model car or plane," Hugh said. "As a matter of fact, I just got a Star Wars authentic Luke Skywalker X-Wing Fighter model that would be perfect for him and me to build together."

Woody felt Vette's transformation as she straightened up. "He was going after Luke. He's preying on Luke. *My* Luke." Her eyes fixed on Woody. "Remember? Remember! You were there when he asked to take Luke to his house. To build models. To ra… my baby. He's after my baby."

Vette shuddered, fighting the images forming in her head. "He was alone with him today. How long was he alone with him? Thank God he's with mom and dad now. I'm going to kill him. If he touched a hair on his head, I'm going to kill him. You have to help me kill him."

"What? No. Hugh? It's Hugh? He's been here all the time? Right in front of me?" Woody shoved the mask back inside the case and latched it shut. "We'll make him suffer. I have one. One last toxic muffin."

"Where? Where is it?" Vette asked.

"My house."

"Let's get it then take it and the case to Hugh." Vette added, "I need a cigarette."

"When did you start smoking?"

"Probably the same time you started with the muffins," Vette said. "No, more like when you started drinking in the back yard."

Tammy frantically rummaged through cabinets in the bathrooms and kitchen, searching for a glucagon emergency kit.

"It has to be here. Has to be here."

When she found him in bed, she knew. He was lapsing in and out of consciousness. His glazed eyes, slurred speech. Tammy was able to get a large glass of orange juice mixed with two tablespoons of sugar down him before laying him back down in bed where he passed out.

Grabbing the bedroom test kit, she pricked his cold finger and waited for his sugar results. The meter registered 57 mg/dL. Normal milligrams per deciliter is 70 to 100.

She ran from room to room rifling through closets, looking in coat pockets.

Going back to Hugh between rooms, she'd re-test his sugar.

53 mg/dL. It was going down. Not up.

Tammy's gaze went to the outside fire pit she'd readied before Hugh came home. They were going to have wine by the fire tonight.

49 mg/dL.

Roberta called to let her know Vette and Woody were searching Hugh's briefcase for the kit. Tammy grabbed a jar of honey and ran back to re-test Hugh's sugar before searching Hugh's toy room, the last room to check.

44 mg/dL.

Hugh was non-responsive. He was falling into a diabetic coma. Tammy rubbed honey on the inside of his cheek.

47 mg/dL.

"That's better. Come on Hugh, we have to get your sugar up. Come back." Hugh didn't move. He'd closed down.

51 mg/dL.

Little Hudson Terry's model of the 1951 Hudson Hornet was on the work table, completed and ready for the shelf that encircled the room. Number 52. And waiting on the table, the box still wrapped in cellophane, was number 53, Star Wars Luke Skywalker's X-Wing Fighter.

The work table's middle drawer was stuck. Tammy yanked hard, making the tools on top quiver, inching Hudson's model to the edge. She yanked again and again and again, finally dislodging the object inside and sending her, Hudson's model, and the drawer crashing to the floor.

The 1951 Hornet's body broke free of its chassis, retching its putrid guts before Tammy. Next to her the bright orange glucagon emergency kit clunked out of the drawer but rather than picking it up, she turned the Polaroid picture right-side up.

There, in their bedroom, facing the north wall was a naked little boy. A naked little boy. The baggie of hair told her his name, and when. *Hudson 2018.*

Her view of the toy room twisted as if she were inside a carnival fun house. Surveying the 51 vehicles on the shelf, Tammy could see it wasn't a hobby room. It was a trophy room stockpiling Hugh's obscene prizes.

Holding Hudson's hair and photo in one hand, Tammy's other arm wiped clean the surface of the work table, driving everything to the floor. She went to the kitchen and came back with a foldable step stool.

Climbing up. Climbing down. Crash.

One by one, Tammy hurled model cars and trucks to the floor. Then she placed each baggie, together with its photo, onto the cleared work table.

Up. Down. Crash.

Up. Down. Crash.

Up. Down. Crash.

There was a pattern. Many of the little boy's names were inside model cars of the same name.

Up. Down. Crash.

Up. Down. Crash.

Up. Down. Crash.

Repeating fifty times, she chose to leave the 1941 Ford Custom Woody Car for last.

Hugh couldn't have done that, she thought. *Not that.*

Climbing up. Climbing down. Crash.

He did.

Her spirit numbed as Tammy stared at the photo of little Woody and Vette standing as all the others, facing a wall. Looking at the baggie, *Woody & Vette 1998,* Tammy calculated the year to be when the Futrell's lived in the trailer on the used car lot.

Tammy couldn't shake the thoughts out of her head as she heard herself screaming, "You took them in their own home. Their own home. You raped your friend's children. They trusted you. How could you do that?"

Tammy leaned over the work table and wept. Her eyes fixed on the unopened model. Luke's model. Luke had been there.

His first boy was in 1966, the year Hugh and Tammy graduated from high school. The model, a 1966 Pontiac Bonneville, triggered a memory from a few years after they graduated, when thirteen year-old Frank Bonneville hung himself from a rafter in a barn.

"How many more of these poor lost boys have you killed? How many?"

Hiding the orange emergency kit in the back of another drawer, Tammy went to check on Hugh.

55 mg/dL.

His blood sugar was coming up. Looking around the room she saw the Polaroid camera, the petroleum jar, the scissors, the towel and the face mask.

She left and came back, this time with a vial of insulin and a syringe. Popping the purple tab off the insulin vial, Tammy filled the 100 unit syringe, tapped out the air bubbles, lifted Hugh's shirt, and began.

"There you go," Tammy spoke to his motionless body while injecting him. Five times. Some in the belly. Some in his thigh. All his normal injection spots.

"I know you feel I'm betraying you, but don't you see? I have to protect you so you won't hurt any more little boys." Half of the vial of insulin was gone. "You can't stop yourself. But I'll help you. I'm helping you. This is better. You see? Better." Silent tears seeped from Tammy's eyes.

20 mg/dL.

Hugh's brain screamed for glucose, though no sound came from his mouth. A moment later his brain was silent.

05 mg/dL.

Tammy wiped saliva from his mouth.

00 mg/dL.

DATE OF BIRTH: 05/04/1948 SEX: M RACE: W WEIGHT: 223 HEIGHT: 600

Date of Death: 09/15/2018

Chapter 53

Still

On the way to Hugh's house, Vette frantically called her mother to speak with Luke.

"Mr. Johnson was fine, Mommy," Luke said. "He didn't want me to play in his toy room though."

Luke answered all her questions. "Did he touch me? Well, he picked me up from the couch and told me we were going in the bedroom, but then he set me right back down on the couch. He looked sick. And he said he was going to go lay down. Then Mrs. Johnson came home and then Grandma came."

Luke wanted off the phone. "We're about to go into the play now mommy. I got to go. This is a big room. Grandpa bought me a t-shirt with a pig on it."

Vette could breathe. Luke was fine. Even so she was taking him to therapy to make sure nothing happened. Woody parked in front of Hugh and Tammy's house.

"Shit. This place battled poltergeists and lost," Woody said.

Everything hidden in closets and drawers was thrown about, littering floors in all of the rooms Woody and Vette encountered. A massive pile up in the toy room left tiny plastic wheels, hoods, engines, grills, headlights, and bumpers scattered and broken.

"Tammy?" Vette called.

They'd been calling for her since they discovered the front door unlocked. Instead of Tammy, they found Hugh, his face absent of color, while the back of his neck that rested on the bed was bluish-purple.

"Hugh," Woody hissed. "Hugh."

Vette touched her fingers to his cheek and felt death's chill. She didn't have to shake him, it was obvious. "He's dead. He's already dead."

"What?" Woody dropped the briefcase and shook the blood-thickening body. "Wake up, you asshole. You can't die that easily. Wake up!"

Flames from the outside fire pit caught Vette's attention. Tammy had been watching Vette and Woody through the window. Their eyes met and with a wave of her hand, Tammy bid Vette to come outside. Vette gently pulled Woody from Hugh.

"Tammy's outside." Vette took the mask from the case. "Come on."

Moving through the kitchen to the back porch, Vette set down the paper sack containing the last muffin on the counter. She thought, *don't need that anymore.* She would shove it down the disposal before they left.

Tammy and Hugh's backyard was a landscaper's wet dream. Mature trees, lush bushes, and seasonal flowers were perfectly placed. Electricity had been run to two crystal chandeliers swaying from branches at opposite edges of the outdoor space to softly light the night. Hollow tones from wind chimes haunted the half-acre space. At the back, a flagstone patio was covered by large oak branches masquerading as an umbrella, and kept the round table and chairs beneath shielded from the moonlight.

Vette and Woody headed to the right under the roof of stars, where fat cushions bulged from the classic but new wicker furniture that surrounded a flagstone fire pit.

Pinpricks of fire sparked twelve feet above the intense flames shooting from a teepee of logs.

"Tammy," Vette started.

"Please sit," Tammy was on her feet, the perfect hostess with a wave of her hand, indicating the available seating away from the fire's smoke.

Vette and Woody obediently took a seat. Jag had their backs, circling three times to lie down facing the most threatening direction, the house that held Hugh's remains.

"There's a bit of a chill tonight," Tammy went on. "Please, do use the throw blankets on your chairs. They're fleece and very soft." She turned to a wicker end table next to her loveseat, lifted a wine glass, and asked, "Red or white?"

"Um," Vette and Woody said in unison.

"White." Tammy chose for them. "White is always good." She emptied a bottle, filling their seventeen-ounce stemless wine glasses to the brim, and handed them to Vette and Woody. Tammy walked under the pergola to the outdoor wine cooler. Vette and Woody heard two empty bottles smash into a trashcan. At least they hoped the bottles went in the trash. They watched her come back into the firelight carrying two fresh bottles.

She stacked another log on the fire, and said: "I saw you through the window. You were in with Hugh." Tammy sat on the edge of her loveseat and took the brass-handled fireplace poker to move a few logs. Creating a small space, she threw in a sandwich-sized plastic-bag with its matching Polaroid picture. The new items irritated the fire to sizzle for the fifty-first time that night, sending sparks spitting to the sky. The smell of spruce and hickory wood overshadowed the faint scent of waxy-plastic and burnt hair.

Vette could tell Tammy was anxious, breathing rapidly. She heard Tammy murmur a prayer.

Moving to the loveseat, Vette took the fleece blanket and covered Tammy's shoulders. "You're right, this is soft." Vette sat with her arm around Tammy. "Tammy have you seen Hugh?"

"Yes. He's in bed."

"Tammy?"

"He's dead. I know," Tammy said, looking all of her seventy years. She took a deep breath. "I was scouring the place for his emergency kit. I just wanted the kit. To bring him back to me." Staring into the fire she added, "Then I knocked over one of his model cars. It broke open."

She looked up at Vette and Woody. "Have you ever known someone, only to learn you don't? That you've been lied to and used in the foulest way? I was nothing more than his cover."

Tammy took a long pull on her wine. "Oh... I've been arguing with myself, telling myself he wasn't all evil. He was good, too. And he was. He was good to me in a friendly way. Not in a marriage way. But still he was kind to me. Though now, I see what he did. What he was."

Tammy held her hands tightly on her lap. "How could I be so blind? You see I found... I found out something about Hugh tonight that can never be unfound. That can never be unseen."

Woody moved to the loveseat, where he and Vette flanked Tammy. Tammy had grown small with age. They sat as parents with a child on the small couch.

"What did you find?" Woody asked.

Crepe-paper skin, dotted with brown spots, sunk into Tammy's brittle hands where blue veins protruded. Her hands remained on her lap, with her left over her right, covering the last Polaroid and sack of hair.

"Fifty-two years. He… he hurt little boys," Tammy said as her tear drops fell. "Why didn't someone say something? Why did they stay silent?" Tammy asked.

"Why did *you* stay silent? How could he do that to you? Why didn't you tell someone?"

"How do you know?" Woody asked. "We didn't know Hugh was the man. We were just kids. We didn't talk because the man knew where we lived. He threatened that if we talked, he was coming back to do it again, only the next time he would do it in front of our parents. And after, one by one, he would kill us all. He used our love for each other to keep us silent. He used our love."

Vette added: "We didn't know it was Hugh. We still don't know that it was him, because the man wore a mask. Tammy, it may not have been Hugh." She held up the white mask for Tammy to see. "The man's mask looked like this. Tonight we found this in Hugh's briefcase."

"Was he the man?" Woody asked Tammy.

"Yes. Oh my God… yes. Oh, my God," Tammy whimpered as she revealed Woody and Vette's picture along with the baggy that held their hair clippings. "This is why I had to do it."

"Do what?" Vette asked.

"I found fifty-two of these. How could he have done this to you… to you? I had to stop him. You understand. You have to understand, I had no choice."

Inside the house, like a cold layer of fat seals the top of homemade stock, Hugh's blood congealed in his veins. Rigor mortis had already begun as Tammy confessed to his murder. Telling them how his blood sugar began to rise, and what she had done to make it plummet.

"Tammy, you didn't kill him," Woody said to her. "His body shut down. He went into a diabetic coma. There was nothing you could do. Say it. Say it back to me."

"Nothing I could do," Tammy muttered. "Nothing I could do."

Vette handed Woody their picture and baggy of hair. Without a second look, he threw them into the pit where the fire converted them to sparks in the sky. Following his lead, Vette dropped the mask on the flames. The white mask turned yellow with a center of blue whooshing from the eyes and nose to pierce the air with the smell of pungent diesel.

"Nothing I could do," Tammy muttered. "Nothing I could do."

Woody covered the dissolving mask with heavy logs, while Vette helped Tammy lay down, tucking a pillow under her head and covering her with three of the warm blankets. Jag moved close to Tammy and laid down.

"Tammy, we're going in the house now to clean up. You lay here and rest."

"Nothing…" Tammy muttered.

Chapter 54

Now

It took only three days from death to cremation to memorial. Tammy sat alone in the first pew. Behind her was Max, Opal, Woody, with Jag at his feet, and Vette next to Carlton. Tammy insisted Jag come. Behind them were Neil and his husband Kent, who was beside Roberta who wore a full length, bohemian regalia of black lace, with fringed sleeves, and her bedazzled head sporting elaborate hair chains of silver dangles.

The entire Futrell Automotive family filled the pews. Max had closed all four dealerships in remembrance of Hugh Johnson, their Chief Executive General Manager of twenty years. Everyone was expected to come and pay their respects, then go off and enjoy their long weekend.

There wasn't going to be a graveside service. Tammy had plans for his remains. She needed to be alone when she poured Hugh's ashes out of the plastic container and into the ditch. No need to waste a good container. She'd put it in the dishwasher when she got home.

Tammy had found a desolate gravel road where coyotes ripped trash bags open and left their rotting contents in the ditch. That's where Tammy would stomp Hugh's ashes into the ground, throw the neighbor's dog shit over him, and then top him off with a gallon of gasoline. She wasn't really going to pour gasoline on the ground. That would contaminate the soil. But the dog shit was real. There was a gallon-sized zip baggie of dog shit waiting in the limo.

Tammy had to endure the memorial service and the church-lady luncheon in the fellowship hall before she could grab his ashes and chuck him in that ditch.

"Amen," said the pastor.

"Amen," replied the congregation.

Tammy stood, and Pastor Buckler guided her down the aisle to the bottom of the curved staircase where all began passing by her, offering their condolences. Inappropriate laughter spilled from her, when she spotted Roberta.

Thank God for Roberta, Tammy thought.

Tammy wasn't grieving correctly. But then how was she supposed to mourn a monster? She was strapped tight to a schizophrenic roller coaster, not knowing what to feel. One moment sick, next sad, then furious, then sick, sad, furious, sick, sad, furious. Round and round, up and down. She could throw up any second and had been doing just that for the last three days.

That awful night, before the coroner tookay Hugh away, Woody called his friend in the mattress business to come with movers and bring with him a new king-size mattress and box spring. Once Hugh was out of the house, the soiled bed followed, and taking its place was a new, freshly made bed.

The movers took away all of Hugh's clothes and belongings. All of the trash from the toy room, all of his medicine, his pills, vials, syringes. They emptied his closets so that when Tammy went to bed it was her bed. Her home was hers alone, and when she woke the next morning there would be no sign of Hugh.

All that was left of Hugh were his ashes in the plastic container, tucked inside the mantel-ready black leather case.

"We're so sorry for your loss," said a lady in a black hat.

"Thank you," Tammy said, not knowing who that was.

"At least he lived a long life. So many people die young."

"Okay," Tammy said.

A woman gave her a big hug, said nothing and moved on. Tammy didn't know who the fuck she was either.

"He brought this on himself. Worked like a dog." The man was already headed for the food.

"You're young. You can find another husband."

"What the hell is wrong with these people?" Tammy muttered.

"I have two pounds of bacon in my car with your name on it," a man said.

"No. Thank you," Tammy said.

The next man jumped in front of her with a big smile, "Guess who I am!"

"What? No. No. I'm not in the mood for guessing games."

"I'm Hugh's cousin, Ivan!"

"Okay. The food is over there," Tammy pointed.

"I can't imagine what you're feeling, but we're here to help in any way we can," Neil said. His husband Kent next to him.

Kent added, "Hugh's in a better place."

"I hope not," Tammy said, then realized she'd said it out loud.

"What?" Neil asked.

"I have knots… in my stomach," Tammy did a quick save. "I think I'm coming down with the flu. Or maybe it's something I ate."

Vette, Woody, and Jag were next in line.

"Did you throw out that muffin?" Woody whispered to Vette.

"No, I thought you did."

"Fuck no. I didn't."

Woody found himself in front of Tammy. He leaned in and hugged her, whispering in her ear, "Tammy there was a paper sack with a muffin in it on your counter that night. I meant to throw it out but forgot. You didn't eat it did you?"

"Oh yes," Tammy said.

Woody inhaled sharply and looked to Vette whose mouth was agape.

"I saw it," Tammy continued. "But I didn't eat it. My mother always warned me to never eat anything if you didn't know where it came from. She'd say, *Could have a roofy in it*," Tammy chuckled. "She was a funny old thing. Always worried someone would drug me up. At the present, I could use some good drugs. God bless her soul, I miss her."

Taking a deep breath she added, "Anyway that muffin went down the disposal and is fish food by now."

My Dear Reading Friend,

Thank you for coming with me on this journey. I began writing *THE URGE* in March of 2017. That's a lie. The shadow of this story fell on me twenty-six years before, where it's been tucked away in my head-closet with the door closed.

I've always loved writing tales. My first recognized horror story was put to paper in junior high. Mr. Johnson, the good-looking teacher extraordinaire, thought my story was so well written he asked me to stand in front of the class and read it. What a glorious day. His encouragement skillfully fueled my passion. I am eternally grateful to Mr. Johnson.

As I grew, I found paying gigs writing articles that were published in newspapers and magazines. This spurred me on to write my first novel, which led me to an agent who back then merely required copying fees, no reading fees. Keep in mind, this was long before the internet.

Yes, there was a time before the Internet, and yes, I'm old. Don't judge.

I sent this agent money in order to make copies of my novel and in turn she sent those copies to publishing houses. It wasn't long before she informed me my work had been sent to every publishing house in existence. I believed her. She sent me a detailed list of the publishing houses. *Damn, I was gullible.*

Months later after the copying fees were paid, a letter came. My agent was dropping me and my book. She explained no one would ever buy my books. It was an overwhelming defeat.

Sadly that's all it took—one letter, one opinion from a faceless person—to quash my dreams. I put away my writing and picked up mind-numbing jobs.

Rifling through my file cabinet years later, I came across that infamous letter, which led me poking around the worldwide web to discover that agent was a thief who never sent anyone's work to any publishing house. She was a dream-stealer. A charlatan.

I have only myself to blame for those lost writing years. Thank goodness there's no age limit for authors.

The moral to the story: Listen to your teachers, and not the back-stabbing, blood-sucking dream-stealing thieves of the world.

Thank you again for joining me on this journey to *THE URGE,* a Devil's Rules series novel.

Talk to you soon,
CL Gibson

P.S.,
I really do need your help. Please go to Amazon.com and to Goodreads.com to write a review of *THE URGE*. It will only take a few moments and it will mean the world to me. Your feedback is so important to me and to future readers. I can't say it enough, I truly value your input into my work. And now with your permission, I would like to quote Elvis Presley, *"Thank You, Thank You Very Much."*

You can also let me know your thoughts on THE URGE via the contact form on my website, ChristiLGibson.com. I look forward to hearing from you. I do read every note personally and every note will receive a response.

Also on my website find excerpts from my other novels, check out my blog, and an upcoming schedule of appearances. The only thing I like better than hearing from my readers is meeting them in person.

Following is an excerpt from **The Grudge**, the second in The Devil's Rules series.

COMING IN THE FALL OF 2019

The Grudge

By
CL Gibson

"For where envying and strife is,
there is confusion and every evil work."
James 3:16

Chapter 1
Saturday, July 8, 1978

I'm barefoot, strolling through their living room with the fireplace as big as my kitchen. I pass the mahogany-paneled dining room, and stop in the rotunda with its three-story spiral staircase.

I really didn't need to take my shoes off. They're busy. Listen to them moaning and writhing one floor up. Did they think I'd walk away and forget it? They're so unconstrained. So careless.

Blankets and sheets are probably kicked to the floor. Bed springs grinding, echoing through the halls. If they knew it was their last time, would they be doing it any differently, trying new positions, taking it slower or faster?

The stairwell consumes and amplifies every disgusting sound they make. I can't help but listen. Hard-pounding staccato gasps grow louder, faster. They're coming to the crescendo, luring me in.

I let my clothes slip from my body, and moist, warm heat slides onto my skin. July's beating down on the main house, roasting it like a well-done piece of meat, but my nipples are erect. Around me chandeliers sparkle, gilt mirrors shine, and the wood work gleams. Being naked in this gaudy, overdone mansion that screams "we're rich and you're not" excites me. Knowing they're going to die today excites me, too.

Right and wrong?

Don't feed me that crap. I know what's right and what's wrong. We were flat-out poor when I was little. Back then I thought good silverware was plastic, and paper plates were reusable, but I learned quick enough. When you haven't got much, you have to fight to get more. I was taught to appreciate people rather than things. They don't see it that way. Everything was given to them wrapped in red foil and gold ribbons.

It's not my fault they were born into a snotty rich class of bigots that taught them to manipulate and exploit people. They didn't have to listen. No, these two are so high and mighty, they figure they can trash anybody and get away with it. Who's gonna stop 'em? As long as they've got pockets full of cash, it's okay. But it's not okay with me. I'm tired of being used like an old wash rag. Like I said, it's not my fault. They deserve to die. And watch, no one will blame me when it's over. No one.

My breath is coming quicker now, working me up, making me ready. Skin slides against skin as I walk to the center of their fancy dome-covered rotunda. The sun is piercing the stained-glass windows three flights above my head, I'm drawn to the banister's base where a bronze sculpture of a wood nymph holds the stems of glass, tear drop flowers. Today, draped over the nymph's flowers, I see her panties. If I step closer, I'll smell her scent. I try to hold my breath.

"In a hurry Ross?" I whisper, but they don't hear me. They're too wrapped up in themselves to hear me.

Protected by surgical gloves, the tips of my fingers lift the pink, silk panties from the nymph and drop them into the garbage sack that holds her purse. Her khaki shorts and white sandals are on the floor, as usual, I have some straightening up to do. I toss the shorts and sandals into the sack, too.

Looking across the room, I see my clothes that I have neatly folded and stacked inside a plastic bag. Hers are strewn all about, a cluttered trail running up the stairs. A tee-shirt. Her bra. Some jewelry. A watch. Earrings.

"Filthy pig," I mumble. Looking up the stairs, I'm a touch louder. "Too damn lazy to pick up after yourself?" I'm growing braver.

All of her things go in the sack. As I turn on the staircase, I hear something drop to the floor below. There's a faint tinkling sound, like loose change, but I can't see anything.

"Oh, ah, Ross." slips from their bedroom and almost ruptures my eardrums. Suddenly I want to drive stakes in their eyes and use a dull razor to play tic-tac-toe on their bodies. I won't. Not yet.

I'm wearing only a shower cap and surgical gloves, and I move my clothes to the bathroom under the staircase and lay them next to the shower. The towel and washcloth are exactly where I'd left them.

"Almost. I'm almost ready."

I arrange the gold pocket watch and note on the mantel, and go to the den to lift the .44 Magnum from its perch on the wall. The cylinder is loaded with six hollow-point bullets. It's so much easier to move without clothes. I'm at the back door. There's no turning back once I slam it shut.

"On your mark. Get set. Go."

Heavy wood smacks together. Like a thunder clap it crashes and ricochets up the three flights of stairs. Every window in the rotunda rattles and shivers with the resounding thud. It pushes me across the large, round room to the pocket watch perched on the mantel. I lightly touch the gold latch, and the ornately engraved cover snaps open to release the music. It's as if a tiny harpsichord had been trapped inside the watch. Music fills the rotunda. "*Shall We Gather at the River*" is swirling notes around me, swaying my bare body, dancing me back to my hiding place under the huge staircase. Everything is in place, and soon they'll be coming down to see me. All of me.

With the gun raised, I wait.

"Come out, come out, wherever you are."

Chapter 2
Back - March 1977

She lived on a farm sixty miles west of Chicago. A farmer's daughter on the porch outside her bedroom,

Clarissa swayed on a cushioned glider with a warm comforter wrapped around her, fluffy slippers on her feet, and Queenie, her semi-feral black cat, asleep on her lap. Queenie should have been named King, but when Clarissa named him she hadn't bothered to look there.

He wasn't fully black either. There was a white spot on his neck, and he wasn't feral, only slightly aloof, which meant he was a tame cat living on a farm that could hold his own with the real feral cats that lived in the outbuildings.

Then again, Queenie never went off the porch, so he'd never been in a boxing ring with a wild cat. But those were just silly details. What was important was Clarissa loved him and he loved her back.

Clarissa pulled the comforter over her head like a hoodie, making Queenie nestle deeper under the warm blanket. Clarissa's thoughts took her back to her second memory.

While others did calisthenics to keep in shape, Clarissa did brain exercises to keep sharp. Her grandma, Addi, taught her the exercises that strengthened her gift.

One exercise was to remember as far back as she could. Clarissa's first memory was of the Christmas tree when she was just furniture walking. The second was riding in the car and feeling really pissed off, which wasn't like her at all.

"You are so bright," her mother would say, although it had nothing to do with intellect. She meant bright as a yard light shining over everyone with joy.

Clarissa was so thrilled with life she would squeal, high-pitched squeals that sounded like a combo-platter of a baby pig being squished under the weight of its mother, and long witch's fingernails scraping across a blackboard. Squealing was Clarissa's way of expressing her love of life. For those who weren't prepared for it, it was disturbing.

In her second memory, the woman in the car was definitely not prepared, but Clarissa had completed the squealing portion of the ride and was now merely sitting in the front seat between her mother, the driver, and the woman overflowing in the passenger seat, who smelled old.

Clarissa was not wearing a seat belt. It was 1965 and even if cars had belts, nobody wore them. Quiet for now, Clarissa held her sacred white blanket that was bordered all around with the softest white tassels. Contentedly, she brushed a tassel back and forth across her right cheek while simultaneously sucking on two fingers from her left hand, always the middle and ring fingers. She snuggled in closer to her mother's side.

"You need to take that blanket away from her," the old-smelling woman ordered.

The memory didn't include any other dialogue, Clarissa just remembered clutching her blanket tighter, glaring at that woman, and daring her to try and take her blanket.

Not long after that incident her blanket was MIA.

Clarissa smiled slightly as she recalled that time in her life some twelve or thirteen years prior, and made a mental note: *Life is hard, don't take away anyone's blanket.*

Pulling the comforter close around her and Queenie, Clarissa felt the first touch of spring in the air. The brown front yard was succumbing to early blades of green pushing upward as dirt-filled mounds of snow melted and grew smaller. Filthy black piles of the icy dirt lined both sides of the lane.

From spring to summer, from summer to fall, and even from fall to winter the seasons merged beautifully. But winter to spring had melting snow slurping filth like brown syrup on shaved ice and turned northern Illinois uglier than shit. Major, Clarissa's grandfather, always said, "You can't shine shit, but you can roll it in glitter." This time of year needed truckloads of glitter.

Even so, it was nice waking early on the farm, especially with the promise of spring. With no corn or soybeans growing in the fields, she could see for miles and miles.

This time of year made her think about how life used to be. Not that Clarissa was old. Hell no, she was only fourteen, but she was a wise fourteen, and a worker. A person pretty much had to be a worker if they were growing up on a farm.

The exception to that rule could have been Clarissa. Her family farm was over nine-thousand acres with lots and lots and lots of hired hands, housekeepers, maids, cooks, and grounds keepers. So yeah, Clarissa didn't really have to work, at all, ever. But back when her mother was there, Clarissa did have to do chores.

Just a year after the blanket fiasco, Clarissa was deemed old enough to get a job. With child labor laws, she was only allowed to work on the farm. Each morning before breakfast, Clarissa's chores included getting the eggs.

Simple enough. Open fridge. Extract eggs. Done! That's not how it worked on the farm.

5:00 a.m. Grab a basket, go outside, cross the farmyard, go to the chicken house, get eggs.

A clear-cut job description that anyone could understand. Rain, shine, snow, didn't matter, that was her job. And as with any job, there were set qualifications to be met in order to successfully accomplish the objective.

Clarissa's mother, the head of HR in their home, should have realized Clarissa did not meet all of the requirements for the position, but her mother had other things on her mind. Regardless, having been assigned the task, Clarissa was expected to complete it. No excuses.

The real problem was in order to open the door to the chicken house, Clarissa had to be able to reach the door handle. She could not. The key criteria she was lacking for this position was the height requirement. On that particular day, the stool, normally there for her to step onto, was missing.

Having lived through the blanket incident the prior year, she was a hardened three-year-old and was not about to let the height barrier stop her from accomplishing her mission. She also wanted to eat eggs for breakfast, which was a great motivator.

She remembered spotting the broken window at eye level with only a few shards of glass jutting from the frame. Viewing the easy entry, Clarissa tossed the basket in, climbed through, and set about her task.

Clarissa was aware that chickens don't take kindly to losing their eggs, and that their beaks are sharp as knives. She knew this from experience.

Like a lion stalking its prey, she silently scanned the multilevel roosting area for sleeping chickens. Starting at the bottom, Clarissa meticulously eased her hand under each feathered creature to extract one egg per chicken, then carefully placed the warm eggs in her basket.

Sometimes, if she was lucky, a chicken would lay two eggs. But she didn't count on it. Consequently, to fill the basket, she had to dig under a bunch of chickens.

Suddenly two sergeant-at-arms crazed chickens, with wings extended, raced toward her. They were as tall as Clarissa, and the only weapon she held was a basket full of perfectly placed eggs. Clearly at a disadvantage it was a fight or flight situation.

Swaying on the glider Clarissa pulled the blanket closer to her chin and remembered choosing flight.

Protecting her breakfast eggs as only a three-year-old could, she threw the basket out the window and hurled herself after it. Mid-flight, she felt the searing pain of her upper thigh being slit open by a shard of broken glass.

Once on the safe side of the wall, she no longer felt the pain. She was the victor. Gathering the salvageable eggs, she'd accomplished her task. They ate scrambled eggs that day, and although over the years it had become smaller, to this day she wore the scar on her right thigh proudly.

Curtains lifted and fell softly in the night on the farm when she was small, in rhythm with the buzz of crickets, the howl of coyotes, and the call of owls. The earlier years seemed brighter, easier somehow, probably because her mother was there.

Many summer nights, Clarissa would lie in the front yard with the stars as her ceiling, and drift to sleep, only to wake and find herself tucked in her bed the next morning. She didn't know if it was her father or mother who carried her to bed, but she did know what it felt to be safe. She was safe there on the farm and grew with a freedom and trust that many never knew.

Although an only child, Clarissa wasn't alone. She had playmates. Garrett, the housekeeper's son, and Joseph, the boy from the farm across the road were like two older brothers to her. They would hop on their bikes to spend the day riding the country roads for miles. If they got thirsty, they'd stop at a farmhouse and ask for water, most times not knowing the occupants.

No stranger-danger there. They would always be welcomed in, given something to drink, and at times treated with a cookie, then sent on their way. All the farmettes and all the land around them belonged to Clarissa's family. Fifteen square miles of land with the main house smack dab in the center of it.

Major always said, "Throw in some pink beaches, add five square miles of land, and call us Bermuda." Bermuda is a little over twenty square miles.

They owned all but Joseph's little family farm across the road. So yeah, they were given water and treated nice whenever they got thirsty. But Clarissa never thought of herself as any different than the next person. She was just a farmer's daughter, growing up in the country.

There were days Clarissa, Garrett, and Joseph climbed to the top rafters of the barn, and swung on a rope to drop twenty feet below into mounds of hay.

Sometimes, Joseph the oldest of the group, hung on the ladder that led to the hay loft, waiting for one of the hogs in the yard below. When positioned just right, he would let go and drop onto the back of an unsuspecting hog, grab its ears like the reins of a horse, and ride it around the pen.

Clarissa and Garrett never tried that. It was a hoot to watch, but Clarissa worried she'd miss the pig and hit the ground. Even as a child, Garrett was a realist who knew it was an idiotic thing to do, no matter the outcome. It was bad for the pig and bad for him, too. Truth be told, the pigs were not thrilled with this practice.

Clarissa was not a fan of having hogs as livestock. They were mean and cagey. They plotted their escape during the days and would make a break for it at night when she and her parents slept. She'd hear her father's frantic call to get up! They would rush out into the dark and have to herd the pigs back to their pens.

"Let them go! Set them free!" Clarissa would yell back to her folks, but her Dad and Mom never listened. Up they'd get to chase the hogs back to their yard.

It wasn't long before her dad moved all the livestock, including the hog set up, to one of their other farmsteads so that they didn't have to deal with the mess, smell, or nightly escapes.

Clarissa softly set Queenie on the glider next to her, and stood to stretch. She looked across the road to Joseph's family farm, thinking: *the true culprit of the pigs's multiple attempts to escape was Joseph. Pigs are not horses. Riding of pigs leads to sleepless nights.*

Joseph and his father raised hogs on their farm and she wondered if Joseph still rode pigs now that he was a grown man. *Nah*, she thought, *probably not.*

That was all so long ago, at least it seemed like it. It had been years since her mother had left them and over a year since her dad had remarried. Everything was different. Lauree, Clarissa's stepmother, was due to give birth to a baby any day now. Although no test had yet to be developed that could determine the sex a baby while in utero, her stepmother insisted she was carrying a boy.

Lauree hadn't had any morning sickness during the first trimester. She craved sour and salty foods, not sweets. And she was carrying low. All the signs pointed to it being a boy. Clarissa was excited about the baby, whether a boy, or a girl. They'd already decided his name would be Nathanial. She couldn't wait to hold him, care for him and most of all to have a sibling so all eyes would not be on her.

Getting used to a stepmother had not been an easy task, although Lauree tried hard to get close to Clarissa, even when Clarissa's dad wasn't all that nice to Laurie.

Holding the door open to her bedroom, Clarissa waited for Queenie to saunter in from the porch. Once in, Clarissa followed and began getting ready for the day.

Chapter 3
Still March 1977

The pain started at 9:30 in the morning. It didn't go away, and begin again like the books, doctors, and neighbors said it would. It came at 9:30 and wouldn't leave.

"Ross, where are you? Ross."

Bounding down the staircase, Clarissa's feet froze on the landing the second she heard Lauree yelling for her dad. *Crap*, Clarissa thought as she slowly moved downward. Up to that moment it had been such a relaxing Saturday morning. She really didn't want to get in the middle of one of their many fights and upset the sweet rhythm of her day.

The easiest thing for Clarissa to do was sneak out through the veranda, but something in Lauree's voice drew her to the living room. With her footsteps muffled by the oriental runner, Clarissa peeked into the room.

"Clarissa, thank God, get in here."

Leaning on to the doorway Clarissa asked, "Are you all right?"

"No, I'm in pain. Go get your father. This baby is coming."

"I don't know where…"

"Clarissa, *please* go find him."

Clarissa bolted as she thought, *the baby. Nathaniel's coming!*

Down the hall, through the rotunda, and out the back door she ran.

Clarissa didn't think as she raced to the network of outbuildings; she didn't want to. If she had, she would see that she was always running from that house. No matter how much time or space she put between herself and that house, she would never be able to run far enough, never run fast enough because what lay ahead would pull her back.

Lauree dropped to her knees and crawled to the phone. Yes, Lauree knew labor would be painful. She'd read all the murky details, heard all the horror stories, but she'd also been told about the breaks. One minute of pain, then a ten-minute break. She'd looked forward to the breaks, planned for them.

But as pain clawed at her body and seared into her brain, Lauree prayed for a break. She clutched the phone. Why don't they answer? It's 10:30. Their office is open.

"Answer. Pick up the phone."

"Doctors Bruck, Hinds and Kelly. Can you hold?"

Lauree cried, "No." But no one was there. Instead, Debbie Boone's, "*You Light up my Life*" blasted from the earpiece. Bile jumped to her throat. Holding the phone, Lauree doubled over.

"Ross. . ." she whimpered.

And YOU LIGHT UP MY… the receptionist cut it off. "May I help you?"

"This is Lauree Trenton. I'm Doctor Bruck's patient. I'm in labor and I'm going to the hospital."

"Let me get the nurse, Mrs. Trenton."

More music screeched through the phone as the wrenching spasms tore at her stomach.

Tears mingling with sweat ran into her mouth. Lauree tried to pant, but breathing exercises couldn't deaden the pain, only a swift kick to the head could do that.

Damn this natural crap. I need drugs.

"Mrs. Trenton, this is Rita. How far apart are the contractions?"

"They're constant, not apart, constant."

"Now, Mrs. Trenton, I understand this is your first full-term pregnancy; however, contractions are not constant. Have you tried to time them?"

"Listen to me, you incompetent moron. Don't you think I've tried to time them? They started at nine-thirty. It's now ten-forty-five. That's an hour and fifteen minutes. This pain isn't going away. There's nothing to time."

Rita let out a long sigh as she thought, *here we go again.* Speaking calmly into the phone, Rita said, "Mrs. Trenton, first-time mothers take forever. We don't want you to go to the hospital until it is close to your time to deliver. You'll be more comfortable at home."

"Do I sound comfortable to you?"

Rita went on as if Lauree hadn't said a word. "I see according to your chart you're not due for another two weeks. This pain you are experiencing is more than likely Braxton-Hicks contractions.

Just yesterday you were in to see Dr. Bruck with the same symptoms and he advised you to rest and relax. I suggest you take his advice and don't worry. These contractions are getting you ready for when it's really your time to deliver."

Pain stripped away graciousness, Lauree snapped, "Do you have any idea who I am? I can have you thrown out of that hospital like a used syringe. Let me talk to Doctor Bruck now."

Rita was aching to tell Mrs. Trenton where she could stick her syringe, but she continued to gauge every word carefully. "Mrs. Trenton, I do know who you are."

And what you are, she thought.

"However, the pain you may be experiencing could be gas or indigestion. Try taking an antacid and call us if you aren't feeling any relief, but do give it time. Doctor Bruck is with other patients. When he is free, I will tell him you called. Now if you'll excuse me, I have other patients to attend to."

The line went dead. Lauree stared at the phone in her hand. "You bitch." Slamming the receiver down, she aimed her anger toward the door.

"Ross."

Heavy footsteps came from the hall. Ross's arms scooped Lauree off the floor like a rag doll and dropped her on the couch. His not-so-tender touch was comparable to being whipped against the wall a number of times.

"Did you call the doctor?" he asked impatiently, striding across the room to light a cigarette.

Moans escaped Lauree's lips.

"Did you call the doctor?" It was more an accusation than a question.

"Yes," she whimpered. "They said to take an antacid. Oh, Ross, I can't stand the pain. Take me to the hospital. I've really got to go to the hospital."

Ross marched back to the couch mumbling something through his clenched teeth that resembled a prayer but clearly wasn't aimed in a heavenly direction.

Grabbing a pack of Tums from his pocket, he threw them onto her expanded stomach. "Didn't we go through this yesterday? Chew those and don't bother me until you're really in labor. I won't sit by your side every time you feel a twinge; so get over it. I have more than nine-thousand acres to plant, and while I'm in here with you, there are twenty men standing around my office waiting for my instructions. It's coming on planting season remember?"

At the door, he turned to glare at her. "I swear, Sarah never whined and cried like you do. She had Clarissa without even batting an eye. All you've done for the last nine months is complain and eat. Eat and complain. You've gotten so fat I can't stand to look at you. Get up and do something with yourself. You look like hell."

The pack of Tums dodged the verbal gunfire by rolling off her belly, but his words made a direct hit. Lauree never thought she could hate Ross, but she was a quick study. During this pregnancy her loving husband had grown colder with each passing month.

Pride stuck in her throat like a hunk of moldy meat, but Lauree forgave him, accepting his behavior, believing it was the pregnancy, not her. She could accept the fact that he didn't find pregnant women attractive. It was common in a lot of men, so when the baby started to show and the compliments came to an end, she learned to swallow it. But allowing their sex life to die was harder to embrace. Ross wouldn't come near her unless she begged.

It had been five months since they made love, if that was what you could call it. At the time, Ross was so thrilled by the idea of being with her, he said, "All right. Let's get it over with."

Even though her body ached for him, Lauree never asked again. It was too humiliating. Lauree knew Ross wasn't the type of man to go without, and she wondered if he was having an affair. Finding it too painful to think about, she put it out of her head.

With each progressive month, Ross became more vicious and hateful toward her, doing things totally out of character. The Ross she knew wouldn't kill a bug in the house. He captured them and put them outside.

But then it started. He pushed her against the wall. He pushed her hard, knocking the air right out of her. She was stunned silent, staring at the man who resembled Ross, refusing to believe it was him. Next, it was a hard slap that left his hand imprinted on her cheek.

Every night she'd open her journal, rationalize, and write, *He doesn't know what he's doing. He has a lot on his mind.*

After the initial shock wore off after each assault, Ross expected her forgiveness, and like a fool, she forgave him. But not this time. This time he brought Sarah into the picture, and she wasn't about to forgive that.

Ross disappeared from the doorway. Driven by rage, Lauree worked her way to the rotunda by supporting her stomach with her arm. Ross was already out of the house on the veranda

Shaking with anger, she opened the back door and screamed, "I'm not your precious Sarah. I never have been, and I never will be."

He ignored her and kept moving.

"The only reason you married me is because I look like Sarah."

This got his attention. Ross turned around smirking, "Not now you don't."

Lauree's shrill voice echoed throughout the farm, "You put that bitch up on a pedestal so high you don't remember why she left. Well, let me remind you. Sarah was shacking up with every man in DeKalb County.

You know this baby I'm carrying is yours, but can you be so sure Clarissa is yours? I'm a better mother to Clarissa than Sarah could ever hope to be. Sarah doesn't call. She doesn't come to see Clarissa. She's abandoned her. I've seen alley cats that made better mothers than your beloved Sarah. So don't you feed me that crap about how wonderful Sarah was. I know better."

As quick as the words flew out of her mouth, Ross was dragging her back in the house, his calloused hands smashing her against the oak staircase.

Lauree tried to pry his hands from her shoulders, but Ross's fingers dug deeper, grinding her back against the hard wood. His right hand locked under her chin, slamming her head hard on the railing.

"You vile bitch," his voice a whisper, "if I ever hear you talk about Sarah like that again, I'll kill you."

His grip slid from her chin and tightened around her throat. Lauree's heart pounded in her chest demanding to split open her head with each thunderous beat. Stretched to her full height, she felt as if a razor blade was slicing its way from her crotch to her navel. Words came out of her in distorted squeals, "Ross—the baby. Stop—you promised."

Ross jerked his hands away, his chest rising and falling with each breath. He backed toward the door, hands held stiff in the air. "Why did you make me do that?"

Lowering his arms, he stared at his hands. "This is what you're turning me into. I've never. But you. You."

Lauree massaged her neck and gulped for air, watching Ross's fingers clench into massive fists.

"You push and you push."

Seconds ticked loudly from the cuckoo clock hanging on the opposite wall. Lauree couldn't move.

"You've got to stop." He took a step toward her. "I'm going to make you stop."

Lauree squeezed her eyes shut.

Don't hit me. Don't hit me, she repeated to herself over and over keeping time with the loud ticking of the cuckoo clock.

Every muscle in her body stiffened as the wooden bird burst from its house. Lauree's body braced against the blows to come, protecting her baby with her arms.

Ross stared at his pregnant wife. It was true. Lauree did look like Sarah. But that was before the baby and a mountain of fat piled on top of her.

When they met, Lauree had the same long legs and tiny waist. She moved like Sarah. He dressed her like Sarah. Her breasts overflowed from his large hands like Sarah's and he could pretend, as long as he didn't look at Lauree's eyes or hair. Lauree's hair was flaming "I Love Lucy" red, and she refused to change it. Red sprang like a sunrise from Sarah's hair, blending gold, red, and brown. Brown... Sarah's eyes.

It was too painful to think of Sarah.

Staring at Lauree's eyes closed tightly with fear, her face pinched and twisted, Ross felt nothing but disgust. Disgust with himself for driving Sarah away and opening the door to this woman. He had searched for Sarah, hired private detectives, everything, but it was useless. She didn't want to be found, so he found Lauree.

Lauree was nothing more than a mirror image of Sarah. A chipped mirror. He didn't love her, he despised her. It was Sarah he loved. But Sarah was gone, and this cringing woman before him was carrying his child, his son. This one would never leave him. He knew that for a fact because he would never allow another woman to leave. Never.

The slamming door blasted Lauree's eyes open.

He's gone.

Clutching at the railing, her shaking legs buckled beneath her. Lauree collapsed under the crystal-bell-hung chandelier. Around her, the cantilevered oak staircase spiraled three stories up to a dome of stained glass windows, but she couldn't see the twisting hues the sun shot down on her. Blanketed by a kaleidoscope of colors, her crumpled body lay still.

Chapter 4
Still March 1977

Clarissa huddled on the playhouse porch trying to keep warm and at the same time make herself as small as she could. It was hard to do since she'd already reached five-foot, ten-inches in height. She was the tallest girl in her freshman class. The tallest girl in Leland High School, but it wasn't something she rejoiced about. Truth was, it really bugged her. None of the boys in her class even came close to her height. None but Stanley Smith, and he didn't count because he was a nerdy loudmouth.

Stanley had nicknamed her the tower of pizza. Stanley wasn't too bright. In any case the title was beginning to stick and Clarissa was not pleased. She didn't like nicknames. They were nothing more than caricatures that exaggerated features she'd been trying to hide all of her life. But hiding the fact that she was tall was an impossible task, especially on the playhouse porch.

Clarissa's grandfather, Major Samuel Trenton, or Major, as everyone referred to him, bought the playhouse from a family in DeKalb. It was built in 1891 for a trade fair parade. The two-story Victorian house with its intricate gingerbread trim boasted many patterns of siding, and was topped with a decoratively scalloped roof. But it was more than a playhouse to Clarissa; it was her escape hatch.

She used to love going to "her house" to have tea parties with her dolls. Whenever friends visited, they'd stand in awe with wonder sparkling in their eyes as they stared at the furniture just their size.

There were rugs on the floors, pictures on the walls. The kitchen and dining room had all the necessary items to complete the picture-perfect house any little girl would cherish.

There were no bedrooms upstairs because there was no upstairs, just very high ceilings. At least they used to be high when she was six-years-old, but at fourteen, the house had grown small.

Now, instead of tea parties, Clarissa ran to her house fleeing Ross and Lauree's fights. The time of day didn't matter. Once the screaming started, she tore out of the main house, which was actually more like a country mansion, to find sanctuary in her playhouse. She was safe there. Crouched in the corner with her hands over her ears blocking the screams, she was safe.

They were shouting at each other again. Near the little door hidden in the shadows, Clarissa wrapped her arms around her legs, pulled them to her chest and rested her forehead on her knees. She could hear them. Everyone could.

CPSIA information can be obtained
at www.ICGtesting.com
Printed in the USA
BVHW09s0150230818
524797BV00005B/36/P